S. A. CLAREMONT

Provoking the Lost

Contents

The Burn Scars and First Sight

Inhaling sharply, my eyes snapped open, and I bolted upright in the cab of my truck. My chest numbs after having one of the recurring nightmares that'd been taunting me since childhood. I sighed slowly as I rubbed at the sleep in my eyes and glanced sideways at my watch, squinting to check the time and fumbling for my phone that was vibrating somewhere on the dash.

I missed my bed. I missed the buttery, soft down comforter and the smooth sheets. I was definitely ready for a glass of my favorite red and a good movie. I even missed that dumb alarm clock that Ethan bought me to wake me up gently using light.

Cracking my neck from side to side, I did my best to stretch in the confined space. It was the final day out in the wilderness. Back to civilization and away from the peace and quiet of the forest.

Hopping out, I stepped through the darkness of the predawn morning. Streaks of sunlight were slowly beginning to rise over the foothills and penetrate the morning haze. I closed the door and caught sight of myself in the reflection of the glass. I wasn't winning any beauty contests, but I always liked my vivid green eyes. I had narrow features, delicate lips that were always a shade of muted red wine, and dark chocolate hair that could pass for black in low-light settings. It framed the ivory skin of my face and fell in thick waves around my shoulders. I was that not- too- short- but- not- tall- enough- to- be- a- model height where no clothes ever fit quite right.

I tiredly pulled my hair into a pony tail and tugged on my thick boots. Jeans and plain white tees pretty much summed up the entirety of my pitiful wardrobe. It was chillier than usual for early May, so I threw on my corduroy jacket and trudged to the edge of the place my campfire had been the night before.

Plucking the silver canister from the ground, I grumbled when I realized I was out of coffee.

"Lovely," I muttered.

My long-range walkie-talkie chirped to life. I left it on the hood of the truck so I could get some sleep last night.

"Breaker- breaker 1-9. It's Blond Panther. Do you come in, Fat Rabbit?" August's voice came in loudly over the speaker.

I grabbed the radio. "Don't call me Fat Rabbit. I thought we were out of the trucker phase?" I called back.

"No, we're not. Over." She laughed as she let go of the button.

"What's up?" I asked, slightly irritated.

"Calm down, grumpy. I just wanted to say that I'll be heading to the rendezvous point soon. Over. Ya whiny bi—" She let go of the transmitter.

"Heard that."

This would be my second year working my dream job as a conservation scientist for a private land owner in the state of Colorado. I loved everything about it. The mountain air and the forests made me feel right at home here.

I inhaled an incredible mix of strong pine, fresh water, and soft grasses.

Darkness still shrouded the service road down the hill. The little light that did break over the horizon burned indigo against the snow-capped peaks.

"You could have answered me last night. You know, I would have filed a missing person report by now if I wouldn't be a prime suspect in the disappearance." She burped into the walkie purposefully.

"Apparently you're still digesting last night's plans." I tossed items into the bed of the truck.

"Lily! Gaming is serious! Those are real people who depend on me. At least I'm not going on *fake* dates with my bed." She honked the horn of her Jeep angrily. "Nice hair, by the way. I assume you've taken the time to do your ponytail look," she chided. "I will see you in fifteen!"

"I'm at least twenty-five away," I chimed.

"Twenty sounds good! See ya then."

The walkie chirped off. I glanced at my watch. I still had time.

I shoved the final items across the backseat floorboards and quickly slipped on my backpack. If I jogged, I could get up there and back before I had to meet her.

I instinctually knew the way there. I set off at a quickened pace. When I saw the outcropping of boulders, I ducked under and rounded to the left. There were no trails here. This was memory I was working from.

Even in the dim of morning light, I could see it ahead. I broke past the tree line and emerged into an opening. It was large and if someone without my background had found it first, they would think they had discovered a lovely meadow. But upon closer inspection, I learned it was so much more.

Perfectly round when I had measured it crudely and roughly a thousand paces across. But that aside was not what had drawn my attention. I sprinted over to one of the large stumps about twenty yards to my right.

Charred.

Clicking on my miners light to see better, my fingertips grazed the burnt bark. I pulled out my phone and began snapping photos. Every twenty feet or so edging the periphery of the space were these damaged trees. Petrified in a perfectly even circle. I found it last fall and couldn't stop myself from stealing away to it every time I was in the area.

I had seen something similar when we studied the effects of radiation and shelling during war time in college and what it did to local forestry. The trees absorbed it like a memory.

But there were two problems with that theory. Explosives of that caliber had never been experienced in the region. Colorado hadn't seen war on that scale and other trees in the area would've been affected if it had. But no matter how far I trekked, this was a singular anomaly. A big one. There would be a smattering of similar instances if that idea held water.

The larger problem —and the reason I had kept this discovery a secret —the event that created this blast radius, according to the tree rings, predated the known history of explosives by *thousands* of years. Far before humans had managed to weaponize anything of this caliber.

This led me down a rabbit hole of searching for natural disasters, but nothing explained what I was seeing here. It simply didn't make sense.

I was eerily drawn to the place after initially finding it. I couldn't explain it other than a feeling that I was supposed to be here.

My watch rang out that I needed to go, I clicked off the timer and turned to leave. But not before turning back to snap one final photo of the space as the morning light began to illuminate it.

***

I passed through a valley with trees that lined one side of the pavement. I drove not a mile longer before spotting August.

She sat on the lowered tailgate of her royal blue Jeep, large wheels looming at its base, her gourmet coffee probably half gone by now.

At first glance, you'd notice her short, lithe stature. She was capped by blond waves that always looked wild and sultry, even when imprisoned by the hurry- up- you're- late ponytail. Unfairly turquoise eyes and hot pink polish graced her nails, pulling you in with her ruffles and pearls until she opened her mouth to let loose a cannonade of curses.

I met August freshman year of college at Colorado State University. We were assigned to be roommates in the dorms.

"Are you her?" the tiny blond asked with a raised eyebrow.

"I'm her," I shrugged. I wasn't sure what to expect, but a miniature Barbie that the makers of Mattel surely modeled the original after was not it. She smelled like flowers and her outfit had two random girls casually commenting on it in the span of fifteen minutes while walking past.

I wasn't sure what I had expected. A hipster who crocheted her own hats and made slippers out of felt? Someone who possibly had way too much macrame and listened to indie music that smelled like vegan cheese? Forestry wasn't exactly a major the future trophy wives of America were clamoring to get into.

"I'm August." She grinned her signature sparkling smile and stuck out her tiny, manicured hand for me to shake. "I hate the smell of Cheetos, I snore when I'm drunk, and if you ever need a study buddy, I make amazing flash cards!"

"I'm Lily." I half smiled and reached out to shake her dainty palm. "I'm told I should smile more, I snore when I drink whiskey, and I'm the reigning Cheeto-eating champion in Hamilton County two years running. Looks like this is gonna be a tough year for the both of us."

We laughed.

August was a great friend for me to have. I never made them, and she always did. August knew, talked to, and liked everyone. She was voted "most congenial and confident" in our freshman and sophomore dorms, and she was impossible not to laugh with. She hardly took anything seriously, was willing to try anything once (as long as it didn't involve butterflies), was wildly quick-witted, and was that girl you wanted to know at the party.

If she hadn't adopted me as her token introverted friend, I might never have had the full college experience she bestowed upon me.

Looking back now, I still smiled. She'd grown up in Washington, the youngest of seven and the only girl, working as a logger alongside her father and brothers. The family I never had. When she had learned I had a vaguely distant mother who I never spoke to back home in Vermont, a father who passed away when I was little, and no siblings, I became the sister she always wanted.

We went home to Washington every few months and I had actively spent every holiday, vacation, and event there for nearly seven years now.

She was, as best I could describe, a conqueror, fearless in every situation except one.

Butterflies. She claimed they flew too erratically for them to be trusted creatures.

* * *

I coasted in behind the small silver trailer attached to her Jeep and hopped out.

"I thought we talked about that shirt." She pulled in a deep swig of her coffee.

"I thought we talked about using so much concealer the morning after a rough night."

"Hardy har. That's it." She threw her hands up. "You're my friend on a probationary period today. I'm going to need you to prove yourself by giving me the day off." Reaching into the cab, she pulled out her tool belt.

"Alright, fine. Get out of here," I replied with a sigh.

"Really?" She smiled with excitement.

"No. Not really." I grinned. "Hardy har."

She laughed and let it trail into a sarcastic sneer as she tossed her empty coffee cup into her Jeep and pulled out a second.

"Oh, thank God. I ran out." I reached toward the java feeling relieved.

August slowly pulled her hand back, a wicked smile embracing her face. "That'll be fifteen dollars."

I paused, crossing my arms, scrutinizing her. "So you're going to steer the four-wheeler while carrying *that*?"

"Yep." She popped the *p* sound.

"Oh, this'll be fun," I laughed.

"Well, at least you can recognize the signs of where you're falling short," she countered as she stepped into her harness. "I can multitask, Lily."

I snorted in reply.

Around the back of my truck, I sifted through my gear. Dropping my harness to the ground and flattening it out before stepping into it. A plethora of tools hung from every loop and knot. August climbed the small trailer, mounted the ATV she lovingly called Grizzly, and stood as she eased the machine down the ramps. Looking over both shoulders repeatedly, she spun full circle and aimed for the trees. She stood ready to get the day going and I climbed on behind her holding the racks at the back of the wheeler. Firmly grasping the coffee, she eased into the thick.

"Getting there later, August, doesn't mean we have to work any less."

August turned her head, taking a long drink of the steamy liquid. She carefully tried to prove her point while gaining speed.

I glanced to my right and brilliant white caught my attention. My eyes snapped up to find piercing blue ones staring back at me from between the trees. My breath froze in my lungs at the sight. A man stood, immense, with raven dark hair, milky skin, and a momentous presence. A second later he was gone, and I immediately thought to pay attention to the trees. I turned too late, and a low-hanging branch caught me right across the collarbone and knocked me back.

"Harper! Wake up, slacker!" August bellowed as she quickly glanced over her shoulder to make sure I was still on the seat. My two best friends often called me by my last name. Only my dad used to call me Lilian.

"Yeah," I answered lamely as I sat upright and glanced back at the spot where I'd seen the man.

Empty.

Or at least I thought I'd seen a man.

The wheeler slowed as I gingerly rubbed the area the branch connected with, and I spotted the small clearing up ahead as we climbed closer. This was the stopping point, where Grizzly could no longer pass with ease.

"Who was that?" I looked around expecting him to reappear.

"What are you talking about?" August reached into one of the two giant tool boxes fitted to the back of Grizzly, pulling out her knife and tucking it into her boot. "Wait! Did you see *it*?" Her eyes were wide, yet serious.

August was convinced Sasquatch was real and she planned to catch him and take him on a traveling fair circuit for money. Sometimes I think she wasn't kidding. She claimed, *If we're out here this much, why wouldn't we look for Bigfoot?*

"That guy back there." I thumbed over my shoulder.

"Guy? Is he hot?" August craned her neck looking for the mysterious man as her sweeping fingers adjusted her hair.

"Yes." I gave her a spurning look. "I'm more concerned with the fact that I just saw a hiker in this area."

"Hotness always matters." She rolled her eyes, ignoring my real concerns.

I was dumbfounded. I hoped she was joking. "I'm going to work." I shook my head at her as I walked away.

"Enjoy your caffeine-free day!" she spouted happily to my back.

I pulled out my recorder and latched it to the collar of my T-shirt, clicking it on. "Good morning, mini memory. It's May 2nd, 7:03 a.m." I cracked my neck sideways. "And it's only Wednesday." I let my head loll back. "Last night's storm clouds have dissipated. Light ground fog is settling around me. Moisture levels are uncommonly low accompanied by a cool breeze coming from the north. Today's focus is the deterioration on the upper ridge."

Due to the ever-shifting climate, wildfire season was becoming longer and more powerful. Great for the undergrowth, not great for slides. August and I were looking over our best options to stem the erosion taking place on the north ridge that was giving Nodean, the land owner, grief. All while trying to respect the delicate ecosystems we had to be mindful of. I had just trekked out into the wilderness hunting for any signs of a Mexican spotted owl said to have been seen in the region.

Today August and I would be in the area tagging trees we felt needed to come down and ones we knew could stay.

I approached a giant Douglas-fir, slowly gazing upwards at my goal.

"Hey, girl." I smiled, placing a gentle hand on the trunk. "I'm going to check out how everything's been running."

I picked up the rope that was dangling loosely in a large loop over my shoulder. Tossing it wide around the trunk, I caught the free end. I ran it through the clip at my waist and readied for the ascent. Kicking a thick, heavy cleat into the unrelenting bark, I managed a step up and matched the action with my other foot. Tightening the knot and grabbing hold of the rope with both hands, I cat crawled up to the lower canopy.

This forest was the passion that consumed my life. I was addicted to the peace and quiet of the woods. The trees muted the world while I worked.

***

I snapped a photo when the radio crackled from my hip. "Finished my last tree! Ready to go home!"

"I'll head down to the meet point in five," I responded.

"Ethan won't shut up. He's been bugging me every day about it. I don't get it. I mean, has he seen your outfit choices?" She laughed as she let go of the button.

"Do you *want* to walk back to town?" I smirked.

"Calm down. It was a jo—" She broke off suddenly. The radio crackled and shrill screams echoed up to me through the trees. I whipped my head backward in the direction of her site.

"August," I breathed.

I wrenched the knot loose and sat into the harness kicking off the tree. In seconds my feet crashed to the earth's floor. I ripped off my gear and began running as fast as I could.

"August!" I screamed into the radio. "August, what happened? Are you okay?" I called yet again.

No answer.

My feet pelted the ground in time with my heartbeat. I breathed hard through my nose, my body saturated with fear.

"Say something, dammit!"

I fiercely shoved branches and debris aside, my lungs protesting loudly. I broke past the bushes where Grizzly was resting snugly and raged up the hill. My thighs were a machine.

"August Bayne, you better not be fucking with me right now!" I yelled into the woods.

I knew her not answering meant this was serious. August was a prankster but knew when to draw the line. This was not her. She would have burst into hysterical giggles by now. I unbuckled my gun we kept for safety against wildlife, ripping it from the holster on my thigh, readying myself.

I erupted through the trees and caught sight of her neon-orange flag tagging the tree she was supposed to be working in. The radio lay a few feet from the trunk. I frantically scanned the awning. That's when I saw her.

"So it would seem that I didn't check my knot again." She sighed heavily, dangling with her safety rope wrapped tightly around her left thigh.

"Well, by all means, belay on," I cracked as I put my gun back into its holster.

I turned and pretended to head in the direction of Grizzly.

"Proof I have more heart. Get me down," she called impatiently while adjusting her T-shirt casually, still self-aware.

"No, you look like you got this," I glanced up at her, my arms crossed and smiling.

"Fine! I will do your stupid weekly report," she bargained with her palms raised outwards in surrender.

I laughed.

"I didn't say I'd do it *well*," she threatened and then purposefully twisted away from me, attempting a cold shoulder, but inertia took its toll, and she slowly spun to face me again as I walked toward the tree trunk.

"Karma, August. Karma," I said with a sly smile.

2

A Mule Deer in a Maserati

"Damn nightmare." Kicking the tangled covers away from my feet and shifting onto my stomach, I buried my face in the pillow as my fingers grazed the mattress. "Good date," I croaked into the wrinkles.

Scooting over to the edge of the bed, I caught sight of the crumbs from the night's festivities and brushed them to the floor. Eyeing the half-full glass of red wine perched on my nightstand. My phone sprung to life. Automatically, I flung myself backward but missed, trying to catch it as it vibrated dangerously close to the edge.

"Crap" I rolled to my back, answering the phone I had plucked from the floor.

"Hey, you." A deep and easy voice replied from the other end, and I smiled. My other best friend, Ethan Monroe. "What are you doing up?" he asked.

"Ethan, you called me." I laughed softly and gulped the second half of the leftover wine after sitting upright on my mattress.

"Oh, right. I couldn't sleep. Bad dream." He stretched through the words.

"Was it the wedding dream again?" I teased.

"You're even cuter when you're jealous." I could hear the smirk in his voice. "How did date night go with the bed? Is he the one?"

"Oh my, you are so…"

"Captivating? Seductive? Completely perfect?" He laughed through his nose.

I rolled my eyes. "Try arrogant, egotistical, and completely consumed," I mimicked.

"Completely consumed by you, my love," he rendered without missing a beat.

"It's late and I have a lot of work to do this week before we go to Washington." I changed the subject.

He yelped into the phone quickly, crushing buttons in response.

"You're not going." His rushed voice was muted as though he was holding the phone at arm's length.

"Yes, I am!" I yelled into the mouthpiece.

"This is not up for discussion," his voice clipped.

"Ethan…" I chided.

"Nope. Goodnight, I love you!"

The phone line went dead.

Ethan was…complicated.

* * *

The thunder of the exhaust trailed behind me. The bike trembled between my thighs and beat against my heels, as I hugged the curves of the road. The heat of the sun warmed the leather on my back. My thoughts were fleeting and hollow as the red bandana acting as a mask filtered the smells of the forest around me. Reaching my destination, I found myself reluctant to pull over as the wheels spit gravel in protest.

Pulling off the small black helmet, I hung it loosely on the chrome handlebar, drawing the bandana down around my neck. Shoving my sunglasses into my hair, with one hand I dialed her number.

It rang twice before forwarding to voicemail. I hit re-dial.

"Oh, hey," she answered softly with false enthusiasm.

"So, what time do you think I can expect you?" Amusement fueling my question.

"About that…" She trailed off. "There was a bear blocking the way to the Jeep."

"A bear?" I skeptically replied.

"Yes, Lily, a bear. We live in the mountains. This is their home too," she huffed.

"'Kay, so where is this bear now?" I mitigated her need to continue the story.

"Funny you should ask. Animal control came to remove it after I called them, you know, and I was telling them, 'Guys I have to get to work. Lily needs me,'" she declared.

"You're at Mason's, aren't you?" August's not-so-secret addiction. A cocky jerk she ran to whenever she was lonely.

"Nope. Absolutely not."

"So you didn't drink too much and then call him and go over to his place last night? I saw you hadn't been home." I raised my eyebrows.

"I told you I was done with him, and I'm done with him," she affirmed.

"Don't forget to look for the pink polka bra you thought you left there last time." I smiled, reminding her.

"Oh yeah!"

"You're on laundry duty for the next week." I rolled my eyes and hung up.

Amusement blended with annoyance as I leaned against the bike, dropping the phone into the saddlebag. I took off my jacket and slung it over the seat, kicking the dirt while I waited. Against my better judgment, I reached for my closet indulgence in an attempt to wash away the irritation.

Lips kissing the end of my vape pen, I drew in a slow breath pressing the button.

Slowly, my hair drifted north in the opposite direction of the mountain wind, splitting around my neck and tangling in front of my cheeks. I exhaled with an ashen breath, bewildered as the silvery trail led south, my eyes drifting in the direction of the anomaly.

"How?" I drew on the vape a second time.

Peculiarity piqued, I noticed the car parked along the road farther down. Had that been here when I arrived? Or did it pull up when I was on the phone? A convertible burnished black and foreign in appearance captured my attention. I squinted for a moment when the undeniable sound of wood splintering echoed from the forest behind me, an apparent force storming through the timber, tearing a wave of limbs downwards in its retreat.

Instantaneously, I swung around, facing the looming tree line. An ephemeral glimpse of a young mule deer flashing by, neck taut, nostrils flaring, hooves hammering the dirt, when he erupted from the woods. He vaulted across the road, letting loose a high-pitched bleat of danger, warning every living thing nearby.

"Predator," I whispered. Enveloped by silence, I pitched my vape onto the seat of my bike. Using both hands, I worked quickly. Seizing the gun from the saddlebag and a clip from underneath the seat, I thrust it into the handle. My index ready, the barrel pointed to the ground, I listened, my breathing inaudible as I focused it through my nose.

"Where are you?" I whispered into the curtain of reticence.

I canvassed, my eyes piercing in attempts to reach beyond the sea of viridian. I saw nothing.

"What was that?" I willed my ears to amplify the sound. Dragging?

I drew in a shaky breath.

"Footfalls," I whispered. But they sounded different. Slow and even. They almost sounded...

"Human." I raised my weapon as the man emerged from the trees beside his vehicle, then slowly lowered it, paralyzed with amazement at the event unfolding in front of me.

My stance was silent as I witnessed the stark impossibility before me, a familiar ambiance shrouding him. I watched as he slid the enormous buck off his shoulder into the grassy soil, the lifeless beast showing no injuries.

His raven hair reflected the sun as he palmed the frame of the car and launched himself into the backseat. Showing complete disregard for the white leather he stood upright on. Shrugging his broad shoulders, he placed his hands on his hips, momentarily surveying his situation. He then bent forward over the side of the car.

"No. He can't," I uttered softly.

Taking a firm grasp of the antlers, he effortlessly pulled the colossal carcass into the rear seat of the sports car. Moving in a fluid motion backward, he exited, hooking the rack over the open edge. He paused as though he were contemplating his next move. Suddenly, his head raised in my direction. I stood still, enraptured as I noticed his hands tightening slightly around the rack he held. Jumping from the vehicle, he started walking toward me. His penetrating eyes creased with curiosity, making *me* feel like the unnatural presence. Our stares were hypnotic at one another until his head jolted to the right, targeting something unseen. He arched his spine pulling his shoulders back in a quick stretch as he started jogging towards the trees before picking up speed just before vanishing.

I blinked repeatedly, shaking my head back and forth from the strange encounter. Looking around, becoming soberly aware I had gravitated closer to the man and away from my bike, drifting in an unknown current.

Unloading my weapon to place it safely away, I assessed what had happened. No remnants of his exit where he had faded into the thick, the only evidence a polished expensive car, its sole occupant an immense lifeless mule deer bleeding down the costly paint job.

Suddenly, a distant rumble of thunder was charging at me, the sound of hooves getting closer. My pulse rushed, lurching panicked through my veins, a symphony of clashes rupturing into the surroundings again. Something fast-moving was chasing its prey. My hands began to tremble as my subconscious moved my feet away from the approaching danger. Like a runaway freight spinning wildly down the tracks and I was standing between the rails. It was coming toward *me*.

A final deafening blow against the dirt and everything went quiet, leaving behind a plume of slowly rising dust that floated to where I stood from the tree line. My shallow breaths were all that was audible. The stranger emerged again, another trophy-sized buck dangling over his shoulder, its antlers swinging with every step as they etched trails into the dirt. No evidence of the kill. I could see he had no weapon.

In an airy whisper, I said, "Hello…" Choking on the remaining words as determination set his jaw. His hand tensed in reaction and the deer's bones cracked under the slight pressure. Awed, I could say no more, as he approached the vehicle and flung the mammoth across the previous corpse.

The engine hummed under the insurmountable stress as the axle hovered dangerously close to the road. He then sped past following me with his bright eyes.

"Predator?" A cold breath escaped my lips, and I was alone.

* * *

I rubbed my eyes as I leaned back. Feet propped against the trunk, I stretched my arms over my head. I couldn't shake the weariness today as the morning replayed yet again. I had decided not to dispel any information to August about the stranger.

"Rebel! I have a surprise for you," August said through my walkie.

"Rebel?" I asked.

"Yes, because you rode your badass bike," she mocked.

"You do?" I asked skeptically.

"Don't act so shocked. I surprise you with things all the time," she said.

"Blind dates don't count as surprises," I clarified yet again.

"Hey, you need the help! Why you turned those cute guys away I'll never know. That Derek dude was gorgeous!" she rambled.

"Eh, I guess he was cute," I agreed lamely.

"You guess? You guess he was cute?" she shrieked.

"Uh-huh," I said.

"*Uh-huh*," she mocked. "I'm beginning to think…" She paused. "Are you secretly seeing someone?" she said excitedly.

"No," I laughed.

"I could totally hook you up with someone I know! Oh shit. Quinn would dig you! You're definitely his type— smart, cute, nerdy," she listed.

"August, I'm not really looking for anyone. Isn't Quinn the bartender down at the Boiler?" August's favorite hotspot. To be honest, I had given up hope that I would find anyone.

"So, you have noticed him! Wait, are you still crushing on Jarrett?" she asked seriously. Jarrett was August's oldest brother, and yes, I was. But I would never admit it to her.

"Jump to conclusions much?" I laughed. "I listen to you babble all day long, August. I just pick this shit up on occasion," I said as I rolled my shoulders and twisted to crack my back.

"Babble? I don't babble! I share vital information!" she babbled.

I rolled my eyes with a smile as I glanced around the forest while she kept talking.

Something caught my eye. My breath caught in my throat. It was the man from this morning. I felt sick, my chest tight.

I blinked twice, rubbed my eyes, and looked again. Intensely blue eyes, creamy skin, and a subtle grin pulling at the corners of his lips. The top buttons of his hunter-green shirt were undone, taut across the expanse of his large chest.

"What are you doing here?" I breathed to myself. I sat in my harness dangling about fifteen feet up.

My chest burned as I watched him. His long and powerful legs kept even strides as he strolled. He wore high-end leather boots more fitting for a London job interview than a light hike through the forest. Hands rested in the pockets of his slacks, pausing to turn his head and look up at me.

"Whoa," I whispered softly as my heart pounded in my chest.

"Lily!" August's yell startled me, and I jumped at the sound of her screech.

Taking a deep breath to gather my resolve, I glanced to where he'd been to find him gone.

"Lily! Are you listening to me? Dammit! You tuned me out again, didn't you? Vital information here! Remember?" she bellowed.

"I'm here. Sorry," I responded offhandedly.

"I have half a mind to leave your ass in the woods. It would serve you right to ignore me when I'm talking to you," she said angrily.

"Yeah, I know. Sorry. What did you say?" I said as I searched the woods for him.

"I said they would kill me if I didn't bring you along. So you can't back out of Washington," she said. "They've been dying to see you since you missed Christmas."

"I'm not backing out. Why would you think I was backing out?" I scanned the trees for him again.

"Ugh! You're impossible sometimes. Didn't you hear me at all? You suck," she said and turned off her walkie.

I frowned and clipped my walkie back to my utility belt.

"What the heck was that? Is he following me?" I asked the trees around me.

Who was this guy? I should have been scared, right? I was definitely scared. Maybe I would tell Ethan about him if I saw him again. This part of the park *is* restricted. Yet I couldn't take my eyes off him. I couldn't shake my desire to find him again.

"Desire? To see a stranger in the woods?" I said softly. "Am I that desperate?"

My heart felt erratic against my ribs. My head swam in a foreign pool of thoughts.

"Weird," I furrowed my brow in thought as the speaker rang out loudly.

"Time to go! On my way to you!" August said happily.

I glanced at my watch and started my descent, browsing the trees for him as I moved. There was nothing to prove that he'd been real. I shook my head to clear my mind of the thoughts of him.

* * *

We sat in a cafe in Old Town eating some dinner, one of our weekly rituals, while August swatted at a butterfly floating near some petunias in a planter.

"They taste with their feet, you know. Little winged bitches are trying to eat me, nasty shits!" she exclaimed.

I blinked at her repeatedly and repressed a chuckle.

"You'll see one day. They're going to take over the world. Flying around snacking on people! Everyone thinks the plagues will be locusts," she continued, shaking her head.

"Take over the world?" I laughed. "I don't think it will come to that August."

"Yeah, right. You'll see. You'll all see!" she said as she turned and pointed her finger at the people sitting around us.

I sighed and sank down in my chair.

"You're so weird," I said as I looked down at my plate.

Her chair screeched over the pavement and I looked up. She was moving across the room toward a guy sitting alone at a table. I perked a brow, shook my head, and then returned my attention to my dinner.

My mind drifted back to the handsome man in the forest. What was he doing there?

I wanted to tell August. Heck, I probably *should* tell August, but no one would believe the goliath strength I witnessed this morning. I decided it best to mute any conversations about him. Knowing August, she would call it in and then take me for a spa weekend. She thinks I work too much.

"Lily! Are you in there?" August's voice penetrated my thoughts as her knuckles rapped on my skull.

"Ow. What?" I said as I swatted her hand away and rubbed the abused spot.

"Spaced out again? What is up with you today?" she asked, concerned.

"I'm fine. Just tired," I said.

"You're always tired. Try sleeping sometimes." She rolled her eyes.

"Good idea! Maybe I'll do that tonight," I said with an excited nod.

"No, you're not. I just found the perfect guy for you! He thinks you're cute!" She grinned and waved in the direction of the guy across the room.

I stared blankly at her and then glanced at the guy who was smiling adoringly at me.

"No, August," I grumbled.

"You don't have to hide it anymore! I get it! You suck at meeting people. I'll find them for you," she said and headed back to the guy in question.

A second later they were both sitting at my table.

I groaned internally as I pasted a smile on my face.

* * *

I stepped out of the shower and toweled off. Heading to the dresser and pulling out something to sleep in. Slipping into the tank and cutoff sweatpants I always donned, I shuffled to the bed and crawled under the crumpled covers.

"Yay, sleep!" I said happily as I bounced my feet against the soft mattress and closed my eyes while pulling the blanket up to my chin.

The man flashed in my mind. Was I going crazy?

I felt a shudder.

I snapped open my eyes and took a deep breath.

There was a strange man in the closed-off portion of the park. Why? He could live in the area, but Ethan would have informed us of residents by now. There were a handful of homes that had been grandfathered into the National Park. The forest is dense though and could easily hide a small settlement. Perhaps he's a hunter? Doubtful considering his attire. Who hunts in business casual anyway? Maybe he was poaching? Did I imagine him? Lack of sleep could be frying my mind. Not that I know why I would imagine a handsome stranger. Maybe…maybe I am working too much.

I shook my head and closed my eyes. "Nah," I said aloud and then forced myself into a fitful state of sleep.

I was interrupted by the shrill ring of my phone hours later.

"Hello?" I droned.

"Lil-lay," she gushed.

"Hey, lush, I was sleeping and you're drunk," I said with a mild grin.

"Sleep is for later! I decided you should date Jay," she slurred.

"I should date Jarrett?" I questioned. "Like Jarrett, as in your brother?"

"Yeah, you agree! It'll be perfect! You'll fall in married and get love and have babies and be my sister!" she said excitedly.

"Slow down!" I said, rubbing my eyes.

"No time! He's gettin' old, y'know! It's far past time for him to settle down. And you're perfect! He's good lookin', smart, and funny. His girlfriends seemed to like him. I mean, yeah, he's had his share of…" She rambled on.

"Your brother's a stud, I know," I patronized.

"Oh em gee! You are so into him!" she yelped.

There was crackling in the phone and I imagined she was literally dancing with joy.

"You're *so* drunk." I smiled.

"No! I had a beer and shots from pretty boys. I'm fine!" she said, punctuated by slurred words and random hiccups.

I chuckled and rolled to my side.

"I'm going back to bed," I said.

"I can see it now! You'll have a huge wedding!" she squealed.

"Goodnight," I sang with a smile pulling an errant pillow over my head.

I groaned as it rang again.

"August, call your drunk self a ride," I laughed.

"'Bout that. Knock knock," she said as a bang sounded at our front door. "I may or may not have forgotten my keys."

I hung up the phone. "Seriously." And chucked the pillow.

The Overprotective Playboy

I barged through the bathroom door. "Ethan Ashley Monroe, so help me…" I yanked back the shower curtain and took in a breath. His beauty sometimes couldn't be overlooked. Blond hair and hazel eyes with wonderfully tanned skin that rivaled honey. He was singing into a loofa and smiling.

"Knew you couldn't resist. Come on in, Harper." He grinned wide and backed up holding out his arms in welcome before he took a second look and noticed my face. "Wait, you used my middle name." He backed up against the wall and protectively covered his groin. "What did I do?" he asked nervously.

"This is *my* house, not *ours*! Quit telling girls you live here." This is one of several tactics Ethan used to throw off his one-night stands. The girl shows up at my door confused and I appear to be the angry girlfriend. Today I admit that I doubted she would ever bother him again. "That's the worst thing to do to some girl. You can be such a dick."

"Lily, in my defense, she was a clinger. The situation was definitely dangerous. She said"— he gulped hard— "I love you. I could see the wedding bells in her eyes." He was trying to use his charming smile.

The one I couldn't help but fold to every time.

"There are better ways. How about try *not* sleeping with every girl you find at the bar?"

He threw the curtain closed and I walked to the vanity, curling up cross-legged on the countertop.

"I can't help myself. I have an appetite," he spoke to me now from behind the veil. Steam was billowing out, a foggy haze suffocating the room. "Lily." He poked his lathered head out, holding back the curtain blinking away the water streaming over his impossibly long lashes. "I told you I have every intention of spending the rest of forever with *you*." The curtain fell back in place, and I listened as he continued with his brilliant and colorful reason as to why he is the way he is. "And until you say yes, I can't help but continue to try and fill that void," he finished. "I love you."

"I think you love my shampoo," I retorted, leaving the steamy mixture of my T-shirts and the scent of his skin swirling behind me.

* * *

"Is this really necessary?" I asked, my face masked with skepticism.

"Your safety is always necessary." With a click of his tongue and a wink, he continued. "My lovely assistant today will be Miss Bayne." He waved his hand and stepped back allowing August to curtsy towards me in our living room.

Ethan did this often. Any trip had with August started with a safety lecture.

I rolled my eyes and sighed. "Whatever, let's get this done. I'm sure that August would like to get to her evening plans of boy hunting."

"Cheers to that!" August yelled, raising an imaginary glass.

"Ladies." He nodded towards August. "Future wife." He grinned, flashing his perfect teeth at me. Unfazed, I rotated my finger, motioning to get the situation moving.

"Okay, the first thing you need to know about car safety—"

"Seriously?" I expressed a need to hurry.

"Lilian Bleu Harper, roughly 35,000 people die annually from car accidents. Since I assume that August here will be doing a majority of the driving, I feel this is a necessary step." He clapped his hands together. This was all due to the incident over Thanksgiving where August lodged her dad's truck in the ditch. "It's common knowledge that we drive better here in Fort Collins than anybody in the whole state of Washington." He shrugged.

"Excuse me, neither of you are Colorado natives. Both of you are East Coast tight asses," August sneered. "Maine." She pointed to Ethan. "Vermont." She eyed me disgustingly.

"Whatever. Would you two hurry up?"

Sensing my frustration, he halted August's instructional motions and walked up to me.

"Babe, I know you think that I'm crazy, but you're important to me. I couldn't survive August without you. How would I get rid of girls? You know she wouldn't lie for me!" he coaxed now with palms holding both sides of my face. "Humor me, please?" he pleaded with those eyes.

"Okay, but make it quick, Monroe." I buckled under the weight of his request.

"Agreed. Assistant?" He wiggled an index finger at August instructing her to stand in place again.

"This is an oxygen mask. You laugh now but if the cabin depressurizes and you lose oxygen, you'll suffocate." He looked at me. "Don't ask me how I got it."

"Probably slept with a stewardess," August mumbled out of the corner of her mouth.

"They prefer to be called flight attendants, August," he reminded.

August was pulling the oxygen mask over her face laughing and making comments as she went.

"And remember to make sure that your mask is on securely before you help your neighbor." She grabbed a pillow off the chair from behind her, cramming it into Ethan's face. "Help your neighbor, Monroe!" she yelled, tackling him to the floor. I laughed.

"I will be forced to restrain you, Bayne, if you don't stop making such dangerous threats," his muffled voice called from behind the pillow. "You're just looking for another excuse to touch me." He wrestled with the tiny blond, pushing her away with ease.

I watched as he pinned her to the floor and gently set her aside as though she were a small child involved in the battle. Another laugh cut through my lips. Ethan's face snapped up and he shook his head slowly back and forth.

"You laugh at me?" He held a hand to his chest and extended the other towards me while still on his knees. "Oh, laugh again, bright girl, for thou art as glorious to this night, leaning tower shy bed."

"You're stupid. If you're quoting Shakespeare, do it right." August sat up, leaning back on one arm, sticking her finger in her mouth pretending to gag. "Just bang her already and get over your delusions of her," she shoved at his face.

"Oh, that is it!" He leaned back and picked her up with the scoop of one arm and threw her to the chair. "Go trolling for your prey already. I need Lily time without the company of *your* comments." He coasted towards me. "I'm going to run to the store and get your favorite." He kissed me on the top of the head and grabbed my truck keys off the end table. "Grape popsicles!" he simpered.

"Those are *your* favorite," I replied.

"Fine, I guess I could bring orange for you, love." He was slipping his shoes on at the door.

"Could you get me some banana ones too?" August asked, sitting on the bench slipping her pedicured toes into sandals and adjusting her jeans accordingly. "I *was* your assistant."

"Worst assistant ever. You put all assistants to shame with that crap. She dies by suffocation, it's on your head, Bayne!" he called, running down the stairs.

"Suffocation?" she mouthed back to me.

I shrugged.

The street lights came on as Ethan and I were sitting on the wooden steps that led to my front door. He insisted that I wrap a blanket around me if I wanted to be outside.

"Will you be careful?" he asked while staring straight ahead.

"Quit worrying so much. It'll give you gray hair." I leaned against his shoulder. "You're my best friend, Monroe. I'll jump out of the way," I placated.

"You better not have too much fun and want to stay there." He sucked on his Popsicle.

"It's the Baynes, Ethan." Wrapping my arms around him, I kissed his neck lightly. "No competition."

He blushed and smiled wide. "Why can't all girls be like you, Harper?"

"What? An introvert? Who hangs out in the woods?" I retorted. "I sound like a creeper," I added.

"Cutest creeper I ever met." Ethan smiled, kissing my temple. "*My* little creeper."

I looked at his doleful eyes and understood. No wonder they chase him.

I met Ethan in the dead of winter cursing a vehicle that was firmly planted in the ditch next to me.

Kicking the tires hopelessly, surrounded by mountains, holding a dead cell phone.

I was beginning to plan for a night in the woods in my car waiting for a passerby. Suddenly, the smooth vocals of a chipper young stranger vibrated behind me interrupting my survival planning.

"Need a tow?" the young man called.

"Yeah, stupid toy of a car decided the ditch would be a better place than…" I turned around and locked eyes with lush hazels staring straight back. Comfort washed over me, and calm annulled all other emotions.

"Good thing I stopped." He was slowly stepping out of his large rumbling truck, a truck that appeared to never worry about getting stuck. He was easily over six feet and wearing an ensemble that suggested he knew his way around a mountain.

"Do you live around here?" I asked to make light conversation with the giving stranger who made me feel okay again.

"No." He leaned over the side of the truck into the bed and pulled out two straps that could assist in a tractor pull. "Work. The ranger station up the way is mine." He nodded in some direction up the road. "So who are you?" he asked, clipping some of the ropes to the front of his truck.

"I'm working in the forest." Using my opportunity to check him out as he lay on his back working his way under my car looking for a place to put the hooks, one knee cocked.

"Ah." Getting up, he dusted off the flakes of snow. "You're one of the tree doc students. I haven't had a chance to meet you yet." He walked forward, pulling off a thick glove. "Ethan Monroe." He shook my hand sweetly, "You must work with Miss Bayne." He pulled down a confused brow. "I figured you to be a little more earthy." He started smiling in a flirtatious manner.

"Sorry?" I answered, unsure quite how to respond.

He jumped back into his truck. "They didn't mention that you were also going to be so cute." He winked and closed the door.

Human nature ruled me for months. Every time afterward that I had seen Ethan, whether it was the flat tire or the day I got stuck pushing

Grizzly when August called in fake sick, I always managed to find myself unintentionally batting my lashes at him.

If I hadn't discovered his devilish ways while out one gruesome night with August, I could have been prey as well.

A bar, a pissed girl, and one tall beer down his back. That's when I learned that Ethan Monroe was quite the playboy. I banished the thoughts of us two ever living happily-ever-after and planted him firmly in the not- marriage- material category.

However, it wasn't easily discarded. He never relinquished his proposals until the day he decided to stop asking altogether and assume our date of marriage was definite.

"What are you thinking about?" he asked, interrupting my memories.

I was pulled back from the past and licked the drips of orange making their way down the Popsicle. "How we first met." I smiled.

"I knew *that* day you were the girl that I was going to marry." He munched. "I couldn't help it. You're who I fell in love with."

"I love you too, Monroe. I'm going to be living on that for the next week," I pouted.

"Always adorable, even when she pouts." He wrapped an arm around me. "I'm worried that Jarrett's going to steal you away. He's always had a thing for you." A look of sorrow cradled his eyes and face.

I laughed. "They don't stand a chance."

"You say that every time…" He trailed off.

"What is that supposed to mean?" I asked, concerned.

"It's just that…when you come home…you're different. Quieter, more reserved," he pondered. "Confused."

I knew what he meant. Being around Jarrett Bayne, something in me changed. I couldn't avoid it.

"Even now when you think about him…" He looked away chewing on the stick of his dissolved treat. "You get this look…like you don't belong to me anymore."

I smiled and hugged him, kissing his cheek. Turning my face into his shoulder, hiding the worry I felt.

4

First Touch

Piles of papers from work surrounded me on the table, anchored in place by stones from the sidewalk. After coming home to the "bang boa" wrapped around the knob of August's bedroom door and the muffled sounds of Mason's voice, I came to the park not far from our apartment.

* * *

"August why is the bang boa on the door?" A pink feathered boa was wrapped around the knob of our dorm room. "We're supposed to be studying tonight!"

I could hear shuffling. "We are!" She swung the door open. She was wearing a baby blue robe and had a towel wrapped around her head. "I forgot to take it off after I showered."

"Do I dare ask?"

"Cute Dalton from the chem lab!"

"Sweater vest Dalton? He always smells like burnt out matches."

"Don't make that face." She pointed at me. "Dalton is very nice and believe it or not, the boy can kiss."

August popped up on top of my loft bed. Sitting cross-legged she pulled out a stack of brightly colored note cards. She was brilliant when it came to studying and if it wasn't for her, I never would have made it through my Biology 102 class.

I sat in my desk chair below the bed and put my feet up on one of the lower rungs of the ladder, doing my best to guess the answers to her neon cards she was reading from above.

"Can I ask you a strange question?" I chewed on the end of my pen.

"If it's about Dalton, I don't know. I think he's sweet."

"No, that's not what I was going to say. I know you chose this major because of your dad's company, but why did you choose Colorado? There are great schools out on the West Coast and with your GPA, you could've went anywhere."

There was a quiet pause and I looked up at the bottom of the bed.

"August?"

"If I tell you something, you promise not to judge me?" she asked quietly.

"Of course."

"When I was a junior in high school. It was like suddenly I knew. I knew this was the degree I wanted and more than anything, *this* was the school I wanted to go to. It felt like I woke up one day and had this feeling that I needed to be here. And I couldn't quite explain it to anyone. It was like, there was a reason I was meant to be in this place at this time."

I knew exactly what she meant. Throughout my entire life I would feel these intuitive whims to do something. Gnawing feelings somewhere that felt so strong I couldn't ignore them if I tried.

"It makes sense. I decided to come here my junior year too," I murmured softly.

"People didn't understand it. My friends, my family, even my boyfriend…"

I mulled on what she was saying. Maybe fate brought us together because it knew I was in desperate need of a real friend or perhaps it was trying to get August out from under the chaos of her infamous brothers. Whatever it was, I'm glad the intuition struck.

"I know it sounds stupid," she murmured.

"Not at all. Sometimes I think all of this is happening for a reason. A bigger picture at play that none of us can see clearly yet."

"Sometimes I wonder…" she pondered quietly before asking the next card's question.

***

As the breeze made me shiver, I reached for the hooded sweatshirt beside me. Looking around as I pulled it to my hips, someone caught my eye.

I gasped at the sight. It was *him*. Barely twenty feet away from me was the stranger from the forest. My heart thundered. My muscles froze. My chest burned. I watched as he strolled along the path, heedless in his movements.

He paid no attention to the commotion around him. Children rushing around the fountain, giggling as they chased a bouncing ball or avoided the hand in a game of tag. Mothers laughing as they sat bunched together discussing the amusement of their respective children. Dogs barking as their masters ruffled their ears upon return from a good fetch. His face was blank despite it all, hands resting comfortably at his sides and his eyes motionless.

He veered toward a lone bench opposite me and lowered his massive frame to sit upon it. He rested his arms across the back, stretching out his legs and crossing his ankles. He turned his head as he glanced around. He didn't seem to be looking at anything in particular. I couldn't pull my attention away from the sheer brilliance that he was.

I hadn't been this close before.

His skin was like flawless ivory and his obsidian hair was short with a hint of soft curls. His lids were lined with thick lashes that shadowed the most startling icy blue eyes. He had thin lips that were a dark red and a strong jaw with the hint of a dimple set into one cheek. He was clean-shaven, but given a day, his face would be thick with whiskers. His clothes looked like the fabrics were imported and an expensive timepiece wrapped around his thick wrist as his only accessory.

I watched for a long time before shifting my eyes to the other people in the park. How could they not see him? Stop to gawk and stare?

A stray ball flew at him, and he raised a refined hand to palm it away. As if he could feel my gaze, his focus turned to me.

Curiosity renewed, I kept watching, disregarding the impoliteness of staring. I watched until the sun dipped below the horizon and the park emptied. I watched and my desire to learn more grew. My determination to know who, strengthened. My need to hear his voice broke down the wall of reservation that had kept me at bay.

I stood and slipped away from the table. My fingers wrapped absently around the typewriter key that was the charm on my ever-present necklace. A gift from my father. My feet seemed to advance themselves as I worked myself up for the confrontation. My eyes fixated on him, and he remained still as I inched toward him.

"Breathe," I repeated. My blood felt thick in my veins. I could hear my heartbeat in my ears. My mouth went dry as I closed in on the man.

"I know you," I said softly.

He cocked his head to the side and narrowed his eyes at me.

"I saw you a few days ago up in Roosevelt," I said with more certainty.

"You don't and you didn't." His face was calm, and his deep voice was soft but firm as he stood.

"But...I know you," I said firmly.

"No." He began to walk away.

"I saw you yesterday morning with those deer. Who *are* you?" I reached out to halt him with my hand on his arm.

The spring breeze suddenly calmed and the evening songs of the insects in the surrounding grasses quieted. The chatter of distant college coeds en route to the bars lapsed and the lamps of the park yellowed with warmth. In a moment of hushed hesitation, the world became still.

We both staggered at the contact. A feeling akin to a warm tingle somewhere between holding a steaming cup of tea on a cool fall day and opening the door to an inviting place that always feels like home flourished as his hand went to the place I'd touched.

"What did you do?" he asked lowly as his eyes narrowed while he looked at his arm.

"I..." Stammering, I cradled my hand to my chest. The tingle slowly soaked my nerves and began to permeate across my flesh, leaving a residue of warmth radiating through me like sinking into a forested hot spring on a crisp winter afternoon.

"Who are *you*?" he asked softly.

"Lily. I'm...just Lily," I answered in a whisper.

He stared at me, concerned anger set in his jaw.

"I have to go," he said in a hushed tone before turning away.

"Why?" I asked, crinkling my brow.

His step faltered in surprise, but he didn't turn back.

"Hey! You didn't answer me. Who are you?" I called to him.

He continued.

"Why won't you answer me? Hey!" I called louder.

Nothing.

I scowled.

"No need to be rude!" I said in annoyance.

His shoulders shook slightly.

"Oh, you think I'm amusing? You won't be laughing when I turn you in for poaching!" I said into the lengthening distance.

He ignored me.

"Jerk," I growled.

Strolling down the path as if nothing had happened, never looking back. I felt a peculiar cold creep into my chest as he disappeared.

I threw my hands up in disgust and strode purposefully back to my table.

"Just wait until I talk to Ethan." I sank onto the bench. "Won't be so funny then."

Framing my face in my hands as I leaned my elbows on the table, my eyes clouded over in concentration.

What was that pulse I felt? Touching him, intense and warm, literally bolting up my fingertips through my arm to my collarbone.

I replayed the moment. Remembered that his hand had covered the spot where mine had been.

"He felt it too," I said quietly.

He'd been amused. What was up with him? Maybe he was homeless? Yes. That makes perfect sense. A homeless man… who must hunt to eat…with his bare hands. And wears cap-toe boots, designer clothes, and drives a Maserati? Or perhaps an eccentric billionaire who hunts with his bare hands?

"All of this sounds stupid," I sighed.

I shook my head trying to clear my mind and remove the unexplainable frustration enveloping me. I threw all the papers into my bag and headed out of the park with a heavy heart.

5

The Bayne Boys

August was bumbling around in her room down the hall. I kept coating the toast with fattening butter. I didn't care. Calories don't count this early in the morning.

"Are you ready yet?" August called from her bathroom.

"Yep, still ready."

"Great! I'm not ready!" She said the last part in one mashed-up sentence and ran out into the hall. "Sorry, just nervous, I guess. Should I bring the red T-shirt that I look way hot in?" she asked quickly, holding it to her chest. Before I could reply, she answered her own question. "No, that'll give the boys an excuse to call me names." And she turned and disappeared.

I walked over to the couch and curled up while I balanced my small plate of toast on my knee.

A muted buzz fluttered against the cushion. She was calling me from her room.

"Hi, you've reached the voicemail of Lily Harper. I'm not available at the moment but please leave a message and I'll return your call as soon as possible." I pressed the five to simulate the beep.

"Is that Morse code to go with the yellow tank top? I'm not following.

You're dumb. Beep that," she called from down the hall.

August was a bit of a procrastinator, so this was nothing new. I dropped the phone by my side. I should be drinking coffee at this hour, but someone needed to remain calm and apparently August had chosen frantic.

I'd thrown on a ratty band T-shirt, pairing it with some leggings while I slipped on some brown flip-flops. I smiled, reveling in the fact that August would chastise me until she was blue in the face for mismatching. How dare I? "Ha!" I cackled. "You're so mean," I chimed at myself in the mirror across from me while smiling.

I couldn't believe that I felt downright chipper. A dose of the Baynes could do that to you. Saturate you with grins and tearful laughs. I could feel the excitement brewing in my stomach like I was going home. The buzz tore me away from my thought tangent.

"The phone number you are trying to reach is no longer in service," I droned.

Click.

"Ha!" Triumph.

Buzz.

"Shit." My head rolled back, "Yes, dear?" I asked forfeiting the small game I had invented.

"Okay. I look like shit. Let's go. Fuck my life." She ended the call and came bustling down the hallway past me.

I gripped the handle and jerked it hard from the top of my rolling suitcase and then glanced around, slowly making sure everything was off and where it was supposed to be.

I practically skipped down the stairs keeping in the spirit of my shining mood. I jogged over to her Jeep and pulled the door open happily. Shoving my stuff in the back, I climbed in while she trudged slowly gulping at her coffee to the driver's door.

"That is the last time I'm drinking when I have a butt- crack wake-up call," she grumbled.

"Bet you'll think twice. Butt crack?' I asked, slightly confused.

"I'm not finishing my sentences. You're already well- versed in my lingo, Harper. Keep up." She coughed, obviously still crawling through her field of hang-over.

"Sorry, I just thought you were hitting on me," I replied sarcastically.

"Ha ha blah…" She gave a fake laugh, trailing it away in a mocking and tired manner.

Her eyes constantly connected with the green clock on the dash as she sped. This girl could beat you to work daily but give her a wake-up call before noon on any Saturday and don't expect punctuality.

Getting up early on weekends went against nature, she would say. Saturdays were a day of rest and reflection, according to her. I didn't bother wasting my breath explaining her confusion about the holy day.

Babbling in my ear, August rehashed the night's events, unaware that my mind seemed to be preoccupied with other thoughts.

The misplaced man in the woods was wafting through my mind on a rerun wheel. The part that ate at my stomach the most was my sick infatuation with his attractiveness.

Even odder was the thought, *what if he never appeared again?* This was stupid. I was crushing on a man who I'd clearly hallucinated and was ignoring the fact that I was fabricating beautiful men in the mountains. There are thousands of rational explanations, I'm sure of it. I just couldn't think of any that wouldn't land me in a psychiatric ward.

* * *

Before I knew it, the pilot was giving us the temperature and local weather while I cracked my back.

August, on the other hand, didn't flinch. You probably could've set her out by the engine, and she would smack her jaws and rollover.

"August, we're here." I shook her. She mumbled incoherently at me.

"Hey. Listen here missy…" She trailed off.

I shook her again and looked up to notice that the sparse amount of people sprinkling the plane heard her vocal REM narration. I smiled politely and shook her harder.

"August, get up," I said through gritted teeth. She rolled off my shoulder.

Opening her eyes slowly, she wiped at the corners of her mouth while sitting upright in her seat.

"What the hell? We're here already? Was Superman pushing the plane? I fell asleep five minutes ago. Now I really look awful. Great. You know my brothers are going to say…" I couldn't hear her rant as she got up and moved forward in the aisle.

She minded none of the people surrounding her as she headed toward the exit. She just kept talking. I vaguely caught something about a rental car and baggage claim.

I followed behind with my backpack slung over a shoulder. The airport was bustling and seemed to come alive as planes arrived and people hurried up to wait near the baggage carousel.

I watched while anxious parents hugged their children and relatives waited with excited smiles. I never had that growing up. Someone who looked forward to me coming home for the holiday, so we could celebrate our favorite family tradition. Maybe one day.

* * *

After watching my best friend play tug- of- war with someone else's bag, a valiant fight to the bitter end I must say, we made our way through the airport to pick up the rental car and headed out.

Traveling with August— in a vehicle she's driving— is an adventure in and of itself. With her mind on the road she was excellent. Unfortunately, her mind was often darting off into multiple planes of the world. Multitasking behind the wheel was never a good idea for her. So, when she pulled out her cell phone after a few miles, I immediately braced myself for the *excitement* we were sure to encounter.

"I'm going to let Mom know we're on our way." She'd read my mind yet again. "It'll just take a second."

"Talking on a cell phone causes nearly twenty-five percent of car accidents" fell from my lips without a second thought.

"Not my accidents," she mumbled as she brought the receiver to her ear.

I laughed softly. I could hear the phone ringing and a muffled voice greeting her on the other end.

"Dad? What are you doing at home?" Her voice was laced with genuine surprise.

Jimmy Bayne was normally hard at work by sunrise, so for him to answer this late in the morning was an oddity.

"Oh, right. I'd forgotten about that. Well, let Mom know we're on the road. We just passed through Ever—" She paused as Jimmy's voice rose from the other end. "Yeah, I'm driving."

I could barely make out the words "dangerous" and "phone" in his rough timbre.

"Ugh, yes, I know all about the danger of cell phones while driving." Her eyes rolled lightheartedly. "You sound like Lily and Ethan. Alright. I'm putting it away. See you in a little while." Dropping the phone in the cup holder, she shook her head slowly. "I blame you."

I turned to gawk at her. "For what? *Your* accidents? How does that have anything to do with me at all?"

"No, for my father and his insane worry about the stupid phone. You're the one that showed him that damn article."

"It made sense at the time. You'd just had that close call on 25. I needed him as support against you." I wouldn't look at her as I said it. Knowing the impending reaction made me want to laugh.

"First of all, it was a near miss, not a *close call*."

"Same thing," I shot at her quickly.

"Secondly, you had Monroe on your side." She had blatantly ignored my comment. "Lastly, you weren't even with me when it happened! So you don't know the facts!" she screeched at me.

"But I have the video." My voice was soft and provoking.

"Lying damn reporters! Editing at its finest." Her hand flew up for a second to emphasize her distaste for the subject.

"They don't edit live broadcasts, August," I interjected.

I'm not sure why it seemed like a good idea to poke at August.

"If you don't stop the shit-talking about my driving, I'm dropping you off in the middle of nowhere so you can walk your happy ass to Maple Falls!"

Have you ever heard a weather siren? Listened to the pitch oscillate and tried to ignore the fluttering of worry in your stomach? Glanced out the nearest window to check the skies?

Her voice did the same thing at that moment. My empty stomach flip-flopped, and I scanned the horizon. Deep down, I knew she'd never actually do what she threatened, at least, not to the full extent. She would leave me stranded for a short time though. I did not doubt that.

"I was kidding. You're a great driver." My voice was confident, eyes focused and icy with calm. Completely obscuring the worry I felt inside.

"Yeah, you'd better be." My phone buzzed unexpectedly from my pocket.

"Tell him this is his last call! You're supposed to be Ethan-free this week." She jabbed her finger into the air.

I smiled as I answered the call. "I'm supposed to be free of you this week. Have you forgotten?"

"My love, I had to get one more call in to make sure you'd landed safely and that August was abiding by our safety agreement. Is she?" His tone was serious.

"Safety agreement? You're kidding, right?" I glanced at my best friend behind the wheel as she frantically moved her mouth in silence.

"What? Don't yell at Jim about the bone? What are you talking about?" I tried to read her lips.

"She was on the phone?" Ethan yelled on the other end of the line.

"Oh, great," August sighed.

"No. Ethan, stop. Everything's fine. She's being perfectly safe. You didn't really make a safety agreement, did you?" I couldn't get past the thought.

"Hell yes, I did. Made her sign it and everything. She's got my favorite part of life in her hands for the week. I expect you to be taken care of. She harms a hair on that little chestnut head of yours again and there'll be hell to pay."

I couldn't help but smile at his words.

***

I stood ten feet back on the flagstone sidewalk behind August. I could hear the noise pouring out from inside the small woodland farmhouse. I felt excited and nervous all at the same time.

She rapped on the wooden screen door and backstepped a few feet.

"Here goes." She exhaled hard and shrugged her shoulders into a strong stance. She turned and I smiled encouragingly.

The footsteps loudly clambered to the door. In the blink of an eye, a flood of burly yet boyish men rushed through the opening all at once. Sweeping past August, I had several arms wrapped around me lifting me off the ground a few inches.

"Lil!" A barrage of deep voices called my nickname. Whiskers brushed my cheeks, smothering them with kisses.

The Bayne boys. Trip and Tate were a set of twins with dirty blond hair and brown eyes, that were two halves of a whole. They were the troublemakers. The Frankenstein inventors of the wild Bayne games to keep their small-town life interesting. Their rap sheets with the local sheriff were tales of legend…or so I'd been told.

"I can't breathe," I managed to say.

Grey and Logan were the playboy twins. A pair of James Dean lookalikes that were tall and lanky. They had grins that could make anyone blush with their bright blue eyes and muddy-brown crowns. They were kings of flirt and could seek out any girl in a fifty-mile radius that needed a shoulder to cry on.

"Sorry!" some voices said in unison. My feet graced the ground, and they released the squeeze they had on my lungs.

"What the hell, guys?" August spouted behind them. "You don't even hug your sister?" she asked.

"We're just kidding, Auggie!" Logan soothed sarcastically. "Always pissy," he jabbed.

"Yeah, Auggie! Don't go crying," Grey chimed.

The four visible boys surrounded her and began drowning her in a familiar pool of hugs. August's mom smiled wide as she came down the steps with arms already extended. She smelled of lilac, cake batter, and lemongrass. I exhaled quietly, smiling.

"Lily, dear. So thin." She clicked her tongue disapprovingly.

"Hi, Nell," I replied warmly. "Your daughter runs me ragged."

She turned over her shoulder. "August Beau Bayne."

August gave a confused look. "What?"

"Hey there, Lily." Jimmy approached.

"I see the ATV is still up in the tree." I nodded in its direction.

"Well, I got it down twice." He paused. "They got it up there, so I figured this time they can get it down."

He smelled of pine and a sawdust mixture, and his hair was prematurely graying like his eyes.

They all felt affectionate, some mellow while others *spirited*.

"So Lil, Grey and I are heading to town to hit up a few bars after work. You still coming?" Logan called as he approached.

"Still?"

"Yeah Lil, you coming?" Grey cut off Logan while walking over to me. "Damn Lil. White is such a hot color on you. Not too many women can pull it off," he complimented poorly.

"Hey! I'm wearing white," August stated while looking down at her shirt.

Grey's eyes didn't break contact with mine. "Like I said…not too many girls can pull off that color," he finished with a wink.

August scoffed, arms crossed, at the bottom of the steps. She muttered incoherently as she bent over and started to gather her luggage.

Logan shoved his brother aside and slung an arm around my shoulder. "Listen, Lil. Ignore Grey. He spawned from the definition *pretty but stupid*. You're an intelligent woman with demanding needs. Needs that I feel I could fulfill." He shot me a weak pick-up line.

"Logan, are you implying that I'm high- maintenance?" I asked, raising one brow.

"Hey, Lily," a casual voice coolly called. There he was. Sandy blond hair cut short with the perfect wavy cowlick, sienna brown eyes that warmed you, and a cocky crooked smile. He walked by with ease. Tall and lean curves were accentuated by a simple gray T-shirt and faded blue jeans. Heavy boots said he was ready for the day. His skin was bronzed.

"Hi, Jarrett," I said softly. I instantly felt my cheeks burn pink.

"Jarrett always gets the girl," Logan murmured.

"Who are you kidding? I almost had her, killjoy," Grey retorted.

"Bull!" Logan grabbed his brother and swung him into a headlock. Knocking Logan sideways to the grass, he and Grey began wrestling. Trip and Tate took one look at each other, shrugged, realizing their opportunity, and spied me with a predatory look.

"Don't look directly at them. It's like fuel for them." I smiled at the sound of Bennett's voice coming down the steps.

Despite the fact that Bennett was the youngest of all the boys, he was the largest. Burly biceps crept out of his cropped sleeves and his thighs resembled the tree trunks that he scaled day to day. He reminded me of Jimmy and Jarrett the most, so naturally, I felt comfortable hiding behind him. He had soft chestnut eyes and a short buzz cut. He could be intimidating if you didn't know his gentle persona though, with a thick neck and deep voice.

Nell swatted at the boys, her apron blowing wildly in the wind of the battle. I caught sight of Jarrett walking towards the big red shop past the mess of cars and trucks crammed in the long driveway.

I automatically tuned it all out.

August shoved past them all.

Jarrett and Jimmy called across the yard in commanding voices. Jarrett lifted a hand and waved lightly.

Words caught in my throat and all I could manage was a feeble wave and half smile. Instantly, I dropped my hand catching the sight of Nell waving in my peripheral vision. He was waving at *her*.

I stood there with my feet locked to the ground, mortified. I haven't even been here twenty minutes and already I've embarrassed myself.

The boys got up off the grass and jogged in the direction of the waiting vehicles. They all kissed their mother standing on the lowest step. Bennett brought up the rear slowly.

"C'mon, Bennett!" Trip and Tate called back. Slapping and punching as they disappeared.

"Alright, Lily. Let's get you settled in for the week." She smiled, warming my shoulders with a mothering arm. I managed up the stairs with the luggage, desperate to find a hole to hide in.

***

"Lily?" I felt a warm and soft hand nudge my shoulder gently. "Lily, dinner's ready." I wiggled my shoulder and turned away.

"Too tired, more sleep," I managed to say. I could see through my lids it was dark outside.

A low chuckle gently shook the bed. My eyes snapped open at the sound. I didn't move. No. The boys are not home already, and I did not fall asleep. Maybe if I didn't move, he wouldn't be able to see me.

"She made lasagna. It smells really good. Do you think you could get up? Because she said none of us can eat until our guest joins us."

I felt Jarrett lean back and start humming. It sounded sweet and I realized I was smiling.

"Go away," I said firmly.

"Can't. I'm hungry and you can't be left unprotected. It was going to be me or Tate and Trip that came to get you and you don't want those two waking you up," he joked calmly.

"Not hungry," I said into my pillow. *My face has fold imprints on it, and you can't see me,* I thought to myself. "You're not that hungry, are you?"

"Yep," he said. I didn't have to see him to know that he was smiling.

I peeked through the strands of hair still trying to hide my face in the pillow. He was leaning back looking at the ceiling, arms behind his head. Legs crossed at the ankle, a crooked smile playing on the edges of his light pink lips.

He looked at me. "So? Are you going to do this the hard way or *my* way?" he asked playfully.

I didn't move. I was staying put. He wasn't supposed to see me like this. I was supposed to have a cute ponytail and nice eyeliner.

Yells broke the small silence between us, "Lily Harper come out, come out from wherever you are," Tate and Trip called up the stairs in unison.

"They're really hungry. I wouldn't risk it. Because I'm betting they're serious. And the two of them would win," he leaned in and whispered.

Footsteps echoed on the stairs. "Lil, I'm not a fan of cold lasagna!" Trip called.

"Me either, Lil!" Tate added.

"They're getting closer." He said the final word slowly.

"They can't force me." I felt mortified. I had lain down on the doughy flannel sheets earlier and drifted off next to my suitcase and backpack.

"Trip called your feet and Tate yelled 'got the head' before I volunteered my less forceful method. But I'm really starting to get hungry," he said teasingly.

"Nope. Not doing it," I said, standing my ground. I probably smelled like airplane pretzels and had bedhead.

They reached the landing and began marching, echoing the song the flying monkeys sang from *The Wizard of Oz*.

"We're hungry, my pretty," they called down the hallway.

Determination washed over me. "Call off your hounds."

"I'm sorry, Lily, but they're already committed." He laughed, feigning helplessness, raising both palms.

They quickly crowded the doorway. Moving slowly in almost a

crouch towards me they edged around the bed.

Jarrett eased off with a wide grin spreading across his face.

I scooted quickly to the center of the bed not minding at this point how I looked to anyone and flipped over. My fingers clenched the sheets with a vice-like grip. I could feel a laugh trembling inside my stomach. This was war.

"Looks like we got a kicker, Tater Tot," Trip called across the bed.

My legs jolted for the chance at freedom. I faked left by Trip. As I was about to pass through the only exit an arm caught around my waist forcefully pulling me backward. Within seconds, a firm grasp gripped both my wrists and held tightly on my arms.

"Oh no, you don't," Jarrett said.

In one swift motion, he lifted me, slinging me over his shoulder.

Crossing my arms, I said, "Jarrett Ichabod Bayne, put me down!" with as much serious force I could muster.

"It's Patrick and now that you're making fun of the Bayne names, definitely no," he said, chuckling, as the twins lopped behind him like laughing idiots.

"Don't you know women are always right, J.P.?" I asked.

"J.P.—" he started but his questioning was cut off.

"Put her down!" Nell commanded as she swatted at the boys who were carrying me through the kitchen. A wave of laughter rippled through the family casually hanging around the room. Trip and Tate listened but Jarrett ignored her until I was placed neatly on a lightly cushioned chair at the handcrafted wooden table.

"Humph," I said with an irritated huff. I firmly grabbed my ponytail and tightened it. "So lasagna?" I asked. "Sounds delicious, Nell," I finished laying one of the cloth napkins across my lap.

Everyone gathered around the table. August sat down to my left and not surprisingly, Grey took up the chair to my right. Jarrett eased down directly across from me.

August leaned in nudging my shoulder. "What was that about?" she asked.

"I don't know what you're talking about," I said calmly.

"You're flirting your ass off with my brother. That's what I'm talking about," she murmured teasingly. "Knew you still liked him."

"Your brothers basically kidnapped me and now I am sitting at the dinner table with bed hair and sweatpants," I retorted.

"Psh. That was a game of slap- and- tickle if I ever saw one," she scoffed under her breath at me.

I rolled my eyes and didn't continue the conversation with her. The smells of the kitchen saturated my lungs, overwhelming my palette. My mother never cooked like this at home. I never resented her for it either. It was too difficult for her to play family without my father there joining us.

My attention stirred beside me. "So, Lil, you're still coming with us tonight, right?" Grey asked seductively.

"Hell no!" I said too quickly. "I mean, I'm not a big drinker," I explained.

"Roll, Lil?" Bennett interrupted, kitty-corner from me. "Mom made them from scratch." He nudged the basket with his knuckles.

"Thanks, Bennett." I smiled politely at the subject change and plucked one from the pile.

"Benny, quit flirting. She's August's age. Don't you think she's a little old for you?" Grey asked.

Poor Bennett was always the butt of the boys' ridicule. Although August was born last among her siblings, Bennett was the youngest of the boys, placing a suffering hand upon his shoulders. They would often remind him to mind his "big sister." His usual response was a frustrated sigh.

Grey quickly turned his attention back to me and pulled up a crooked smile. "Lil, don't be worried. I'll protect you from yourself," he continued. "I would never let you be embarrassed or anything but the classy woman I see you as," he said while a gentle finger reached up to brush my loose bangs aside.

I rolled my eyes. "Grey. I'm kind of…not really available right now," I poorly explained.

A spark caught his eye. "Are you seeing someone back in Fort City?" he asked, slightly concerned.

That's when I noticed Jarrett's head lift slightly, perking his ears. Jarrett was listening for my answer. I repressed a smile and my fingers felt fuzzy. I set my fork down and attempted not to show my hand. I wasn't imagining his excited anticipation, was I?

"It's Collins. Ass! "August chimed, reaching around me to whack him in the back of the skull.

I carefully calibrated my answer. "There's no one in particular, but that doesn't mean I haven't noticed anyone." I kept my head tilted down towards my plate but watched through the strands of hair hiding my face to catch his reaction. He smiled warmly while he looked down intently at his food.

Was he smiling because the thought amused him or because he was truly interested in what he was hearing? I couldn't be sure. But I was hesitant to test the waters.

I'd had a crush on Jarrett since the first time I visited August. I was her quiet friend, and he was her charming older brother. I vowed never to act on the impulses, but every visit seemed to get harder and harder.

"Who you noticing, baby girl?" Tate called from one end.

"Boys, leave her alone. She is not a toy." Nell promptly turned to me in an attempt to change the conversation. "So how is the research going, Lily?" she asked as though she were truly interested.

"Well, Nell, it's moving along."

"That is so great," she said, not sure of what to ask next.

Jimmy interrupted with questions to some of the boys about work tomorrow. Conversation broke out around the table ending the spotlight interviews I was being forced to endure.

Dinner ended slowly while people moved from the kitchen. I stood alone, with Nell as my company, carrying dishes.

"You leave them, Lily. I'll take care of that," she stated.

"I don't mind. Really," I said with a warm smile.

"Nope, get yourself outside and enjoy the swing Jim fixed." She laughed lovingly at the thought of her husband's help, nudging my shoulder while we stood at the sink.

"Go now." She shooed at me.

I paused for a moment as she flitted with her hands while I walked to the door. August had gone up to bed. Grey and Logan were becoming "man pretty." Their words, not mine. Trip and Tate were out in one of the barn sheds that had been renovated into a loft and Jimmy had taken a stealthy walk to avoid more of the crowd. I assumed Jarrett had turned in for the night.

I pushed the screen door open to the porch and welcomed the cool night breeze on my cheeks. I strode to the wooden swing that hung from the thick beams and began gliding back and forth.

The mist that spun and swirled in the night air was mysterious. It was like dreaming while being awake. I closed my eyes for a long while.

The screen door edged open, and Nell crept out eventually. "Did I catch you off guard?" she said, witnessing my alert response in body posture.

"No, I was taking in the place," I said. She wasn't wearing her usual apron. Her bare feet caressed the wood of the heavy porch as she approached.

"Do you mind if I join you?" she asked although she was already beginning to sit.

"Not in the least," I said, inching over to make room.

She exhaled, closing her eyes and becoming lost in the world that was veiled in the fog. For several minutes she said nothing, and we enjoyed it together.

"Have you talked to her lately?" Her soft voice broke the thick air.

I wasn't surprised that she had waited that long to bring her up. After all, it had been an entire day.

6

My Hero

I paused, unsure of where to go next with the conversation. I stepped cautiously as my lips began to form words. "Nell, it's difficult. A woman who sends money for Christmas and no card or call isn't someone you chat with daily," I replied.

"Lily, every situation needs someone to go first, and it can't always be expected of the other person," she said quietly.

"I called her on *my* birthday last year, but she said she was late for something at the museum," I retorted coldly.

She and I said nothing. It didn't surprise me that she spoke to her frequently. Nell had no problem doing what she felt was giving a helping hand. I understood that she meant well. Yet it still frustrated me thinking about it.

"We're working really hard right now. That means a lot of long hours," I explained.

"Folks are only that busy when they have something to say but don't want to bring it up." She rubbed her wrist habitually, which pained her over the years. I think it became a calming motion for her.

"Do we have to talk about her every time I come here?" I asked, slightly exasperated.

"She loves you. Maybe not the traditional way you thought she should, but she did the best she could. Bottom line, Lily, we don't get to pick our parents and she's your mother," she stated.

"Keyword: *mother*. She's not a parent or mom. You're a mom. She quit after Dad died. She was a shell of her former self. That's bullshit. I was still here, Nell. I suffered as much as she did. It was my loss too. I couldn't help that I resembled him. I didn't force her to cry every time she looked at my face. Do you know what it's like to look in the mirror and see the memory of someone in your own face?" I shot coldly as blood surged violently in my veins. Anger had started to become apparent on my face.

"Shh, it's okay." She began speaking to me with kid gloves. Leaning over and wrapping her arms around me lovingly. I was trembling slightly from the overwhelming anger. I could never explain to people the dislike for a woman I was obligated by nature to love.

She'd done everything necessary to provide for the two of us. But when Dad died, she went with him. Not a piece of her, all of her. The thought of moving on to someone else was an outrageous suggestion that simply didn't exist for her. I couldn't imagine loving a person so completely that without them, you would cease to be you.

"Let's not talk about it anymore. I really didn't mean to upset you, sweetheart," she soothed.

"I'm going to take a walk, Nell. I'm sorry," I explained, adding a tender smile. I was already backing my way down the steps to escape the situation.

I set a quick pace across the yard towards the trees. I could feel their comforting limbs outstretched like arms inviting me into their loving shadows. The brume caressed me and recklessly churned in my wake. If it were capable, I'm sure it would have parted ways for me.

Twigs cracked under my feet as I reached the edge telling me I was close. A distant soft whimper resounded through the dim light. It pulled me from my irritable trance.

I slowed down and turned toward the sound. Claws scratching wood followed the spotty cries.

Sitting at the back door to the twins' man pad, which was a garage remodeled as a guest house after Jarrett moved into the cabin on the back half of the property, was Copper, the twins' springer spaniel.

He turned, spotting me, and leaned into the door, wagging his tail impishly. As though he were caught doing something wrong and didn't know anything more to do than wave. I gently held out my hand and spoke in soft tones, allowing him to sniff.

"Hey, boy, you need to get inside?" I asked the black- and- white spotted spaniel. It was funny how people always talked to dogs and paid no mind that they wouldn't answer back. I always thought it was because, deep down, you hoped that they knew what you were saying. Something that could be so much like family couldn't co-exist in a world of unknown language.

"Alright, I don't know where your idiotic masters are, but I'll let you in," I said as I turned the knob and laid a calming hand on the dog's head, more for me than him. I navigated around the vehicles parked neatly in the puzzle of machinery and headed towards the door. In large red letters a crude sign was painted:

No Girls Allowed

I rolled my eyes and smiled at their immature comedic entertainment. I pushed the door open and laughter erupted while Copper shoved past me and ran across the shag carpet, leaping over the arm of the couch and rammed into Tate's side.

"Hey, boy! Who let you in? I thought you were out enjoying the evening, looking for the ladies," he spoke to the dog as he ruffled his ears.

My clothes devoured the unexpected murky haze of potent marijuana as I began to retreat my way back outside. When I was ten feet into the yard, hysterical laughter erupted and someone yelled.

"Gardetto's!"

I rolled my eyes and kept walking away, heading back towards the house, an apology already ebbing in my stomach.

A loud continuous banging rang out ahead of me, and Nell's voice reached me through the open windows.

"No! You boys stay on this side of the border. And for Pete's sake, don't bring any girls here," she shouted.

"Mom, we don't like pooping in our own cage," Logan explained. I could hear the smile in his voice.

"Do not compare girls to fecal matter!" she yelled.

"He wasn't. He was comparing sex to crap," Grey laughed.

"Oh, gracious, you two have your own place! Take the poor things there!" she scolded.

I watched as the screen door swung open. The boys were quickly backing down the porch steps, their mother's dish towel corralling them closer to their vehicle.

Grey and Logan raised their hands in surrender. They both wore polo shirts and bootcut jeans. Their boots untied at their feet, dark brown hair unkempt crowning their heads.

"This isn't your bachelor pad. And stop telling girls you own this house!" she insisted heatedly.

Logan attempted a subject change. "Where's Lil? We were going to bring her with us," he asked, turning to scan the yard.

Crap! Freeze!

"Leave her alone, you two!" She swatted.

I spotted the yard shed and ran to dart behind it. I twisted, pressing my back against the wooden planks, willing to achieve chameleon camouflaging.

A warm hand caught my wrist and started to tug me deeper into the shadows. I turned and was about to yelp when I saw who my kidnapper was.

Jarrett crept with a finger pressed to his lips.

I smiled and took my place beside him. He had his back to the wall. Our shoulders connected in silence.

After a moment, footsteps thudded hard and the boys jogged past, heading straight towards a large black pickup.

Jarrett grabbed me and pulled me around behind the shed. Holding a tall stance directly in front of me, my heart sounded like an anxious thunderstorm caged in my ribs.

His palms pressed against the wall on either side of my head. He leaned close to my ear and whispered, "Wait a second or they'll see you."

The truck rumbled to life and the headlights spotted the place we'd been standing moments earlier. They faded and eventually took the playboy twins and loud music with them.

His head poked around the corner and grinned. "You're safe," he said. But he didn't move. To be honest I didn't really want him to.

I gathered my thoughts. "Um, Jarrett, they're gone." I drew his attention.

He was staring at me. "Come with me," he spoke quietly.

He turned and was walking away before I could even answer him. I stepped quickly to follow at his heels. Surprisingly, I could smell his scent that trailed him. I smiled idiotically as I strayed. A shock riveted my chest when it hit me where our destination was.

He climbed the steps to his small cabin set in the far end of the backyard past a few of the trees. He pushed the screen door open and flicked the light switch as he strode through the front door.

I wasn't moving, just standing at the bottom of the steps. He turned and looked at me. "Are you coming or do you have to be invited in? Oh God, you're not a vampire, are you? Dead girls creep me out." He suppressed a smile.

I laughed but still stood there. My feet felt locked to the grass. He was so good- looking I was afraid I would throw up.

* * *

I'll never forget the first summer I came to the Bayne's farm. The porch creaked as we stepped away from the house's screen door and I looked around the yard. Various vehicles lined the edges of the driveway, tucked carelessly between the wooded boulevard and the wide gravel pathway.

"As you can see, their parking skills are shit." August nodded in abject appreciation at the four-wheeler in the high limbs of a tree outside the house.

"It's out of the way up there, I guess?" I nodded as I said it.

"They do it to keep it away from Bennett."

I smiled as she leads the tour. Her manicured fingers pointed out a couple of looming workshops and a few smaller outbuildings that peppered the yard. A classic monitor barn, although showing its age in the discolored wood, it was in good shape as far as I could see.

"Tate and Trip turned that Quonset into their place a while back, so they won't bother us the whole time we're here. Hopefully." She was practically skipping through the grass, successfully dodging divots that I stumbled to avoid.

"Sorry about the yard there. A few years ago, Tate and Trip convinced Grey and Logan there were geodes out here. They dug for weeks to find crystals to give to girls at school. It was during their twin wars."

"Twin wars?"

"Yeah, that's where they got the idea to dig the pool that summer. The whole yard stunk!"

"They're all twins, right?" I asked as her informational rambling stopped.

"Two of them, yeah."

I huffed as my worried eyes tried to keep up with her pointing and take in the beauty pulling at my attention. Thick moss blanketed most of the buildings I could see, and the graying of the cedar wood was stunning.

"Jarrett's cabin is down that little path. He's been building it since he was seventeen though. He put a shower outside and it doesn't even have a hot tub." She shook her head as we continued around the corner of the house.

"He's the…" I paused trying to recall the order of birth she'd told me.

A low tenor voice surprised me as it swept in from somewhere around us. "Oldest and Mom's favorite."

"I'm the favorite and you know it." August led us over to a couple of parked trucks, where the hood stood open on one of them.

"Favorite girl maybe." A grease-stained cap slipped out from beneath the hood and the guy wearing it stopped me abruptly in my tracks.

He had the warmest sienna eyes with hair to match. They looked like the silt of a creek bed on a summer afternoon that I wanted to swim in. His jaw added to his boyish charm, but his russet whiskers gave way to a rakish appearance. Sparse freckles dotted the edges of his down turned lips. He had a lean build that towered over August.

He hastily wiped his hands over his thighs and stepped forward. His well-worn flannel hung open, and a glimpse of V-shaped hips cropped up over the top of his belt line.

"Hi, I'm Jarrett." His smile pulled a distinctly teenage giggle out of me.

I blurted out a hello in order to cover the embarrassing outburst I hoped he hadn't heard. Feeling my ankle roll as I leaned toward the outstretched hand. His hand was rough in mine as I toppled toward him, and he steadied me using my bicep. I cringed as August laughed loudly.

"That did not just happen," I whispered as my eyes closed.

"It did though." August laughed merrily.

Taking a deep breath to calm my racing heart, absolute perfection of manhood in front of me, I was bathed in the scent of him. Boys in Vermont had not prepared me for this.

He smelled of vetiver and was rugged, like sex on legs.

I was doomed.

"You alright there?"

"Ugh, she's fine, Jarrett. Quit sweating all over my friend!" August scoffed.

"Yeah, fine," I replied as she pulled me away by my sleeve.

I didn't look back over my shoulder as August continued her "unique" tour, but I could feel his gaze following me as August and I crossed into the tree line.

* * *

"Hello?" he called. "You okay, Lily?" he asked, becoming worried because I hadn't moved.

I blinked. "Yeah, fine." I had never been in Jarrett's cabin before. I had known the Baynes for six years and never once stepped foot in his place since he moved into it two summers ago. I exhaled and timidly made my way through the front door.

The cabin was simple but held a manly, yet elegant taste. Walnut wood floors spread from one end to the other. French doors were at every entrance, to the small kitchen that faced off to my left and the bedroom to my right. Straight back was a beautifully decorated bathroom. Dark blues accentuated the comfortable deep taupe sectional that filled the room. Everything that could be handmade was. Nell's paintings hung from the walls around the entire place. It smelled of him and instantly felt like home.

I was still standing there silent when he interjected.

"You like it?" he asked.

"Yes, it's beautiful. Nell really has an eye for some things."

"Mom? No. I did this. Finished the floors after Christmas," he replied smugly.

"What website did you rip this off from?" I joked.

"I know what I like." His tone turned serious.

I ran my hand along the back of the couch, bravery brimming in my throat. "*What* you like or *who* you like?"

"Both." His voice was coolly confident.

"Lucky girl," I quietly stated.

"She doesn't know yet." He stared directly at me.

Stupid. This is August's brother. Her brother! Why do you do this every time you're here?

He was moving away from me and ducked into the bedroom quickly. "So I was thinking for your sanity and the sake of privacy I'm offering you this." He casually threw a hand up.

"Your couch?" I couldn't breathe. Him and I… alone, in this three-room, tucked away in the woods cabin, away from prying ears.

"No," he laughed. "My bed. I'll sleep in the house so you can have this place to yourself. It's clean, bathroom and all."

"Oh, I couldn't do that. Kick you out of your house just to avoid mild harassment," I told him.

"I wasn't asking." He smiled wide. "Get comfortable. Remote's on the coffee table. I'll go get your things." He had turned and was out the door heading towards the house without another word.

"Apparently this wasn't up for negotiation," I spoke aloud to myself, and wandered to the bathroom. One thing on my mind— finally a shower.

7

Don't Break Lily

Walking to the house, I took in the scents that surrounded me—conifers, moss, and cherry blossoms. My lungs feasted on the large array of airy tastes. The sun edged mildly through the thin coating of clouds but nothing worth wearing sunglasses for. As I got closer, I began hoping that I might be lucky enough to snag some coffee before we headed to some Bayne-influenced adventure.

I still wasn't sure what today's—or even this week's plans were—but I did my best to maintain an optimistic attitude. Surprisingly enough, I could still recall my first sprained ankle from Bayne bungee jumping. Which was, basically, homemade bungee jumping out of trees off a platform, but kind of blended with hot potato.

I shook a little at the thought and wiped it from my memories. The Bayne boys were no joke. The winter I came for Thanksgiving, they invited me to play a fun-loving game of *touch* football. Well, never again. That's what happens with six raucous boys in a town of 322 people. You get creative.

The small kitchen light shone above the sink. A dark figure hovered over the countertops. I discovered I was wishing Jarrett standing tall and alone, crowding the kitchen with his overwhelming presence. I automatically drifted to daydreams of him and me alone walking through the woods, smiling, laughing uninterrupted.

I flowed up the steps, my heart pattering harder as I walked with a purposeful hope clamming up my palms of conversation with him. A playful smile tickled the corners of my lips. I pressed nervous fingertips to the screen and glided through.

Dark coffee scents evaporated my thoughts and my motives slightly altered.

"Mornin', Lily." A warm smile greeted me.

"Good morning, Jimmy." I smiled, semi-disappointed.

"Ah, not the face you were hoping for." He sipped his coffee, the smile never fading. "Still sweet on the boy, huh?" he asked rhetorically.

"No," I replied too quickly. "Just August. I was hoping that I would be able to talk to her without the spectators commenting."

"Hmm." He hummed in understanding, aware that he had been right but felt no need to press the matter. That's why I liked Jimmy. He reminded me of my dad in so many ways. A quiet and calm person whose feathers were rarely ruffled.

"Thanks" was all I could muster. "So we're the first ones to get the worm I see?"

He handed me a mug filled with steaming coffee. "Nope. Boys went out to get the trucks ready. We're headed up the mountain," he spoke softly as he leaned casually next to me with his back to the countertops.

"Mountain?" I sipped curiously.

"Yep, August and the boys insisted the tree doc gets to watch how the loggers sling a chain. They've always wanted you to come along." He turned and placed his empty cup in the sink. "I told 'em you could come as long as they behave." He smiled, smacked his lips, and turned to sit in the chair.

"Behave? Jimmy, when have those guys ever behaved?" I asked as I watched him lace up the boots.

A loud motor started to echo out front. "Boys are back." He slapped his thighs and stood heading towards the door. "Better get a move on if we want to get home before the sun sets." He was outside pushing through the door, turning to spit sideways mid-stride before I responded.

I sipped my coffee nervously. It's their job. They can't possibly warp this into something. They have to take this seriously, right?

I set my mug down and followed suit. August met me halfway across the porch and thrust a pair of work boots into my chest similar to my own that I used back home. A grin gripped her cheeks.

"Alright, Harper, are you excited? This used to be me before you!" she exclaimed. She had been begging me for years for this. I vehemently refused after discovering the boys' predilection for all things adrenaline-infused.

"Pumped." I pulled up a sideways sarcastic smile.

"Ah, Lil, you're my friend. I won't kill you. I don't love you enough to do hard time for you." She patted me on the shoulder reassuringly. "I've been asking Dad if you could do a day with us for years!"

"Ah, August, I wouldn't do time for you either." I smiled and leaned in, shouldering her.

"Alright, girls, time to go," a smooth voice called up to us.

I looked over the railing of the porch to catch sight of Jarrett before he turned, a warm smile filling his entire face. My eye contact was quick but enough to fill my stomach to the brim with nervous liquid.

"Lil, you can ride with Bennett, August, and me in my truck," he spoke back to us without turning. My chest began to waver rapidly, but I ignored it. I noticed August was watching me out of the corner of her eye. She didn't say anything, only smiled caustically. I rolled mine at her and kept up with the crowd to avoid conversation.

* * *

Riding in Jarrett's truck was quiet. Jarrett and Bennett held a small conversation on the way there about some upcoming game this week. They never mentioned anything more, so I wasn't able to ask inquisitive questions. I didn't want to stammer through an entire conversation, so I smiled politely and remained quiet.

I watched out the window as the dense forest turned and twisted. I was naming some of the rarer trees I could spot in my head.

"Alright, Lily, we're here. Grey and Logan got ahead of us, so they probably already have your gear. They were up and raring to go awfully early today." He turned with a shrug of his shoulders.

"Damn it!" August spat, opening the door to exit.

"What's wrong?" I quickly asked.

"Damn sons o' bitches are getting ready for *log tag!*" she spoke back quickly, closing the door behind her before I could get another question in.

I slowly made my way from the vehicle and chanted internally, "Jimmy said they had to behave. He said it, so that means they have to listen! Don't they?"

"Lil, get over here. We have your gear!" Logan piped. The trouble quad was standing alongside a rig next to a tailgate getting ready, similar to how August and I do most mornings. The four of them were in a suspicious line all facing me, wide smiles cracking through all their faces.

I walked up slowly. Hoping by the grace of humanity that my jeans and T-shirt would be insufficient and I would have to go back to the cozy forest farm and listen to Nell's sweet hums and conversation about people I had never heard of all day.

"Pop said we have to maintain an easygoing profile with you today,"

Logan said with hands behind his back. I'm sure this had something to do with the incident at the winter bonfire roasting marshmallows that had turned into a game of capture the flag which broke my pinky toe.

"Yeah, kid gloves, you know," Tate followed.

"Play nice," Bennett chimed as he walked by. "You guys can never water things down when we have company." He was almost out of earshot when he finished with, "I bet that's why Lil's the only girl that Aug ever brings home with her."

Jarrett nodded, walking next to him.

My eyes were following him faithfully against my will. His head was down, and he kicked through the dirt in the sexiest manner. I did my best not to stare.

"So we decided to be careful with the glass version of Lil today by taking extra precautions," Grey piped.

Logan swung his hands out from behind his back. "We got you a hard hat like ours, but we made it brighter to make sure that everyone can see you, Lil."

My mouth hung slightly agape at the shoddily spray-painted hat. "Hot pink," I said, unsure of how to reply. "It's so…bright." Bright was the only compliment I could muster.

He placed it on my head, smiling wide. "Wow, that's perfect . You can definitely see you. But that's not everything." He turned to Tate. "Go ahead, Tate. Put it on her."

A poor tie-dye catastrophe of hot pink and neon green colored the mesh vest I was gracefully pushing my arms through.

"We thought you would like these colors, being they're kind of girly and all." Grey beamed.

I looked to August for help, but words were apparently failing her at this moment. She was suppressing laughter, tears in her eyes.

They looked on in wait for some response of gratitude.

I looked down. "So…pretty." I swallowed hard.

"Knew she'd like it!" Trip called out, punching his brother as Logan clapped his hands together. I sighed in relief. That wasn't so bad.

"Thanks, boys." I smiled.

"Nah, Harper, that's not everything!" Trip's face radiated excitement.

I immediately looked to August again for help. "No, Lily, that's not everything," August replied, giggling and nodding.

"Yeah, Dad said that since we broke your wrist last summer with the whole lawn dart triathlon we're not allowed to hurt you this vacation. I mean, you're a special person to us—" Trip was interrupted by Logan.

"A way hot special person that we want to make out with. Go ahead, Trippy." Logan ushered with his palm face up in an encouraging motion.

"And we don't want to break you because, like Logan said, some of us would like to make out with—not me though. I mean, I'm a gentleman with heart. I care, Lil." He placed his hand over his chest and smiled warmly edging towards me. "I'm not like those other brothers. I'm a giver. Like today, I gave you a safe skull." He gently patted my head. "Brains are important. I like your brain…a lot," he finished, turning and winking at the others. "Girls like when you compliment their minds." He tapped his temple.

"Thanks." I took a step back. "I…like my brain too."

August grabbed my arm and started dragging me towards where Bennett and Jarrett were getting ready. All efforts to stop the staring at Jarrett failed me now. He had a tool belt gripping his hips and he was pushing his arms through a neon mesh vest. He was squinting in the direction of the rising sun and rolling up the sleeves of his button-up shirt. Then he rubbed his hands the length of his thighs using the washed-out faded denim like a rag. A wrinkled plain white handkerchief hung loosely from a back pocket.

I inadvertently bit my lower lip as I couldn't help but notice the glow of appeal radiating at me.

He rubbed his cheek and chin with his left hand, his fingers pushing against the whiskers in thought. He tilted back and sighed. I was tempted beyond belief to ask him what stressed him.

"Is it my back? They put something on my vest, didn't they?" He was beginning to take it off.

"What? No. I was just thinking." *About making out with you.* I finished the thought in my head. "I didn't mean to stare. I do that a lot." I looked down, ashamed of my apparent gawking.

"When do you *ever* stare?" August belted. "You almost never make eye contact with anyone unless you're pissed."

"I do too. I stare a lot," I meekly added.

"Like when? You wouldn't even look at the eye doctor that time you fell from the oak when we worked down in Georgia and they needed to check your pupils," she retorted.

"August, shut up," I mumbled sideways at her. "You're just too busy being self-absorbed to notice anyone but you."

I glanced up to see that Jarrett was still watching me, smiling, as he had last night over dinner. Two times. Was this a coincidence?

"You can stare at him all you want. I'm not against you two being in love," August blurted.

"In love? You just want a day off," Jarrett corrected.

"Yeah right, don't act like you haven't been asking if I was bringing her." August puffed out her chest and scrunched up her face. *"Hey, August, so, um"*— she kicked the dirt and kept looking at her feet —*"you think Lily might head this way when you come? Hey, August, do you think Lily might like it if I asked her to go hiking?"* She exhaled and relaxed from her mocking tone. "Don't act all *whatever.* You asked about her for the last three weeks," she finished as she walked away.

I decided to avoid the situation altogether and began to follow her again. If I hadn't wished I was home yet, the moment had arrived. I did my best to shield the obvious blushing that was burning through my cheeks. You could always count on August Bayne to tell you what everyone else was thinking, even if it cost you.

I exhaled and reminded myself that it could be worse. Somehow with this family it could always be something worse. Their creative outlet survived from lack of populace. Grey came up behind me and slapped me on the back of the shoulder. Tate came up on my opposing side both still smiling idiotically.

"Grey and Logan were thinking last night, and they came up with so much to aid you today," Tate explained.

"Yeah, we figured that we needed to make you as safe as we could, so Jimmy doesn't scalp us. So, after we left the bar and made out with our chicks goodbye, we got to thinking. Which is the best time to think because—" Grey was explaining when Logan came up and chimed in.

"Because we're at our best when we have a few beers under our belt." He smiled and nodded.

"Right. So we decided that we couldn't just do a vest and call it a night. We needed to make your experience super memorable." He grinned wide.

"Ta-da!" The boys spread their arms showcasing their doings.

"A lawn chair?" I asked, confused.

"Well, you can't be near a chainsaw because that would be dangerous. So this is the keep- Lil- safe zone." Grey ushered me closer with his hand. "Stand here. We'll get the rest." He walked over to another truck that was sitting next to a massive piece of machinery that I hadn't a clue the purpose it served.

I looked over to see that Jarrett was watching what I was unwillingly adhering to. I tried not to think about what had happened minutes before. I turned and paid attention to Logan, who was now on the ground rummaging through a bag similar to what hockey players tote everywhere on their backs. I tried to catch another glimpse of Jarrett slyly but was quickly interrupted.

"So today we are going to be playing log tag and we'll need a ref. Usually one of us does it." Logan gestured to himself and brothers.

"But he ends up cheating and giving points to himself when he ends up losing as usual," Bennett called.

"Benny needs to be burped. He's already crabby." Logan nudged Trip.

"He's just pissy because I put him down without his pacifier last night," Trip replied without missing a beat.

I smiled at Bennett sympathetically although the others hadn't turned.

"We could see who the losers were last time we played," Bennett snorted.

"Anyways, we got you this stuff to protect you. Guys?" Logan motioned to the others as he pulled the large bag up to my feet.

Before I could understand what they were doing, my arms were out to my sides and Tate was kneeling on the ground wrapping something tightly around my knees and shins. I watched as they strapped skateboard pads to my wrists, elbows, and knees. Then they duct-taped shin guards to my shins. When Tate pulled the next item out, I jumped back.

"Whoa, no! I'm not wearing a cup and you are absolutely not putting it down my pants. Sorry guys, that's enough," I demanded.

"Okay, but your parts are important. We tried to figure out how to make bubble wrap work, but we thought that you would get too hot," Logan said in defense. "But you do have to wear this." He held up a mouth guard.

"Are you serious? For what?" I asked skeptically.

"You have very pretty teeth. I like your teeth. I want to keep them safe." Grey turned and grinned. "They also like when you compliment their teeth," he finished, winking to his brother.

"Thanks, Grey. I brush them frequently." I smiled. They were competitively complimenting me. Maybe this day wouldn't be so bad.

I sat back from the job site in the lawn chair, and they pulled out large cans of bright spray paint.

"What are those for?" I asked exasperatedly.

"People need to see you," Trip explained, shaking up his can of yellow.

They began drawing large circles out around the chair and an odd design of arrows pointing away from me. Finally they boxed in the whole masterpiece and wrote in large letters.

Stay back! Don't break Lily!

"Is this all really necessary?" I questioned with a slight groan.

"Don't worry, we promise to make this fun for you," they explained.

"Today we are going to be playing log tag and you will get to be our ref. So for once, this game might actually be fair. Our goal is to cut down as many as possible while still having fun." Logan was starting to pull the last remaining items out of the bag. "You'll need this." He handed me a walkie-talkie, megaphone, and a small white bag filled with large, folded scraps of paper. "Here's how it works. We cut a tree down, but before we do, we have to do whatever's in the grab bag before the point counts. Every tree is worth one point and that includes de-branching it and getting it picked up for loading.

"You'll call out the points through the mega-phone and commentate on the game through the walkie-talkie so people can stay posted. Don't be afraid to let baby Bennett know how bad he's sucking. And August thinks she is better than all of us because she was built all tiny for the tree- climbing thing but she's wrong…as usual," he finished.

"Okay this is our grab bag. When we finish with a tree, we have to make it back to you and pull a slip of paper out of the bag and try to decipher Logan's chicken scratch before we can go back out. The papers are non-refundable, and unfortunately, what you get is what you get." Grey shrugged his shoulders with a hidden meaning I wasn't quite sure how to interpret. "You announce what anyone is being forced to do because that is where it can get interesting." He smiled wide. "Are you ready, Harper?" he asked, raising his brows.

"I think that I can manage. Does everyone cut down trees?" I asked.

"Everyone but Jarrett. He'll run the trucks since he is still faking a busted shoulder." He turned quickly to gauge his brother's reaction. "Kidding," he soothed, pulsing with his palms face out towards Jarrett.

He turned to face his other siblings. "Okay, people, let's remember that Lil is glass today and we have to do whatever it is to keep her safe. Now, remember if you get caught cheating, we all know the price." Everyone cringed at his statement. No. I didn't know the price but apparently I didn't want to either. If this family was half as creative with consequences as they were with their innovative games, then I would rather remain in the dark.

"Okay, Mom will be here in five hours. Let's get a move on. Bennett, don't die or Mom might cut us out of the will." Grey pointed.

"She threatened that before when we filled those balloons with sunscreen that one summer —the greatest hour of my life with sprinklers and girls. And don't kill Lil. She's hot and I won't forgive you because I think that's like a sin or something. God might smite you since I'm going to marry her. So with that all that being said, get ready…get—"

"Go!" Trip and Tate hollered together and took off before the others realized what they were doing. They all started yelling and mushing down the hill.

I exhaled and pulled the mouth guard out that was squished between my teeth.

"You know, if you want to go home, you can let me know and I'll give you a ride back." Jarrett's smooth voice poured down on me.

I turned, realizing how ridiculous I looked, and tried my best not to voice anything that would match my appearance.

"Thanks for the offer." I smiled.

"Nice get up." Jarrett motioned up and down with his hand.

I smiled flirtatiously and tipped my hardhat at him. "Thanks." I smirked.

He was walking away, his shoulders shaking with laughter slightly. "Oh, um…" He paused, taking a few steps back in my direction. "I didn't want to ask while everyone was around but August wasn't lying. I *was* really looking forward to seeing you." The corner of his lips pulled downward nervously as he gritted his teeth bracing for his next question. Anxiously, he rubbed the back of his neck, head tilted sideways, his elbow pointing skyward. "You can say no, you know," he forewarned before even asking what I think he was still pondering.

"Well, you sort of have to ask me first," I nervously suggested.

He chuckled. "I suppose I do." His arm dropped to his side. "So I was wondering if the day after tomorrow you would want to come…out with me?" he questioned, still unsure.

"Um, it depends on who and where?" I tried not to leap at his offer.

"It's a surprise and it would be just you and me going out," he clarified. "If you're okay with that," he finished.

"Sounds delightful," I whispered in an airy manner that I couldn't help. "Of course, I don't want to be rude, but wherever we go, I'm allergic to pecans," I offered.

"No, nothing like that. Something I'd like to show you," he laughed and started walking away. "Okay, so it's a date. You, me, no pecans. Are you really allergic to pecans?" he asked, his brows pulling down curiously.

"No. But I tell that to people because I really don't like them," I said.

He broke up into a little laughter. "Okay. I can't wait. Oh, and"— he stopped turning to face me— "can you not tell the boys about it?" He jerked his head in his brothers' direction.

"Yeah, I won't tell them." I blushed.

He nodded and then strode off without another word, rubbing the back of his neck again. I exhaled when he was far enough away.

"A date with Jarrett," I pondered aloud. "Definitely not going to tell August about this one." I shook my head.

* * *

The sun was high overhead. Despite the massive red beach umbrella and small handheld fan they had put in my safety bag, it was still hot and I was beginning to get tired.

The walkie buzzed to life and August screamed out.

"Olly olly oxen free," her small voice echoed off the trees.

I picked up the megaphone and hit the siren in the air while I kept it at arm's length. Standing it up in the dirt next to my chair, which looked like the middle of a landing zone, and picked up the black walkie-talkie.

"Boys," I spoke with a twinge of southern twang to it, "August takes the lead, kicking Bennett out of first place. The rankings so far are…" I hesitated to take a drink of cold water because they insisted that I remain hydrated. It was a small issue earlier when I got up to use the restroom and the boys went wild trying to come and guard the porta potty. Thanks to Jimmy for rescuing me from that stage fright I couldn't get past. "August is in first, Bennett is in second, Trip and Tate are tied for third while Logan is holding strong onto fourth. Grey, unfortunately, is still disqualified for the grab bag paper that had instructed him to kiss me and, I quote, folks, 'long and hard,' which was not what I signed up for," I recapped.

Logan and Grey during their drunken stupor of brilliant brainstorming the previous night on how to keep me safe also hit a spark of creativity in writing down things on the grab bag requests that would mainly benefit them. The kiss was one of many examples.

A horn honked behind me as Tate was not twenty feet in front of me hopping like a rabbit and his hands pulled up in a manner that would match. He was still serving his penalty from the incident earlier. Despite their abilities to turn just about anything into an extreme activity, they were definitely good at what they did, a well-oiled machine that kept beating to a drum only they could hear. However, I was finding myself longing for a quick phone call home and a nice long nap to soothe my aching back.

More than once during a lull when they were all working hard to be the best, I drifted back to the thoughts of Jarrett, carrying me to dinner last night or pulling me into his cabin when I was in distress. Not to mention our secret *date* the day after next— his words not mine.

I never admitted it out loud to August, but I had had a crush on her oldest brother since that first time she brought me home. I always found myself automatically smiling and turning away abashed whenever he spoke to me. Every summer, holiday, or quick weekend we flew in August would encourage the not-so-secret crush, but it never felt right. The Baynes were like family to me and I didn't want to do anything to muddy that water. And Jarrett always seemed to have a girlfriend whenever I was around, and I didn't want to get into the middle of that.

This was the first spring that I had come where I knew he wasn't seeing anyone. August made a point to tell me before we came. I was glad she wasn't looking at my face when she told me. I had to admit the excitement brewing in my chest had me giddy.

Nell's horn rang out again from behind me and my thoughts were quickly interrupted. She jumped down from the truck, turning it off followed by her sweet voice reverberating off the bark with a knowing demand.

"Boys! Time for lunch!" she called out to her missing ducklings.

"How you holding up, dear?" She placed a sweet hand on my back as she walked up. "I see they decided to take Jim literally today." She wiped what little sunscreen was left over on my nose from Trip's earlier no- skin- cancer campaign.

I figured that this would be my chance to escape. Despite how awkward I abruptly ended our conversation the previous night, I weighed out my options and decided that I would rather be back at the farm than suffering through more grab bag what- ifs?

"Do you think that I could ride back with you?" I asked in a slightly pleading tone.

"Sweetheart, I assumed that you would be waiting on the side of the road for me." She smiled warmly at me and then hesitated before she continued. "I was out of line last night. I had no right sticking my nose in your family business. It's hard not to think of you as my own, I was only trying to help." She smiled sweetly.

"Water under the bridge, Nell." I wrapped my arms around her lovingly. I hated when I was angry at her. It wasn't fair.

"Well, then let's get you some food and you can sneak off with me! We won't tell the boys." She put a finger to her lips.

"Oh, thank you," I replied, exasperated. I didn't want to deal with their scrutinizing and disappointed faces. I stripped off my ridiculous attire, laying it on the chair and heading for the tables, feeling grateful for my savior.

8

Fishing with Guns

"Don't you just love it here?" August beamed walking beside me.

"Yeah, I would have loved it more if you'd let me sleep in."

"We only have a week here, Lily. We can't be wasting time sleeping." She practically skipped to every word.

"Today scares me," I spoke honestly.

"It's going to be so fun." She grinned.

Before I knew it I was standing confused in the shop outside Tate and Trip's door. The guys were all scrambling around gathering items that didn't make sense to me.

"Lil, you're going to love this!" Tate said, grinning widely.

"Fishing?" I repeated the question for the millionth time. "I am not really good at fishing," I tried to explain.

"Good? At fishing?" Jarrett asked from behind me. "You drop a line and sit there ."

"It's not that. It's more like bad luck tends to seek me out with you guys. Worse when I am trying to learn how to do something new," I explained as I recalled the many injuries I suffered during previous

Bayne events.

"Well, listen up. All you have to do is stick close to me and everything will be fine," Logan said, smiling sarcastically at me. "I'll keep you safe. Scout's honor." He held up his hand.

"In what realm were you ever a Boy Scout?" Bennett chimed as he casually strode past heading towards the endless wall of tools.

"Yeah, what kind of Boy Scout? You were just a *boy* who *scouted* girls," August added.

"Right, I'm with August on that one," Bennett agreed.

"Bennett, don't talk back. Mind your big sister!" Logan retorted, completely ignoring August's remark.

"For the millionth time, she is my *little* sister. Hence what that means when people point out the fact that she is the youngest." He sighed heavily with frustration. "I know you're a slow learner, Logan."

"Benny needs a nap, Grey. He's getting cranky already. Hope you packed a bottle in his diaper bag," Logan shot.

"Right, don't forget his pacifier or he cries," Grey egged him further.

I decided that this might be the best time to interject again. "Fishing?" I asked out loud. This had to be some Bayne game. Fishing seemed to be too serene a hobby for the Evel Knievel crew.

Trip marched over to me where I still stood frozen in the doorway of the early morning light. "Yes, Lil, fishing. Fish are these various sized aquatic creatures that swim through all kinds of waters, like this." He palmed his hands together like he was praying and snaked them in a waving motion towards me demonstrating how fish swam. "People catch them for sport, and we like to eat them," he finished. "Now put these on." He instructed as he threw oversized and faded black waders at me.

I held them up the length of my body and stared. I have to walk in the water. I thought that vacation was all about relaxing. Not going on a death fish trip with Bayne boys who are unaware of the value of life.

Six years ago, I made the mistake of going four-wheeling with them one day. Needless to say, my butt was sore for a week and the mud kept my eyelashes glued together for days. They referred to it as *extreme wheeling*. I will never look at nylon rope the same. So ever since, I've been hesitant to take anything at face value.

I pulled on the waders that came up to my collar bone and tried my best to tighten the suspenders. I grunted in frustration.

"I can help you with those, Lil," Grey smarted at my struggle.

"I can manage quite fine," I continued through my grunts.

A hand came up behind me and pulled on the metal, trapping the thick fabric. Helping me twist and adjust until they were almost comfortable. I glanced over my shoulder and smiled.

"Thanks," I spoke softly as I looked up at Jarrett.

"It's tough to hold your own with this group. You do it pretty well. No point in making it worse." He smiled and walked away.

I tried not to grin idiotically. I looked pitiful. I had on these giant black waders, a messy ponytail, a long sleeve thermal undershirt, and not a drip of makeup within a mile of my face.

I was pulled from my daydreams when I noticed that Trip and Tate were both in the act of loading rifles. I began to look around and saw that there were many other firearms and various guns being loaded by the boys.

"We're going fishing…with guns?" I paused.

Trip and Tate both shared a look that I couldn't quite interpret and shrugged their shoulders in sync. "They're big fish?" Tate said it like a question.

"Is that even legal?" I asked, becoming nervous.

"Lil, 'legal' is such an ugly word," Trip said, finger-quoting around the word *legal*.

I stood there. This can't be right. Jarrett clearly said that all you have to do is "drop a line." That's what I had heard him say. Unless…Oh God. The line was only for bait. I swear to God if this is some version of *extreme fishing*, I'm going to run.

Tate stood in front of his twin after his gun was ready and caked camouflage face paint on him. The others were following suit. Tate then approached me with a handful of small circular tins he was holding.

Do I even ask what this is for? "Why do we need face paint? How big are these fish?" I asked, trying to appear nothing but confident.

"There she goes again, Trip, asking all those questions," Tate spat back to his brother.

Great, he didn't even address that question. I'm not going to ask if I should be scared right now because I think I already know the answer.

***

We were bumping along in Logan's black suburban, working our way towards an unknown destination with some form of deadly fishing as our awaiting sport. Trip and Tate were at the helm of the vehicle, one driving while the other navigated all while singing some random pump them up song. Logan, August, and Grey were occupying the middle seat all arguing about which of them did the best at their ridiculous logging competition I had witnessed yesterday. While none of them let off the slightest hints of what was to come.

Bennett and Jarrett were packed in tight next to me and I was rubbing shoulders with a window and Jarrett. He was silent. Not even adjusting movements to try and find comfort next to his burly baby brother. I stared straight ahead trying not to make contact or too many glances to my left.

Worry jarred me as I slowly became aware that this was really happening. Every time the Baynes throw some random *uniform* at me and tell me how much fun this is going to be, I should know that's not going to be the case. I need to make a key of some sort with words. Example, fun equals scary, deadly, risky, and stupid. When asked to wear this I should know that that means this is something requiring safety gear. How August with such a scientific mind could swing with these boys boggled me. That led me to only one possibility. It's bred into them. Adrenaline runs at a higher rate in their bodies, simply. It's in their blood to be insanely unaware that they're not invincible.

My body swayed into Jarrett, and I blinked back to the present. We were turning into the forest, onto an unmarked trail. Trail! This was clearly not a road. I looked backwards at the fading blacktop and the encroaching trees that were filling the opening.

"Um, guys?" I spoke. "The road is that way." I pointed over my shoulder.

"Fish don't swim in roads, Lily," Jarrett spoke softly next to me.

"But the road…it's getting further away," I replied meekly.

He laughed, giving my knee a comforting squeeze. "You'll be fine. You heard Logan. Stick close to him and everything will be okay," he soothed with a sarcastic undertone.

I looked straight ahead and swallowed hard. He let out a breathy chuckle beside me. Fear was the icing on my face as I quickly glanced out of the corner of my eye at him and back again.

"Quit your crying, Harper. Jarrett's got it so bad for you that I doubt he would let a trout gob up your dainty hands with scale slime," August stated as her hands went to her shoulders, flitting her fingers.

"What the hell, August? You can't call who wins her. She chooses!" Tate called from up front.

They can't hear when I mention we're drifting away from the road, but they can pick up August mentioning that? What the hell?

I looked over at Jarrett and winced in embarrassment. A cocky crooked smile pulled the corner of his mouth up. A hint of pink pulsed at the tops of his ears, a subtle reaction that he followed with a swift slap to the back of August's head.

"Ow, shit stain!" August grabbed the back of her head and ducked forward. "Don't hit a woman…ass!" She twisted and punched him square in the chest.

"You're not a woman. You're my sister, even though you hit like a girl," he quipped, lightly rubbing his chest.

She ignored him and he didn't turn to make eye contact with me again. I always felt that changing the subject was the safest route.

"So I noticed we're not making a crescent route back towards the road?" I phrased it as a question.

"Correct. Stop worrying. You'll get gray hair," Bennett pacified leaning around Jarrett.

We came to an abrupt stop with no rhyme or reason to the choice in location. Fear enveloped every nerve. There was no water. Anywhere! I never learn.

The doors swung open, and I sat, my body fixed to the seat. After all had exited and the trunk popped open behind me Jarrett poked his head back in the door. I peered at him timidly from behind the headrest in front of me.

"C'mon, sweetheart, you won't catch anything sitting in there." He held up a hand attempting to coax me out.

I sighed lightly before I hesitantly maneuvered my way out of the vehicle, standing in the crowd of brutish boys shoving around me as they got ready.

"Alright, heads up, everyone! Focus! Remember, big game are not our foes today so be ready to avoid." Trip was spilling out commands as he started tossing aerosol cans of an unknown substance and a kazoo to everyone. "Spread out thin but never alone. The team with the most fish can ride back with their clothes on." He winked at me. I rolled my eyes.

"He's kidding," Jarrett whispered to my right.

"We all know the wager. Least fish in hand when we get back cleans waders before dinner tomorrow." Trip pointed a serious finger at the awaiting faces. "Okay, four hours starts in one minute. Ready? Look alive, Harper! Get set! Bennett, do you need to potty before we go?" Trip joked.

"Eat shit," Bennett grumbled.

"Go!" Trip yelled. The group scattered, including myself following Jarrett's step. "Guys, don't forget, heads up, pay attention, and if you run into company, spray like hell, blow your kazoos, and remember to *play dead!*" The group all yelled the words play dead in unison. He laughed while still lagging behind us.

I flipped my can over in hopes of a better understanding of what I was dealing with.

"Bear spray!" I screamed out loud and stopped.

"I will piss my pants if Grey craps like that one fish trip," Tate yelled. The crowd laughed as they splintered into predetermined groups.

"Seven years ago, asshole. Let it go!" Grey retorted.

"Still shit yourself!" Tate called becoming inaudible through the trees.

"Jarrett, I don't do bears!" I spat breathlessly, ridden with panic standing solid in my spot. Hell no, I wasn't going to join this game! I knew it! Extreme fishing!

"Calm down. I have no intentions of being mauled today and definitely not bringing you back to my mother in any condition besides mint." He smiled and started walking with purpose, sidestepping rocks and downed limbs.

I leaned my head back, shaking before I began stomping off towards whatever hell we were working towards. If there was one thing I knew about the Baynes, it was that they never stopped at unsafe. It always had to be taken one step further.

I looked down as the can shifted beneath my fingertips. I stopped and twisted the somewhat large tube in my palm. Why was the can so poorly labeled? Like a child had written it themselves. My fingernail caught at the rough black speckles of color coating the can. Was this spray paint? I scratched at the dull exterior encasing it and reflective purple shined through. I began to rub vigorously.

"Hair spray, Jarrett? This isn't even real bear spray! Oh my God. I think I am having an asthma attack." I began to fumble and reach out like I was trying to sit.

Jarrett turned around and came jogging back to me. "Do you have an inhaler?" he asked worriedly.

"No." I started breathing frantically.

"Did you leave it back in the Suburban?" he asked desperately.

"No. I don't have one," I said, panic weaving through my words.

"Um, I don't know what to do? I can blow my kazoo and Tate can give me the truck keys to get back to your stuff at the house?" He rushed through the words.

"There isn't one. I don't have asthma. But I can't breathe so I'm assuming that's what this is!" I inhaled sharply.

He stood upright and laughed lightly. "Calm down. You'll give yourself a panic attack. Or worse, you'll hyperventilate and the guys will come fawn over you. Trust me, Lily, you'll be fine. Nothing can happen to you when I'm around." He grinned.

I let out a small laugh and began to stand upright slowly. "I can't do this, Jarrett. I can't go on some extreme invented Bayne game. I'm not a thrill-seeker like you guys." I paused after I spoke, trying to choose my words wisely. "I don't want to do this. I want to go home." I surrendered with my words and scrunched up my face in eminent worry. "I'm sorry. I'll clean the waders, so you don't have to," I begged.

"How about this? I'll go slowly, keep you close, and if you *try* what you're doing once and don't feel totally exhilarated, then we will turn around and head straight back to the cabin and *I* will clean the waders?" he proposed.

That's when he reached out and slipped his fingers into mine. He started tugging at me in the cutest and most impossibly irresistible manner. I didn't want to let him down. He flicked his chin the direction we were headed and looked at me while smiling.

"Fine," I groaned and smiled at our hands still connected while I followed. He handed me the net and I didn't bother asking what it was for.

Yells came back to me from up ahead. I gripped Jarrett's hand a little tighter and would be lying if I said I wasn't scared. Their was the rush of water and I could smell the pungent odor of fish in the air. The trees thinned as we neared the rocky edge to the river. Jarrett turned and smiled wide. That could only mean one thing. This was it.

Laughter resonated from the bark and splashes of water. He stopped before we stepped onto the rocky beach of pebbles.

"Okay, I have the gun. I'll stand on the beach and watch you as you jog into the river with the net. Scoop up what you can without being greedy," he instructed.

"Isn't the idea to get as many fish as possible?" I asked, not beginning to understand.

"Yes, but we have to be aware of our foes." He held up the bucket that he had been carrying with the gun and continued to explain. "Our goal is to fill this. Last year Logan crapped himself. He said he didn't, but we have reason to believe that he did. I don't want to clean the waders." He chuckled at some joke I wasn't aware of yet.

"Foes?" I hung on to that word tight. "Like the police?"

"Well, not exactly, but keep your eyes peeled for them too. The sheriff gets pretty ticked at us when we do this. That's why we try never to do it at the same time, so we should be alright." He began guiding me towards the river's edge.

An out of place groan rang out of the trees and I couldn't quite figure out what it was. Gunshots hit the skies and yelling quickly followed by laughter through everyone. I jumped a little as the rifle popped.

"Shit. Crap. Mother son of a fried chicken!" Tate hollered as he ran back to the water's edge. A net filled with thrashing fish so brightly reflected from the sun that I couldn't place what our prey was.

"Alright, we're starting from behind. We want to get as many as possible. You go first and then I'll be all over that, so we can take turns. Run, dip, and get the hell out of there. The current isn't usually too rough as long as you stand firm and stick shallow. Then get back to shore without falling," he started, readying our position, and I walked out to meet him on the slippery, moss-infested rocks.

I looked to our left and saw Grey and Logan working out their technique among themselves. I couldn't understand how hours wouldn't be enough time to get us as many as possible. Waiting for them was probably the key.

I turned where August and Bennett were standing to our right and the rest of the teams were scattered about along the banks. A solid moment interrupted my assessment of what didn't seem to be so bad after all. Then the realization hit all too clearly. I screamed the words at the site of what was occupying upstream.

"Fucking bears! Hell no! What the hell? There are bears here?" Panic didn't even begin to describe what I was feeling. I looked into the glistening water and saw why the *foes* were so necessarily close.

"Oh my shit. It's fucking salmon season. You have got to be shitting me, Jarrett. No! I will not go into any water where I cannot move quickly away from feeding bears!" My breathing was labored.

"Oh, hush, I have a gun. There are more of us than them, and you have bear spray. So relax and breathe because we need to fill our bucket." He adjusted the gun. "Get ready." He was rolling up his sleeves glancing every so often up and down the stream at the slightest movement.

"For what? Going home? Okay, sounds fantastic. 'Cause its fucking Aqua-Net, Jarrett." I was shaking. Of course I'm going to be the one to shit my waders.

"Harper, relax. I'll go with you since it's your first time. It's tradition, we've done this every year since we were kids and we're all still here." August grinned. "Line up on the bank with me."

"Except for Kip!" Trip hollered to me.

"Who's that?" I panicked.

"Oh, you didn't know. So August never told you we used to be triplets? Damn, Auggie way to show respect," he called, lining up for another run. I noticed he was drinking beer. They all were. No wonder they were so calm about it.

I kept my eyes pasted to the opposing bank where I saw a large brown shaggy bear lazily glancing up at us and then back towards the ground just behind the tree line.

I couldn't pinpoint my nervousness, however, I knew that it was very much present. Jarrett gave me encouraging looks. I knew inside his head he was thinking, *Maybe she isn't the girl I want to go out with after all.*

Baynes' bravery eclipsed the strongest of gallantry.

August was speaking beside me, but my ears were ringing making it difficult for me to hear everything I'm sure she was instructing me to do.

"...the kazoo. Step high. Here we go! Now run!" August threw the can of beer she swigged from hard at the ground, wiped her mouth with the back of her hand, and crashed into the water like a tiny blond hurricane.

It took me twenty seconds or so to realize that high-pitched tone was me screaming like a terrified idiot but what held my attention more was that I was following suit. Dear God, I was running into the water! *This is happening*, as August would say.

I was gritting my teeth so hard that I'm sure any added pressure would probably break my jaw. Both of my hands were wound tightly around the end of the thick metal net, and I tried to retain the instructions to step high. I brought my knees to my chest and stomped viciously into the water constantly repeating, "Don't shit your waders. Don't shit your waders."

The water was cold, and I could feel its force against my legs. My head immediately went to a different place. There were no bears around me, only the overwhelming thoughts that the water was cold, rushing, and I could feel dozens of fish beating against my calves and shins.

I swooped down hard with my net at the water, not paying attention to what my goal was and accepted that I didn't have a prayer for catching anything in these conditions. I thrashed wildly. A voice rang out somewhere behind me.

"Keep your head up, Lil!" Bennett pointed loudly.

"Lily, get out of there," Logan called somewhere from the bank.

I looked up in time to realize what they were talking about. The large shaggy bear across the river was staring at me and making his way slowly into the chilling water headed in my direction.

I looked down at my chest automatically screeching internally for help. I started backing towards the bank, fear quickly paralyzing me from the hips down. A kazoo blew hard behind me.

"She's got it. Give her a sec!" Jarrett yelled.

"Jarrett, she's freaking out," August belted.

Another kazoo, the bear started stepping faster in my direction. My small frame was an appetizing entree compared to the weak fish that slapped in the water at his gargantuan feet, more and more kazoos.

"She didn't blow it!"

I stepped backwards and my foot caught a rock. I slipped in haste as terror shook my nerves. My hands went out behind me instinctively. The net caught against a large, mossy, soaked slab and slipped jabbing my right side. I yelped at the pain and collided with the rushing white tips of water biting the air. Jagged stone impaled my spine, and I arched my back quickly crying out. A wet snarling growl snapped its jaws closely in reply.

I was prey.

Pain bit at every nerve masking the hands that pulled hard at the top of my waterlogged waders. Gunshots fired in rapid secession from several rifles. A loud hissing I couldn't quite place followed.

"There. That should do it!" Tate and Trip both stood at the water's edge holding up their cans of hairspray spraying wildly towards the water.

The immense beast lumbered away, chuffing in reaction to the discharge the rifles sent skyward.

Jarrett was staring down, on his knees next to me, both his hands lightly cupping my head, worrying, creasing his brows closer and closer together.

"Great, you killed her!" August slapped the back of his head.

"Way to go, Jarrett. You killed the hot girl!" Logan piped.

"The one good thing we had to look forward to when August comes home," Grey added.

"Hey!" August turned and slapped him.

"You're my sister, not a girl. That means brother code allows me to hit you." He raised a fist. August raised the net in response.

"You always cheated growing up. Weapons." He walked off grumbling smugly.

My stomach felt like butterflies were hammering the walls. Jarrett was nothing but worried.

A giggle.

I couldn't hold it anymore. I burst into a fit of laughter, my shoulders shaking against the slippery bank.

"I know she is laughing but maybe we should do mouth to mouth just to be safe," Grey piped in from above me somewhere.

I started to get to my feet as the crowd scattered back to their places. I took one look at Jarrett. "You were right —completely and utterly exhilarated." I smirked. I dusted off my elbow nonchalantly. "Mind if I take a second crack at it?"

He stood his mouth slightly agape.

"Yeah, and I am going to need one of those beers." I winked at him, and Jarrett smiled.

"You're crazy, Lily, that's for sure. Maybe that's why we like you so much." Bennett smiled from beside August.

"That and she's pretty! Best damn gift Auggie ever gave us!" Tate chimed.

"Idiots! I am not giving her to you. She's my best friend, not yours. Find another toy to play with…" August trailed as I rushed back out into the water for my second attempt. This was going to be a tough day, just remember, *don't shit the waders.*

9

The First Date

The rain spit on the windshield and I sat dazed, wondering what it would be like to be a raindrop. Then my mind began wandering wildly among my thoughts. How could people smell rain? I thought I could smell it, but I was never truly sure. How can you smell water? I smell nothing coming from my faucet when I get a glass of water. With that being said, perhaps that was because it was purified. I could not smell this smell that so many would look to the sky, inhaling deeply, and foretell that rain was coming.

"What are you thinking about?" Jarrett asked, smiling lightly.

"Rain. I can't smell it," I blurted. I could already feel my cheeks beginning to tint pink.

He laughed. "I can. But that's probably because I live in a place where rain is a constant," he explained.

His arm rested comfortably on the console between us. The other hand hung over the steering wheel limply. It was hard not to take him in. Admire him. He was wearing a washed-out red T-shirt that had the sleeves cut off, making holes down to his hips exposing his sides and ribs. Without thinking, I began to bite my lip nonchalantly.

"Now what are you thinking about?" he asked, noticing the action.

"You," I whispered.

"Good things, I hope." He looked amused.

He was sitting up straighter looking in the rearview mirror, his fingertips grazing over the tops of his adorably swirling cowlicks. The big rough and tough logger cared how he looked despite his disheveled outfits, ripped T-shirts, and muddy jeans.

"I have great hair. It's one of the few things that I can say I beat Grey and Logan on. My hair gets the girls," he told me.

"No, it's your eyes and when you smile with the sideways smile." Oh. My. Shit. What the hell did I just say out loud? Is my brain not connecting with my mouth today? *Get it together, Lily!* Turning towards the window, maybe he didn't hear me.

"I like you," he said softly.

I didn't even have a chance to blink. My heart turned to liquid and exploded past my ribs.

"Like...*like* you," he continued.

"Me too," I spoke before thinking yet again.

"I always mean to ask you out when you come to visit, but I didn't know how that would be with August being your best friend." He sighed.

"I felt the same way." *Be brave*, I chanted. Swallowing hard. "But I kind of don't care about that anymore," I whispered.

"Me either," he replied gently.

I didn't know what to say. I felt obligated to fill the silence after his admission. My throat seemed to be tightening. My mouth's moisture evaporated instantly.

I looked at his knit shorts and pondered my return words. My lungs squeezed shut whenever he walked within a ten-foot radius of me. I babbled like a dumb idiot speaking in tongues when he would attempt a conversation. I reverted to being a teenage girl and not the intelligent, cool woman I prided myself on attempting day in and day out.

I began to open my mouth slowly. Not sure of what to say.

"We're here," he said with a tinge of excitement.

"And where is here, since you won't tell me where you are taking me to?" I asked as relief washed over me that the subject had been dodged.

"If I told you, it wouldn't have been a surprise," he said as he looked right out the window past me. He pulled into a narrow dirt drive. We bumped along a thin line of fir trees that shielded what appeared to be a field from the road. They'd grown so tall you could see below them and easily past what was beyond.

Massive logs acting as benches were cut in half and smashed into the ground along the edges of the unkempt sidelines. Cars were parked all at the far end in no order. A very large group of men were all standing close to the farthest corner of the field talking and laughing. All of them were wearing similar loose-fitting clothes. T-shirts and shorts and most had tall socks on as well. Were those shin guards?

"Soccer?" I asked, surveying the men.

"Nope. Again, it's a surprise," he urged. A smile was lighting his face and I couldn't be irritated with his insistence on surprising me. He was utterly adorable at this moment.

We parked at the opposite end, and he hopped out, reaching into the back of the cab pulling out cleated shoes. I wasn't keen on sporting shoes, so I still was clueless, but I was sticking to my guns assuming that he was in some friendly weekly soccer game.

"Get out. I'll show you where you can sit," he spoke, closing the door before I had even moved.

Apparently, this wasn't going to be an option. So I did as I was instructed and pushed open the heavy door hopping out. He was waiting with a cocky smile plastered on his lips, lips that I wanted to kiss, a lot. I realized I wasn't moving.

"What's wrong?" he asked, confused that I wasn't going anywhere after closing the door.

"Oh, nothing! I was thinking about your lips." Shit! My hand flew to my mouth. Seriously, what the hell was wrong with my mouth today? I mean *really*. It had a complete mind of its own.

I walked over to him feeling like more of a moron than ever. I stood there unmoving at his side.

"My lips, huh?" he asked, obviously unchanged by the overwhelming embarrassment I had just suffered. "You're cute," he stated as he began walking forward towards the other players. But not before he reached down and took my hand.

My hand was on fire. I wish I could have yanked it from his and rubbed it vigorously down the side of my jeans before I placed it back. I was such a bumbling dork sometimes.

He must have sensed my hesitation.

"Is it my butt this time?" he asked, stopping his casual walk towards who knows what.

"Okay, smarty pants. And before your head floats away I was thinking they were chapped. Maybe how gross it would be to kiss them," I retorted. "Seriously though, I was thinking I don't like not knowing what's going on. I am not big into participating in physical contact sports. Or any sports for that matter. Not that I don't enjoy them, but I have a tendency to twist things and I'm a bleeder," I explained, remembering the purple and black bruise that was canvassed across my ribs from fishing. Something I would have to hide from Ethan when I got home or he might murder August.

"Stop. You're just a spectator today. I promise," he explained as he was facing me, still holding my hand. He leaned in slightly and whispered, "You're my cheerleader." Backing away, he smiled and still refused to explain what sport I would be spectating. "Come on. We don't want to be late. Nathan has to work at six."

And without a moment's hesitation, he quickly bent and kissed my forehead. Like it was nothing and he had done it a million times. He started walking again. "So, you were thinking about kissing me, huh?" he asked in a semi-rhetorical manner.

I dug my nails into the back of his hand slightly.

"Kidding!" he shot quickly.

I followed behind nervously. The slew of massive men collected at the other end of the field were intimidating. Jarrett's six-foot-two frame was something that was overshadowing enough. However, some of his fellow teammates dominated him with ease. Their voices were deep and reached me several yards away.

We stopped less than halfway, and he turned to me. "You can sit here and watch from the sidelines, cheerleader," he explained, setting me down on the half log masquerading as a bench.

"Rah-rah," I joked, pumping a weak fist upwards.

"I'll get you poms for next time," he said sarcastically. "I'm going to go figure out who's playing today. You're going to love this, I promise." And with a charming wink, he was off.

I watched him jog and gather with the others. He reached them momentarily and I was careful not to smile too wide or send any implications that we were something other than close family friends.

The rain was falling intermittently. There were two other spectators. One was the man I assumed to be Nathan, who had volunteered to rotate out and leave early for work, should the mystery sport game run long. I was still betting on soccer, and a petite girl wearing an oversized rain poncho with the hood pulled low over her face, hiding most of her shimmering blond hair. Skinny tight jeans stuffed into sheepskin boots, she sat quietly on the opposite end. Keeping her face on who knows what boyfriend.

I turned my attention back to Jarrett and glued my eyes on him as he adorably strode forward. He tugged on the cleats and laced them upholding a lively guy talk conversation with three men standing in front of him.

"Okay, whatever, Cap," One called down to him.

"Hey! You voted. Not me," he rebutted, pointing a finger at himself.

So, Jarrett was captain, huh? Well, of course that would make sense being that he was captain in everything else in his life, to his brothers, and apparently now of the mystery sport that I was going to be witnessing shortly. He glanced over at me, and our eyes fastened on each other. He flashed his perfect teeth in my direction and jutted out his chin in a nod at the action.

The players began to run out onto the field and take places. Stretching arms back behind their heads, pulling on their elbows with the opposite hand. Nathan started clapping, leaning forward and yelling weak cheers at the guys.

"C'mon, girls. Let's get this going!" He chewed his gum and sat back putting his arms out behind him.

Jarrett pointed an index finger in my direction and mouthed the word *cheerleader*, nodding. I rolled my eyes in response and shot a stupid thumbs up. My eyes went back to the girl down the way. And that's when I recognized the man that came to stand in front of her.

She stood up immediately with a bright smile lighting her tiny face. I was transfixed as Bennett stood in front of the girl. He didn't look like himself. He looked like a man. He was wearing white shorts that were once sweatpants, now long cut-offs, a charcoal T-shirt that complimented him well, and matching cleats like the rest of the team.

He ran a gentle palm down her shoulder and finally swept up her hand. Exchanging wide grins, her face glowed when he laughed a little and quickly bent and kissed her on the cheek, his lips turning them red in the aftermath. She sat down, bliss gracing every inch of her being.

Huh. So baby Bennett had a girlfriend— one that he kept secret from everyone in the family that could embarrass him...except his private, mature, overly understanding oldest brother. She seemed sweet. Judging the book's cover, she seemed adorably perfect for him. It appeared that he agreed.

He jogged backwards blowing a sweet kiss and ran to the other guys. None of them were mocking his public show of affection. Did they understand what he endured at home?

The men took a football stance and gathered in a starting play that looked very confusing and honestly like nothing I could say I'd seen before. A tall and handsome dark-complexioned man ran up, tossing a football to another. It was of vintage dark brown leather and had odd laces for a football, but perhaps it was a game tradition that I felt shouldn't be questioned.

Some yelling began slightly, and the unusual play became still. I watched in wonder where they were going with this made-up sport. It would be just like Jarrett, in something that he and several of his other small-town buddies invented. I didn't say anything.

A loud yell that seemed to make sense to the huddle was called and violent shoves pulsed throughout the men. I couldn't tear my eyes away, and amazingly, it wasn't Jarrett I was ogling but Bennett. His head was down, and his massive arms were wrapped around the wreck of men.

A volatile roar ripped from his chest, and he drove them to the ground without effort. Nathan cheered and a small voice yelled "Good job" from the other end. I guess that meant it had started. My question was…

"What the hell was that?" I pondered out loud.

Bennett rose and a proud smile smeared his face. Several hard slaps on his shoulders came down from the other players. That's when I realized the reason he wasn't teased for his sweet sideline kisses. It wasn't that they understood; it was respect. This gentle giant at home had an outlet for his unmatched force. Jarrett came into view and gave a brotherly sideways five. Bennett shrugged and took his place yet again.

I sat for many minutes as the ball was tossed backwards over players shoulders and tackling with no pads ransacked the field. They neared my side and did something in the unfamiliar sport that immediately helped me realize what I was watching.

As the ball was being tossed in such a complicated manner, several men from the other team surrounded one of their players and fluently thrust him to the sky for an interception, upwards of ten feet above the ground, the move familiar to me in my passing knowledge of the known sport. It dawned on me.

Rugby. The guys were playing rugby.

The breeze kicked up and blew my hair wildly around my shoulders. I pulled it away from my face and continued to try and understand the game. A difficult feat when you had no ground to stand on.

Jarrett jogged up to my side of the field and called out to me, "Umbrella or poncho in the truck if you need it!"

I smiled and shook my head no. I was fine. I didn't mind the dampness.

I found my eyes drift down the log benches to notice that Nathan had disappeared and all who was left was Bennett's tiny girl. Her small hands stuffed in the pockets of her jacket under her poncho. Eyes attached to the men sloshing through the field while her petite feet were cemented to the ground in front of her. The rain was starting to come down a little harder and it was impairing my ability to see her clearly.

I began to imagine what her name might be. I thought it would be prying if I were to introduce myself to her, being as Bennett opted not to. She looked like a cute name— Annie or Emma.

I turned my eyes to the game. I didn't understand if there would be a halftime, innings, or quarters perhaps? Anytime for them to re-group and further their game plan giving me a chance to talk to Jarrett?

The rain was coming down in sheets. So thick that my vision was fogged enough so I wasn't able to see the other end of the field. Some men were blurred outlines standing in the distance.

My clothes were becoming sticky on my skin. I started to second guess my earlier decision for the poncho and umbrella. As I thought the word umbrella, Annie Emma popped a mauve one the size of Texas open and sat smiling dry underneath. Not fazed by the climate change, her gaze was still attentive to the sport.

I reached into my pocket and pulled out the truck keys that Jarrett had slid me when I took my place on nature's bench. I stood pushing out my chest stretching my back a little way before I made my way quickly towards the truck. What good it would do now that I was wet made no sense but hopefully would stop me from becoming saturated to the bone.

I yanked the dark blue poncho over my head and grabbed the black umbrella he mentioned. It was quite large and kept most of the rain from pelting my face. I plopped back down on the bench and continued to let my eyes wander the field.

I watched Jarrett as he jarred the other men with his force. Tossing the ball and running despite the growing sloppiness of the playing surface. He was sexy. The way he would shake his head sideways quickly to get his hair away from his eyes. Or the way the wetness on his skin was alluring. It made him shine and for whatever reason, it was appealing to me. I twisted in my seat, sitting up a little straighter.

His body hit the ground hard and mud caked his clothes along one side. The plays didn't stop despite the relentless rain that assailed the players. Sludge that clotted the men's clothes made it increasingly difficult to tell the teams apart. Now everyone wore shades of brown and far enough in the distance appeared nothing but a mass of fighting slosh. I pulled my knees up to my chest to keep as dry as possible.

My mind began to daydream about him. Kissing him and touching him and talking to him.

A loud yell ripped me from my internal wanderings. I noticed that Annie Emma was standing peering with intensity at the cluster huddled together apparently around something. One man turned his head and hollered unintelligibly to the sidelines. Annie Emma leaned backwards and grabbed a small black case behind her bench and started jogging to the men.

So it would seem that Annie Emma was a doctor or first responder? Team respect was further understood. The only spectator besides me was a contributor. I stood as she had and watched with intensity. Sidestepping slowly down the field towards where she had been sitting trying to gather a better look.

She was kneeling next to a mass on the ground. A man whose face I couldn't clearly see. My heart raced in fear at the thought of Jarrett or Bennett lying there. My eyes transfixed on the event.

I counted the seconds in my head as minimal movement plagued the group. Should I go over there? I didn't know them that well, but it seemed rude not to. Then again it seemed rude to stand and stare at a stranger as well.

The figure began to sit upright. Evenness returned to my breathing. Some of the men bent and placed gentle arms around the injured. He stood and limped with Annie Emma following closely behind talking to another man. The rain was ridiculous by this point.

Jarrett emerged and headed in my direction walking and talking seriously with Bennett at his side. He looked up and smiled.

"No autographs, please, ma'am," he said jokingly, holding up a hand.

"Fans. Psh," Bennett said, shaking his head as they passed by. "Never know when to be considerate."

Jarrett was nodding.

"Jerks," I muttered more to myself than to them.

"What was that?" Jarrett asked, turning around eyeing me skeptically, taking a few steps back in my direction.

"Just pointing out the obvious," I stated sarcastically.

"Really? Are you sure about that?" he asked, standing directly in front of me at this point.

A smile crept out the corners of my mouth. "What are you gonna do about it?" I crossed my arms trying to stand my ground.

"Oh dear. You know I can't fight with you. How about a hug?" he asked. It was too late his arms were out and draped around me in a muddy embrace before I could say no.

My hands pressed against his dirty chest, and I mumbled incoherently trying to avoid it. It was hard to pretend not to like it. I wanted to hug him. But for the sake of the show, I turned my head and flashed a disgusted face sticking out my tongue.

He backed off and smeared two streaks of mud under my eyes like a football player. "Adorable," he said, his face taking on a more serious look.

"Ahem." Bennett cleared his throat a foot from us. "Alright, well, I am going to ride with the guys down to the hospital. You're cool with driving my car, right?" he asked Jarrett.

"Yeah, I'll have Lily follow me in my truck so you can be dropped off at the house later," he answered.

"Alright, I'll see you later. It might be a while because Adele thinks he has broken ribs. Good thing she's on-call tonight," he said. "EMT," he answered my question that I hadn't asked out loud but apparently was showing on my face.

"Ah. I see. Way to go, Bennett. She looks nice," I complimented him on his catch.

"Yeah, I think so too. Can you do me a favor? I plan to introduce her to everyone at the barbecue this weekend. They can be a little intimidating and kind of like..." He trailed off unsure of what name to place on them.

"Vultures when it comes to fresh meat?" I offered.

"Exactly." He pointed a finger at my face. "This rain is stupid. You better get back to the house. It's late and dark. Lily doesn't know these roads in this weather so drive slowly for her." He winked as his brother had earlier and smiled encouragingly at me. He patted me on the shoulder and jogged off in the opposite direction.

"Alright, you have the keys to my truck. Follow me and be careful, sweetie. The roads are slick when it's raining like this," he explained.

"Sweetie?" I asked skeptically.

"Dear?" he asked, raising his shoulders in question.

"How about you just call me—" I was cut off.

"Fine, sweetheart sounds good! You can be so difficult sometimes, Lily Bear." He jogged away.

"Lily Bear?" I questioned more to myself than to him.

"I think that's the one!" he called back over his shoulder.

I turned and put my head down against the wind. The sinking sun made the temperature chillier now that it was accompanying the rain.

I climbed into the cab after folding up my umbrella and tossing it on the floor next to me as though it were my vehicle. I paused for a moment, pulling in the smell of him that bathed every inch of the interior. I shook my head and let out a slow breath.

A horn honked behind me, and I knew it was him in Bennett's car. I put on the reverse lights and maneuvered my way to the road. I followed the car through the forests, finding it easier to be more aware of my surroundings when I wasn't right next to him. His smell lingered in my lungs and pulled at my thoughts.

I tried to divert my daydreaming by thinking about Bennett and his secret girl. What was her name again? Adele is what I think he said.

My mind wandered back home again. The stranger I had seen was walking through my memories. Worry etched at my already frayed nerves. A shred of yearning made itself present. I had forgotten about the black-haired man in Colorado. The feelings that he wouldn't return started to tear at my stomach once again.

We pulled into the driveway. It seemed that no one in the house was up and from what I could see through the heavy rain Trip and Tate were sleeping too.

I hopped out after I parked behind him and started jogging back towards the cabin. I passed him without a word. Anxiety was on my mind the entire drive after remembering the elusive man, but towards the end, all I could think about was the fact that I hadn't *thought* about him since I'd been here.

I rushed inside and struck the light switch by the door that illuminated all the lamps in the room. An orange and blue glow glossed over the walls. I stood wet from the small jog into the house.

"Lily are you okay?" Jarrett's voice startled me.

I jumped. "What?"

"You kind of ran right past me there. Are you mad at me or something?" he asked, looking nervous.

"No, I was thinking about something that I forgot back home," I sugarcoated my explanation.

He eyed me momentarily and finally said, "You're shaking. Is it something I can help you with?"

I realized that he was closer to me than before, directly in front of me now. Violating every inch of personal space I possessed. I looked up at him and did my best to breathe more calmly. "It's nothing that can't wait until I get back home. It's going to be sad that I have to leave after tomorrow. I never feel I could be here long enough. It's never as much as I want," I breathed the words. If I simply leaned forward our chests would have been pressed together.

My hands were balled into fists at my sides, and I was trembling against all my will, as my desire drove my need to reach up and kiss him. I was a statue. Our eyes connected.

For once his face was solemn, showing no hints of sarcastic smiles and I did nothing to break the tense moment. I was nervous about what his thoughts were right now.

He was leaning closer, and I realized at that moment I was ready. I began to let my eyes close with the raw emotions. The ends of my nerves were frayed, and it seemed any spark would send me across the room.

I thought I heard something outside, but I ignored it. Copper could wait. This was Jarrett. That's when it hit me. *This was Jarrett.* A man I had crushed on and became a breathless dork around for the past few years. A man that lowered my relentless guard without even trying. A man that sent my heart into palpitations teetering dangerously on a cardiac event at the sight of him.

He was so close now that I could feel his pulse racing across his chest. I leaned closer and without a doubt, he did the same. Our lips were fractions apart and I turned my chin upwards in drunk anticipation.

All too quickly, before I could react, his hand swept upwards into my hair, knotting the strands between his fingers and pulling me so tight I was forced to hold my breath.

The door burst open, and a drunken Grey stumbled into the room filling it with the scent of beer and liquor. "Hey, Lil. Logan's being a girl and is pissed about some chick I shucked face with next with… darn…" He mumbled incoherently before walking through the doorway and the sound of him collapsing on *my* bed, followed with "juice-box." I had assumed that he had meant *jukebox* but now wasn't the time.

Jarrett had let go and had a gentle arm placed slightly above my elbow. He kissed me on the forehead as he had earlier at the rugby field. "See you tomorrow, Miss Harper," he whispered into my hair at the top of my head. My thoughts weren't even able to register. I could barely see his silhouette walking slowly down the front steps.

All I could hear in the distance was…*intoxicating*.

"So, Lil, did I cock block ya?" Grey was standing in the doorway he'd stammered through. Shirtless and wearing one boot, one arm above his head resting on the door frame and the other trying to unbuckle his belt.

"Don't even think about it!" I shuffled off to bed, slightly irritated at my unwanted guest.

"So yes then? How 'bout we cuddle? That might make you feel better?" He turned to follow.

"Not likely!" I scoffed and headed to the shower, making sure to lock the door.

I almost kissed Jarrett, and it was good, and I didn't care that he was my best friend's brother.

10

Kissing My Best Friend's Brother

I awoke to sun streaming through the wooden blinds and the reek of beer filtering through the house. Grey had passed out face down on the couch appearing to have collapsed there.

The day before yesterday, Jarrett and I came in second out of the four teams fishing. Grey and Logan's logic failed and when they started losing, they gave up altogether, starting to sabotage Trip and Tate's attempts at winning. Bennett and August's margin of fish from ours was massive but we were still able to avoid cleaning the waders, which I was grateful for after Tate's close call that had us all rolling in laughter on the banks.

Last night's rugby date had me slightly less confused about Jarrett's intentions. Our luck at getting alone was minimal though. All day we crossed paths, running errands for Nell, lining up the picnic tables outside for the entire town of Maple Falls. Nell insisted on cooking up the fish for a spring barbecue and goodbye to August and me. Our eyes would meet momentarily, and before a few words could be spoken, Nell's dish towel was swatting us in opposite directions.

I was standing placing the table clothes over the tops of the wooden picnic benches, while the boys were hoisting a canopy over everything to avoid the rain. Jimmy was hanging lights around the edges, August was in my wake placing a plate of candles on the table I had completed, and Nell was ordering everyone around in a fluster through the open kitchen window. The aroma of delicious homemade recipes drifted towards us all.

"Do you think that I should wear my hair up tonight?" August asked from behind me. I wasn't really paying much attention. My stare was fixed on Jarrett standing with his back towards me on the top of a ladder. "Harper, can you pull your eyes away from my brother for a second and answer me?" she asked now right next to me.

"What? Yeah, sure," I replied.

"Yeah, sure what?" she asked skeptically, eyeing me.

"Yeah, sure, I don't care. I'll finish the tables," I spoke through a daze. My mind daydreaming about last night's almost-kiss. Our time had passed, and I was becoming more and more disappointed by the hour that I wouldn't be able to talk to him about it.

"Oh my God. Why don't you stop ogling my brother and answer what I really asked?" She shoved me aside leaning over a table setting down another plate of candles.

"What did you ask me?" I turned blinking away my daze, finally noticing the irritability.

"Never mind," she huffed.

"I'm sorry. What did you ask me about your hair?" I pressed again.

She turned with a hint of worry behind her eyes. "I asked if you think I should wear my hair up tonight." She looked down and that's when I caught it.

"Why are you acting like that?" I asked skeptically.

"Like what?" She lifted one shoulder, acting as though she didn't understand my meaning.

"Nervous," I highlighted. That was very unlike August.

"I'm not nervous. Just a lot of people that I haven't seen for a while."

She laid down another plate, continuing to walk along.

I wasn't imagining this. "Anyone in particular?" I asked her.

"No." She flipped her hair with her hand and set down the last plate quickly and walked away ending our conversation.

I stood with a brow raised at August's odd behavior but decided not to pursue her. I took off in my own direction yelling back through the window at hurricane Nell.

"Nell, going to shower and get ready. That should do it with the tables." I pointed behind me smiling sweetly.

"Thank you, dear!" Her voice yelled from somewhere near the oven.

I retraced my earlier steps towards the cabin and quickly glanced under my lashes to catch Jarrett leaning back watching me just in time before I was lost behind a shed. I lowered my head and smiled wide. He had to have been thinking about last night as well.

* * *

The oval mirror that was suspended in the corner of the room of the small cabin reflected my frustration.

"I know I'm being ridiculous," I spoke aloud to no one. "This is my best friend's brother!" Saying his name and repeating it, hoping that would help. "Jarrett." It came out with a tone of longing. I squeezed my eyes shut and clenched my fists at my side. Who cares what I'm wearing? It's like I'm trying to do everything in reverse this week. Now I try to impress him, after he's watched me fall in oversized waders, get soaked in a monsoon rainstorm and that catastrophe of a Halloween safety costume when I followed them to work.

No matter how hard I try right now, August could find something to kill my preparations with one word.

I decided on some plain jeans and a faded white blouse. I shook my head in frustration.

"This is August's brother." I cracked my neck side to side. "What are you doing, Lily?" I eyed myself in the mirror.

The thought of Jarrett sent shivers across my chest. I couldn't help the way I felt. There was obviously something there.

* * *

"You're weird right now," Ethan stated skeptically.

"No, I'm not," I shot over the phone quickly as I lay on the large couch safely back from my hellish day watching the loggers.

"Don't lie to me, Lily." His voice firmed up. "Are any of your appendages being suspended or splinted in some way?" he pressed pointedly.

"Heck no," I shot. "Honestly, Ethan, do you think that August would do hard time for me?" I asked, repeating her statement from earlier in the day.

"You're right." I could hear his lips smack together in thought. I could picture him leaning casually on his countertop. Phone wedged in between his ear and shoulder. His hands firmly gripping his Xbox controller.

"Turn off the TV," I instructed softly.

"I'm fine," he replied with slight irritability at my obvious subject change. "I've only been playing for five minutes."

"Five?" I told him without even being present.

"Maybe ten." I heard him rustling.

"Well, I wanted to check in." I could tell he was frustrated that I was being seemingly weird. Without letting on about Jarrett, I attempted a diversion. "I miss you, blondie." I smiled through the words.

"I miss you too, babe," he replied warmly through the shell I'd broken. "Don't be weird when you come back," he added quietly.

"Never," I comforted him with the confidence I didn't feel.

I looked at the expression printed in my eyes.

"Are you being weird, Lily?" I asked myself in the mirror. "Why does he even care about Jarrett?" I started to pace. "Why do you care if he gets a little jealous?" I asked myself, rolling my neck in circles.

Jealous, I stopped walking back and forth.

Why would Ethan be jealous of anything? It's not like he's ever actually been interested. Well, forget about Ethan. Tonight I was going to be focused on Jarrett.

* * *

"Intimidated?" Bennett asked, standing next to me on the edge of the huge crowd gathered under the tent.

"A few more than I expected," I spoke breathlessly, arms crossed nervously, staring at the people milling about laughing and conversing loudly.

"When Mom has a spring barbecue, usually people are itching to get out of their houses," he explained, smiling. "The people of the PNW love to seize any ounce of sunshine."

Cars were parked a half mile down the road on both sides each way. *A few people* were an understatement. My chance to be alone with Jarrett all day was a complete failure. August had dragged me into a multi-hour prep time for this.

"Should my hair be up?" she yelped nervously. "If you like this skirt Lily, I know it's wrong." Nervousness I hadn't witnessed in her before. I couldn't figure out why though.

"What's with August?" I turned to look up at Bennett. His eyes out of all the brothers matched Jarrett's the closest.

"Ah, noticed that, did you?" he asked, laughing a little.

"Yeah, I've never seen—" A small voice interrupted the conversation.

"Hi, Bennett." Adele's blond hair spun in large wispy waves around her shoulders. A fitting brilliant blue blouse clung to her thin exterior matching her eyes wonderfully.

"Del, you made it." Bennett beamed.

"Hi, Adele. I'm Lily." I raised my hand to be polite.

"Hi, Lily. I saw you at the game last night." She smiled wide. "I know who you are, Bennett told me all about Jarrett's crush on you." She smiled at the sound of Bennett's name leaving her mouth, pausing momentarily to make eye contact with him. "Six years. Wow. I wish that I could have someone that had waited that long to tell me their feelings," she finished.

"Well, I better get this going." Bennett began to usher her away towards the family littered about for introductions. The softest of hands was on the small of her back. A tower compared to her little stature.

"Don't let them eat her alive," I called to Bennett.

"Definitely won't." He smiled, disappearing into the crowd.

I tried not to let him see the excitement that I wore like a bow. Six years? That's something to live up to. I had to find him. Talk to him. Frustration bit slightly at my edges.

I turned and glided quietly around the rim of the crowd. Jarrett adhered to my thoughts when suddenly I caught sight of August. Not just any August— a *blushing* August.

Who was that?

August was tucked away from the crowd around the corner leaning against the porch. A handsome guy in front of her, palm pressed against the wood next to her head.

He had shaggy brown hair and eyes to match. A wide jaw and toned muscles that explained he really worked for a living. A nice white button-up and jeans would tell you he had put just as much thought into his appearance as August had.

Jimmy was at my side. "How you holding up there, kid?" he asked, smiling lightly.

"A little intense." I sucked air through my nervous teeth.

"That's Maple Falls. Little place that loves to eat." He smiled warmly.

"Who's that?" I asked, nodding in the direction of August and her obvious crush.

"Bobby Swiss. Just moved back to drive truck for us." He smiled wide. "Good boy. Just finished his time in the military. He and August were pretty sweet on each other in high school…" He trailed away.

"What happened?" I asked, completely ignoring my need to find Jarrett and intrigued about this mystery August I had never known. She had never mentioned Bobby. Not once. In all the years I knew her, she was always someone who seemed flippant when it came to love. It never occurred to me that an old flame was behind her behavior.

"Broke each other's damn hearts." He turned to camouflage an emotion I couldn't pinpoint. "She begged him to go away with her to college and he begged her to stay. Became a moot point. Didn't stop them from loving each other though," he said. "Damn shame too."

We stood watching them curiously. So August had a great love. How unlike August. The girl that couldn't be tied down forever had a dedicated heart that couldn't let go. A sense of sadness for my best friend took over. In all our years she only said she had a high school sweetheart and that they grew up. The countless lectures of love were all too well-known. She had taken them all with a silent understanding. I felt the need to apologize.

"Better get to finding Nell. Sure she needs my help by now." He walked off quietly.

I stood in his wake still observing August completely saturated with her lost love. My brows pulled together, and I wanted to reach out but I knew better. August wasn't someone who did well with sympathy. She hated to be pitied. She was too much of a realist. I learned that my first summer with her at school when she caught a boy she'd been dating kissing Megan Harris outside a house party. Instead of getting upset, she actually thanked him for showing her his true colors. She then proceeded to tell Megan how beautiful and deserving she was of someone that warranted her time. They were friends for two years until she transferred. I decided to turn and continue my mission.

I circled the yard many times, but there were no signs of Jarrett anywhere. Anyone I asked shook their head no in response. He'd disappeared.

I started walking towards the shed that he had saved me behind the first night I'd arrived when I was hiding. My shoulders hung low, and I looked down at my ridiculous attempt at attractiveness. At least August was too busy to add insult to injury.

I plopped onto the ground pressing my back against the red flaking wood.

"This stinks." I slapped the dirt with my hands. I didn't care that I was getting my jeans a little dirty. The temperature was uncharacteristically warm all day and the mist had subsided allowing a dense ground fog to replace it as the cool night approached.

"Hiding?" a soft voice called into the darkness beside me.

"It's a little much." I smiled abruptly at the sound of Jarrett's voice so close to me. My heart recognized him, and my pulse began to rise.

"Let's go." A hand reached down, and I placed mine into his. "Mom saw us today. Gave me some asinine excuse to leave." He was smiling as the yellow torches near the party danced across his tanned cheeks.

"I couldn't love your mom more right now," I blurted.

We started walking carefully behind the buildings and going around the opposite side of the house watching for other people about to intervene. I followed his steps hopelessly. I didn't care in the least where our destination was. The thing that mattered was that we were together at this moment. A late spring night, the low sunset barely creeping through the gaps among the tree trunks. We arrived out onto the pavement and his pace didn't slow until we reached a bend in the road.

"I love walking down the middle." He smiled while still holding my hand.

"Me too," I spoke nervously. I had prayed for this moment all day. To talk to him. To ask him about last night's *almost* instance.

"Lily, I gotta ask you something before I do this." He paused in thought, slowly walking, never letting go. "Is there something with you and Ethan?" he asked in a rush.

"What? No," I replied quickly. "Why would you think that?" I asked worriedly.

"The way you two talk. I've met the guy. There's a sync between you two I couldn't match." He looked down with a slight sadness reaching his expression.

"He's my best friend, Jarrett." I decided not to think about it, just say it. "Jarrett, I've had a crush on you since forever." Nervous of his reaction at the confession, I drew circles in the pavement with my toe.

"You were wearing this shirt actually." He paused as I grew silent. "What are you thinking about?" he asked, eyeing me.

"I can't believe that I've owned this shirt for that long." I looked down, plucking at the corner of the fabric with my fingers.

"I love that about you. How you speak your mind without trying." He stopped and started to face me in the middle of the road. "How beautiful you are."

My breath was weak.

I looked down the black river of concrete ahead.

No one.

The noises of the party were barely audible behind us. The sun had dropped so low the temperature was conflicting with its environment. Thick steam was billowing up from the pavement surrounding us up to our waists.

"Lily. Would you be mad if I…" He stopped, staring me directly in the eyes.

I wasn't breathing.

"If you kissed me?" I spoke softly, swallowing hard to hide my nervousness.

He reached his palms up holding both sides of my face gently and without another word slid his hand back and twisted the strands into his fingers pulling me into him, my whole entire body obeyed.

No interruptions.

My lips caressed his lightly, then more passionately as the fear melted away. I didn't care who's brother he was. My arm reached around his waist, the other pulled him towards me by his hip.

He mimicked me, pressing harder. A low growl rose from his chest in approval. His kiss strayed as his hand dropped to the back of my neck. Intuitively my head fell, and his lips went wildly down my neck that bordered the heat brimming within.

He slowed and came to a stop at my collarbone, kissing more and more lightly. My body felt like a current was running through my veins, our breathing, both strenuous.

"Completely worth the wait, Lily," he breathed into my ear.

"More than." I smiled happily.

"I've been wanting to kiss you since the first time I saw you," he murmured. "That first time you came here, wearing that little white sweater, walking across the yard at August's side. I tried not to look at you. Not to notice my little sister's best friend, but I'd be lying if I said I didn't daydream about it. Daydream about…you." He whispered the words into my hair.

"Me too." A smile played at the corners of my lips.

He started walking back towards the house. Not without taking my hand first though. He walked a little closer and a little slower, and honestly my thoughts were nowhere near anything coherent.

11

I Can't Think When You do That

"I'm going to miss this food, Nell," I groaned as I took another bite of egg.

"Well, honey, I'm hoping you'll be back for Christmas." Her smile was the warmth I had no desire to leave.

"Hell yeah. Aug's room is empty most of the time," Tate offered.

"It's my room," she defended.

"We'd rather have you in it anyway, Lil," Trip threw an arm around my shoulders and squeezed.

"We could get bunk beds, August." I smiled at her as I pulled away from his hand.

"Don't encourage them!" she urged as she reached across and stole the last biscuit from my plate.

"Frankly, I don't know why you always complain about your brothers. They're not nearly as annoying as you say." I blinked innocently, the mischief obvious behind my eyes.

Jarrett chuckled beside me as I sat back in my chair glancing at him, a pleased smile on his face. I could vaguely hear playful bickering among those at the table and I watched as Jarrett's lips formed words, but they didn't reach my ears as thoughts of kissing him replayed in my mind. Suddenly, it seemed like everything I needed was right here.

A commotion at the other end of the house echoed into the dining room, a silence fell among us.

"Shh." A dainty voice carried the soft command to the table.

"Do you really think we're getting away from this house secretly?" a smokier voice said in amusement.

I watched as the chairs around the table tipped on their rear legs and the entire clan of Bayne boys craned their necks to catch a peek of the source. Following their gazes, I turned to see for myself.

Two young women, one tiptoeing while the other strode proudly through the house. One bent at the waist to slip a heel onto her bare foot. Her mahogany locks spilling over her shoulders in a tousled mess. As she righted herself, she ran her hands over the wrinkles of her dress and tugged an errant strap up over her shoulder, eyes downcast throughout the entire promenade.

The second looked straight ahead as she smiled at her cohort, amused by her shyness. Her hand swept through the disarray of strawberry-blond curls that fell around her face. She wore sleek black pants and a plum shirt, heels clicking against the floor without apology.

"She's back again?" Jimmy said softly, pulling my attention away from the girls.

"I told you that she would be." Nell nodded.

He seemed impressed and resumed his breakfast.

As I turned, I saw Logan taking long strides to catch up to them. His hand went out and wrapped around the red head's elbow, tugging her to a stop just beyond the door frame, essentially blocking everyone's view.

So naturally, they had to tip further back in hopes of catching a better peek.

While they were distracted, Jarrett inconspicuously leaned in close to me and whispered in my ear.

"Are you all packed?"

I felt a sadness wash through me. I was going back.

"You should go finish. I'll help." His seductive grin was inviting.

I gave him a quick smile and pushed away from the table.

"I think I'm going to go finish packing." I picked up my plate to take it to the sink.

"I'll get it. You go ahead," Jarrett said as he stood beside me and took the dish from my hands. His fingers lingered over mine briefly.

"Thanks, Jarrett." I smiled.

"Jarrett! Stop with the chivalry!" Tate grumbled as I turned to walk away.

"It's called being polite." He laughed.

"It's called showing off," Trip mumbled as I headed off to the cabin.

As I made my way through the house and out the back door, all I could think of was getting a little time alone with Jarrett before we had to leave. Stepping into the cabin, I took a slow deep breath as my eyes closed trying to paint my memories with the aroma of his place. It was neat. His work boots were set next to the door caked with mud. I could get used to this place.

"You don't have a whole lot to pack do you?" his voice called from behind me as the door closed.

"No, but I still don't want to do it." I turned to face him as he stepped towards me.

"So don't." It was a simple solution.

"And how do you suppose I'd get my things home?"

He reached out to me, and his hand slid around my waist. "Either you'd come back to get them or I would bring them along when I come visit." He smiled confidently.

Mine was radiant. I vaguely wondered if a grown woman should squeal like a child.

"I don't know when I'll be able to come but I *will* be there." The gentle pressure of his hand at my back compelled my body to fall against his. I didn't want to wait two months until the Bayne boys came for the Fourth of July. I wanted him for myself.

"I would love that." My voice was a whisper as his hand tipped my face up to his.

"Me too." His lips descended on mine as he spoke and the excited flutter in my stomach was replaced with a burn that engulfed every nerve in my body.

My hands, resting on his chest, pulled the fabric of his shirt into fisted fingers. On their own accord, my heels rose from the floor, and I stood on the balls of my feet. Trying to get as close as possible to the delicious caress of his lips.

"Now that I know what I've been missing"—his voice was thick with hunger— "I won't be able to talk myself into staying away anymore." His lips brushed against mine.

"You shouldn't listen to yourself quite so much." It wasn't nearly as witty a statement in the breathless timbre of my voice.

"Lily Bear, you've been the..." He paused with a deep breath through his nose. "How do I say this? For guys, there's always that one girl who lays the foundation for every other girl. Some guys it's a childhood crush, the girl in high school, or that hot teacher they had in sixth grade." A low chuckle drifted from his throat as I watched his Adam's apple bounce. "His vision of the perfect girl."

I never realized how sexy that was, a man's neck.

"You're *mine*." It fell softly on my ears, and I took a step back as I looked into his eyes.

Shocked was an inadequate description of what I felt.

"Auggie raved about you. It didn't take long for all of us to realize you were something special. By the time you came for that first visit, I was sure she'd forgotten to mention some detrimental trait you had." His head shook in disbelief.

"She raved about me?" That was new. She never did that while I was around.

"Oh yes. I thought she made you up. You were everything she'd said, and more than I'd imagined." He dipped forward and kissed me softly.

"Didn't she tell you I can't cook?" Was I trying to talk him out of this?

He kissed along my jawline. "Mm-hmm."

"I can't think when you do that." My eyes closed as my head dropped towards my shoulder to allow him easier access to continue. Had I said that aloud?

"Me either."

And as his mouth covered mine.

He let out a groan. "God, woman, I want you right here." He pulled my hips to his, "I'm going to come see you soon," he promised with sincere eyes.

"I'll be there." I beamed.

* * *

I adjusted the grip on my bag as I drug myself through the terminal.

"Come on, molasses. Baggage claim awaits," August called over her shoulder.

"It's not going anywhere," I mumbled.

"But we are. So come on!" she urged.

"What do you mean *we* are? This part of *we* is going home to nap," I said.

"Lazy ass. Bayne-cation is over. Back to the real world now," she said.

"Real world?"

Exhaustion was the description that seemed to fit how I felt. No vacation should exhaust you this much. Although it was a *Bayne-cation*, as August had called it. Any sane person would need rest after a week with the Baynes. I yawned at the thought.

"Harper! Lily! Hey! Hey, you're walking!" A voice echoed from across the claim area.

I smiled as I searched for the source of the voice.

Ethan stood waving a gigantic sign over his head. Large bright pink letters read *Lily!* across the front of it. A smile graced his lips. The smile I hated to adore.

"Of course, she's walking! I took perfect care of her all week. We didn't even do anything exciting," August said as she winked at me.

I faltered a step when I heard that. Nothing exciting? My encounter with a bear or the stolen moments with Jarrett would beg to differ. My lips were sealed, and I had no intention of telling Ethan about any of it. I knew he would be upset. He never liked Jarrett, but I couldn't put my finger on why. He always claimed it was how I was around him. Whatever that meant...

"Well done, August! I wouldn't have believed it if I hadn't seen it myself. She even looks rested!" he said happily as he walked towards us.

"I know! I made her behave," she said proudly.

I choked on the air around me.

"You were right. You win," he said.

"Of course I was. Pony up!" She grinned as she held out her wrist.

He sighed as he slipped his lavish watch over his hand and dangled it out for her.

"You guys may have a gambling problem," I interjected caustically.

"Damn it," August swore sideways through her teeth.

"That will be a first-round pick during our fantasy football draft, commissioner!" Ethan smiled broadly while he shot at August with finger guns.

Apparently, they bet on my safety during the trip *and* my reaction to the bet. These two were moronic at best.

He stepped in front of me, pressing a soft kiss to my temple. "Missed you," he said tenderly as he took my backpack. His free hand reached down to wrap around my own as he strode easily beside August, tugging me behind.

I smiled at the gesture and then watched as his hand rose to her shoulder and patted gently.

I felt like laughing.

"Jerk, you owe me dinner for that horribly crafted sign. You can barely see *my* name!" She slapped at the poster board he'd folded and slipped under his arm.

"If I'd known you'd take such good care of her, I would have made it bigger. But let's face it, you're a selfish flake sometimes," he said.

"I am not selfish! I care, Ethan! It matters to me what happens to her! God, I wouldn't risk her coming back injured! Do you have any idea what that would mean for me? Working alone! Bored! Alone! By myself!" she said, appalled.

"Who are you kidding? You'd never show up," Ethan jabbed.

"Holy shit, I'd get to be my own boss." The epiphany unfolding in her little blond head.

"I'm actually still right here," I interjected.

"I don't have to listen to you. You're not my boss anymore," she said as she flicked her hand in my direction.

"Great, I guess it's going to be you and me for dinner, Monroe." I shrugged.

"Just because I fired you doesn't mean the custody agreement is up for negotiation." Waving a finger at me. "You're still mine during daylight hours and every other bar night."

"I'd like to propose an amendment that—"

"All requests must be submitted in writing." August pursed her lips, nodding.

"To whom?" I asked.

"To the board members, Harper," she stated as though I should've known that already.

"No one of sound mental capacity would appoint you two to any position of authority," I said.

"Babe, trust the system. I don't want to fight anymore. Why don't we go home and have make-up sex?" He smiled.

"No fraternizing with the board members!" August proclaimed.

"Wha—?" My mouth agape. "He's fraternizing, not me!"

"Yes, I am. Want to go fraternize in the bathroom right now, honey?" Ethan eyed me devilishly.

"Despite what you think, Monroe, your penis is not the answer to everything," she derided.

"Why, you want to find out, August?" A crooked smile played across his lips. "Too bad. I'm committed to Lily Bear here."

"What did you just say?" I stopped, Jarrett's face coming to the forefront. The pet name he dubbed me, consumed my thoughts.

"The thought of you procreating, Ethan, is an abomination." She smirked.

"Whoa, August. Calm down. That's me and Lily's kid you're talking about right now!" Ethan said.

I trudged forward in disbelief that they were blatantly ignoring me and talking about me at the same time.

"I'm right here, you know," I called out.

"We know. We can smell you," August said.

"What?" I scoffed. "Do not!"

"Too lazy to shower?" Ethan asked with a knowing nod.

"Yeah. It's bad," my crappy best friend answered.

"I don't smell," I said defensively.

"You'd smell better if you'd showered this morning," August said.

"Someone used all the hot water," I said accusingly.

"It was probably those harlots," she said, referring to the two girls Logan and Grey had brought home.

"They obviously weren't showered," I recalled.

"Don't worry, babe. You smell fine." Ethan squeezed my hand.

"Don't call me 'babe,' and I know I smell fine!" I retorted.

"Cranky today, isn't she?" he asked August.

"Yeah, she's still mad about breakfast this morning," she said.

"You stole my biscuit," I blurted.

"Hey! I called the last biscuit before you even got up. Just because my evil brother had them hidden away for you doesn't make them safe from the claim," she said with a toss of her hand.

"I give up," I said as my shoulders drooped.

"God, I missed you guys," Ethan smiled as he wrapped his arms around our shoulders.

I strolled along listening to their chatter. It seemed strange to be home. I'd been so wrapped up in the Baynes that it flew by. I couldn't tear my mind away from thoughts of them. Of him. Of us. And as much as I looked forward to being back with Ethan, I wanted to see Jarrett's face again.

"Daydreamer, get in the car," August said as she slipped into the back.

I snapped out of my reverie in time to step aside as he opened the door for me.

"What's up?" Ethan asked.

I miss Jarrett. I want to go back to him. "Nothing, glad to be home," I said with a smile.

"Aw, you missed my company," he said and wrapped me in a hug.

I laughed softly. "Not too much," I said.

"Lies. I know better." He grinned, still holding me tightly.

I squeezed him softly. "Of course I did," I indulged.

"I missed you. It sucks not seeing your face for a whole week." He pursed his lips.

"Let's go, people! I have a date!" August called from the back seat tapping her new timepiece.

"How do you have a date? We just got back," I asked as I ducked into the seat.

"She got two numbers while we were in baggage claim," Ethan said in amusement before he closed my door.

"I know it's hard for you to understand, but popular and lovable people, like me"— she rested her hand on her chest for visual effect— "are in high demand. We have to plan things weeks in advance. Especially dates," she spouted.

"Oh, right. Of course," I agreed with a quick nod. How could I have been so silly?

"I mean, I'm pretty great," she continued jokingly.

I simply nodded along.

"And if I'm not home by 3:00, I'll be late for dinner with Evan. Then I'll end up making Eric wait. We'd miss the 7:30 movie, and then we wouldn't make it to karaoke by 10:00," she babbled on.

"Two dates, August?" I questioned.

"Well, it was supposed to be a sampler night, but hottie Hank had to cancel," she said sadly.

"Sampler night?" I repeated curiously as Ethan slid into the driver's seat and closed his door.

"Ah, Harper. So innocent. I love that about you," Ethan said with a smile.

I glanced at him briefly with a look of annoyance.

"So naive. You can't jump right into a full-blown date, Lily. It's like a good meal. You have to know what you like. So, you try a little bit of everything until you're sure," August explained.

"You can't plan two dates in one night," I said.

"No. *You* can't. I most certainly can. I mean, have you met me? I'm quite talented," she answered.

"Oh, right," I said softly.

"Pay attention, kid. You'll learn something." August smiled at me with an encouraging nod.

I turned away and rolled my eyes playfully.

"Let's go eat," Ethan said.

"Oh, thank goodness, yes. I'm starving," I groaned.

"Not me. Straight home, James," August commanded as though he were a hired driver.

"We should maybe stop by my place so you can shower first," he suggested.

"Don't you start," I warned.

"I'm just saying." He shrugged.

"I concur," August sang from the back.

I threw a glare at her. "You know, Ethan, it's an hour's drive home if we're lucky, and I'm not sure I can go that long before eating," I said sweetly.

"Aw, babe, we'll eat before we leave Denver then," he said with a smile.

"Don't…" I paused and held back the denial of the nickname. "Don't worry about it. Wouldn't want August to be late for her date," I said.

"Dates!" she corrected.

"Like I care about her dates." He gave an unimpressed glance.

"You should care that my first date knows a lot of your exes. I'm sure they would absolutely love to have your private number," she threatened.

"Lily needs to eat." He grew annoyed.

"Eat in the car," she begged.

"Marilyn does not allow eating," he said seriously as his hand reached out to caress the sleek black dashboard in front of him.

I laughed at the car's name.

"Freaking hell. If I'm late, I'll strangle you, Lily," she said in annoyance.

"No strangling necessary. You won't be late." Ethan shrugged.

"I might do it anyway," she said.

"I'd like to see you try," Ethan laughed.

I looked at him in disbelief.

"Oh, you think I couldn't take her, huh?" August questioned.

"I've sparred with Harper a hundred times. She'd kick your ass," he stated matter-of-factly.

"Oh, really? I bet you'd change your mind if you'd seen her piss scared and falling all over herself trying to outrun that bear!" she blurted triumphantly.

My eyes went wide, and I turned to mouth a *shut up* in her direction.

"Bear?" Ethan said seriously.

"It was a good fifteen feet away from her and she was scrambling to back away from it. Fell on her ass in the river, crawling like crazy and everything. Like a little scared pansy," she embellished as a look of accomplishment took over her face.

"I don't understand. You mean like a teddy bear? Or perhaps a bear skin rug? Because you told me you kept her safe all week, 'didn't do anything exciting,'" Ethan said as he turned to look her directly in the eye.

She froze. "She was perfectly safe! We had kazoos…and bear spray… and"— August gulped— "stuff," she finished lamely.

Ethan stared at her for a moment before turning back to face the front.

"Well, that's it." His lips in a hard line.

"That's what?" I asked.

"That's the last time I let you out of my sight," he declared.

"Ethan. She's exaggerating," I said calmly.

"No. Sorry. Too dangerous," he stated.

"She didn't even get hurt!" August shouted.

"She could have died!" he yelled.

"It was fine," I quickly pacified.

"I wouldn't let her die. God! Can you imagine? That would be horrible!" August cried.

"Yeah, it would. Not only would life cease to have meaning, but I'd have to hunt you down and avenge her death," he noted darkly.

"Can we change the subject? No one's avenging anything," I said.

"I'd have to plan a funeral! Could you imagine! Invitations. Catering. I'd have to hire a band," August rambled on.

I gave her a strange look. "A band, August? No. And you don't send out invitations for a funeral," I informed her.

"And I'd have to wear black! I don't want to steal your thunder at your own funeral! Don't you dare die on me!" she insisted.

"Yeah, I'll do my best," I said with a shake of my head.

"Oh God. The boys would tie me to a tree again. Jarrett would disown me. He hasn't even gotten that kiss he wants yet!" she continued.

I sank into my seat a little more and turned my face to look out the window. A little part of me felt bad keeping things from her, but she'd never let it go. It wasn't like we were that serious. It was just a kiss. A great kiss. Twice.

"Your brother?" Ethan asked with an edge in his voice.

"He wants our Lily hardcore right now, Ethan, especially after he took her to that little T-ball game of his. It's pathetic," she laughed.

"I forgot about that," I lied.

"Oh, crushing. Well, of course he is. Lily is highly desirable," he said as he reached over and patted my knee before pulling out of the parking spot.

I looked at him briefly. The differences between the two men in my life were easy to see. Jarrett was sincere when he talked to me. Mature. When he complimented me, it made me blush. When Ethan did it, I felt no sincerity behind it. No romantic meaning. Jarrett said things when he meant them. It was a refreshing change. Ethan said whatever would sound good. There always seemed to be an angle he was working.

"I wouldn't say it's a crush. The boys have a crush on Lily. Jarrett is being all selfish and concerned. He even got her alone!" she exclaimed.

"Alone?" Ethan repeated as he sat up a little straighter in his seat.

"He was only trying to save me from the rest of you," I chimed, hoping this conversation would die.

"It's eat-or-be-eaten in the Bayne household. If you can't handle it, don't come along," August scoffed.

"You don't give me a choice," I laughed.

"What? I have never forced you to do anything, Harper," she said, appalled at the suggestion.

"Well, you did go through her closet and steal all the clothes you didn't want her to wear," Ethan mentioned.

I turned to face her and dropped my head to the side.

"That was for her own good. Nobody in their right mind should wear things like that, and I didn't want people to think my best friend was crazy. Besides, I didn't take everything," she defended.

"True. There were things you left that rightfully could have gone," Ethan said with a nod.

I smacked him on the arm.

"Don't encourage her," I said in disbelief.

"Harper don't get me wrong, I appreciate a nice bit of leg peeking through, but not in jeans," he admitted.

"They're comfortable! Good jeans are hard to find," I said emphatically.

"Well, that's true! You don't understand how hard it is to find the perfect jeans, Monroe. It's a process like no other, and when you finally get the right ones, they stop making them!" August threw her arms up in disgust.

"Every damn time." I sighed.

The discussion continued through appetizers. I couldn't help but laugh through it. The fact that we could debate on a good pair of jeans for thirty-five minutes was amusing and heartwarming, and it made me feel good being at home again.

As the waitress brought our meals, August made a face of disgust. "I can't believe you ordered that. How are you going to share with me if you order something I don't like?" she asked.

"That was the reason I did it." I smiled as she set my plate in front of me.

"You shouldn't expect her to order based on what you like," Ethan said as he reached over and switched half of his burger with half of mine. "You said no onions, right?" he asked me.

"Yeah," I answered with a laugh as I realized he and I did exactly what he'd said.

I happen to love onions. But knowing that he couldn't stand them, I ordered my burger without onion. In turn, he did the same with his. No mayo either, per my unspoken request.

"Well, that's fine. Leave me out of your little ritual then. I'll sit over here and enjoy my very own food. I didn't want to share with either of you anyway," August said as she plucked an onion ring from her plate and took an angry bite.

"You still want to split dessert, right?" I asked.

"Well, I certainly can't let the two of you finish it by yourselves. You guys really need to watch your weight." She gestured up and down to us with her hand.

"What? Seriously? I'm going to have to start working out more," Ethan said self-consciously as he ran his hand over his stomach.

I shook my head and began to eat. The conversation was light, Ethan asking questions about my health after the "trauma" in Washington. August regaled us with what she thought were hilarious stories concerning the humiliation of me. I finally gave up and pretended to listen.

*****

"It's not happening, Harper," Ethan said as he dropped onto the couch.

"Ethan, this is not necessary," I called from the bathroom as I dabbed lotion on my elbows.

"I'm staying. Anything could happen in the next twenty-four hours. You could spike a fever in the middle of the night and need an ice bath," he answered.

"It's a scratch! It doesn't even hurt," I said as I stepped out of my room.

"After the week you've had, your immune system is obviously compromised. Even that scratch could lead to trouble," he said as I opened my closet door.

"You're worse than usual," I mumbled.

"Normally I could overlook it, but it's infection season," he said as I threw the overnight bedding at him.

I blinked at him. "You're making up illness seasons so you can spend the night," I said matter-of-factly. "Just let me sleep."

"Will do!" he said as the TV switched on behind me.

"And don't order anything!" I said as I glanced at the screen to see the guide open.

It closed a second later.

"Right. None of that," he said curtly.

I padded over to my bed and crawled under the covers. My last conscious thought was that Ethan had better see flames before he wakes me up to drag me out of a fire.

"Lily? Are you awake?" he whispered through the darkness.

Unfortunately, I was. "Yes. What's wrong?" I asked.

I listened as he made his way through my room.

"I had a nightmare that a bear had eaten your beautiful legs," he said softly as he reached to rub his hand down each of said appendages.

I laughed. "Nope. All intact," I whispered sleepily.

He was quiet but did not turn to leave.

"What do you want?" I asked.

"Well, honestly, I was debating how to convince you to scoot over to the other side of the bed so I could sleep by the door." He picked up the blankets and sat on the edge of the bed.

I sighed and moved over, and he slipped in beside me and patted his chest.

"Come on," he said.

I rolled over and draped one arm over his waist. His arm came down to cover mine while his other hand made short, soft trails along my spine.

"Back to sleep. I'll keep the nightmares away," he said.

"You're the scared one," I said softly.

"Shhh. Shhh. Don't tell stories," he whispered.

I smiled as I drifted back to sleep. Safe in the arms of a man who was anything but safe.

12

Being Petty with the Playboy's Girl

"No, that's not at all what I'm saying," I said in exasperation. I paced beside the truck as I looked down to the pavement beneath my feet. Mentally berating myself for the lack of information we'd been able to offer lately to my boss. It was becoming blatantly apparent that the controlled burn we were hoping to avoid this summer was going to be necessary.

"I can't make promises, Nodean." I paused as he mentioned some asinine comment about margins of loss. "I understand that your cattle depend on..." I was interrupted.

I dropped my head back in frustration. What did he expect? Honestly, if he wanted the truth, I didn't think he'd like what he'd hear.

"Of course, I'll keep you up-to-date. As soon as we find anything we'll report it right away and get the proper permits in place. Thank you." I tapped my phone.

I took a slow deep breath as my eyes closed. I tried to cool the heated blood in my veins with visions of calm water, and the earthy aroma of the forest. A hand on my back startled me and I jumped.

"Whoa. Are you okay, Harper?" Ethan's soft voice asked.

135

"Yeah, sorry. Are you ready?" I asked as I swung open my door.

"You're really tense lately, babe. You need a good massage," he said with a waggle of his fingers and a grin.

"No." I gave a half smile.

"Your loss. How about a trip to the boulders instead?" He suggested as he turned to walk over to the other side of the truck.

"Oh, we haven't been there in so long," I genuinely smiled.

"Let's go tomorrow. Make an evening of it. I'll bring the food if you bring the beer," he said as I slipped behind the wheel.

"Deal."

Ethan proceeded to ramble on about his latest conquest and I'm fairly sure I agreed to a double date of sorts.

I felt off. Initially, I'd thought it was the natural withdrawal symptoms after the Bayne high I'd been on, but it'd been two weeks since Washington. I should have been back to normal. I shouldn't miss them anymore.

But I did. I missed them—well, him. We had spoken every evening. His simple presence was enough to cloud my mind and brighten my eyes. Turn up my lips in a giddy smile. Make me lose track of every question I've ever had and not care. All that mattered was that he was there talking to me. It was intoxicating, and I wanted that back. I wanted to get lost with him.

* * *

"What are you wearing?" I could hear the grin in Jarrett's voice.

I blushed impossibly bright and tried to sound casual. "Lingerie, of course. That's all us girls lounge in at night. You didn't know that?"

"I'm going to pretend this is the truth!"

It started with one phone call and now it seemed to be our nightly ritual, when I wasn't with Ethan at least. If you would have asked me three months ago that Jarrett Bayne would be eating popcorn as we streamed the same movie together from our bedrooms, states apart, I wouldn't have believed it.

"What are *you* wearing?" I quipped.

"Lingerie. Guys can be sexy too!"

I rolled into my pillow in a fit of laughter.

"What color are they?" I giggled.

"Blue, of course…to accentuate my eyes…"

"I think any color would look good with your eyes." I smiled.

"Lily Bear, if I didn't know any better I'd say you're hitting on me right now." His voice was low, and I could hear the smirk behind his words.

"Maybe?"

"You sure know how to make a guy blush."

God, I missed him.

* * *

I slapped my hands against the steering wheel as I realized where my mind had drifted. Frustrated that the weeks apart and miles between us had done little to calm the effect he had.

"Lily?" Ethan called softly from his seat.

I glanced at him momentarily and then shook my head. "Sorry," I apologized.

"Are you sure you're up for this today?" he asked.

"Yeah, I'm fine. A nice long and quiet jog will be good for me," I said with a nod. I had agreed to run the Thanksgiving 10k with Ethan this year. We had been jogging together a couple times a week for a while now.

"Quiet. Yeah," he said slowly as he turned to look around the lot we'd pulled into.

"Really nice, actually. Maybe I can clear some of the distractions from my mind and concentrate on work again," I continued as I parked the truck.

"Distracted? Nah, you just need a fun day with friends," he said.

"Fun day?" I repeated as I stepped out onto the pavement.

"Yeah, I mean, a good workout. Great company. A laugh or two," he said enthusiastically.

"I want to get lost for a little while, Monroe," I sighed.

"I wish you'd told me that," he mumbled.

"Hey, there you guys are! I've been waiting," a chipper voice called from behind us.

I smiled.

He merely shrugged apologetically.

"I am so ready for this! What are we doing today? A mile?" August asked as she jogged in place.

I couldn't bring myself to respond to her. Aside from the fact that she was my best friend and the sister of the man I wanted to lose myself in, she was also the most competitive person in the world sometimes.

She looked like she'd been dressed by a military surplus store. Her gray sweats, which must have been a child's size since they were overly form-fitting and came to a stop just below the knee, sported ARMY in large black letters down the thigh. Her T-shirt was knotted in the back to expose her stomach. Her long hair spilled out from under a baseball cap, with the Marines *Semper Fi* creed embroidered on the front.

"What are you doing?" I motioned to her outfit with a flippant hand.

Her face brightened. "Cute, right? I know." She turned to model the outfit proudly.

"Unnecessary," I scoffed.

"Jealous much? Just because you can't make sweats, a tee, and this hat look as good as I do, doesn't mean you have to spew your hate at me." She rolled down the top of her sweats.

"Well, you're barely wearing them so that helps," Ethan said.

"You don't have the security clearance to handle this piece of machinery, Monroe," she said as she strutted away.

I groaned.

"Oh, is that what you're telling yourself these days?" Ethan asked and then turned to me. *Delusional*, he mouthed.

"Can we run please?" I begged.

"Let's go. This part of the path is dead. I'll never get any play if we don't catch up to the real runners." August clapped her hands together.

"Real runners?" Ethan questioned.

"Yeah. You know those guys that run like marathons? Real athletes! Not wannabes like you two." She cocked her head sideways.

I looked at Ethan at the same moment he looked at me.

I nodded with a smile.

"I've got a bet for you, August." A sly smile pulled at the corners of his tanned jaw.

"What's that?" She leaned forward intrigued.

"If you can keep pace with us today and finish, I will buy your dinner tonight. Wherever you want." Brows raised, he had his hands on his hips.

She turned to give him a serious look. "My entire dinner?" she asked suspiciously.

He nodded slowly.

"Deal," she agreed.

Ethan grinned.

"Alright. Let's go then." I smiled and started at a slow warm-up pace.

For the first mile or so, she was energetic enough to run backward while winking and flirting. For the second mile, she merely glanced over her shoulder. The third mile was when she realized we weren't stopping and simply let them pass by unnoticed, as she got quiet.

Until Ethan started badgering her. "You alright there, August? You look winded," he antagonized as he kept pace with her while running backward.

"Army strong!" she said, sounding winded.

I glanced back at her.

"Well, we're going to break out into our normal pace then." He smirked and turned back to face the front.

She stumbled on the path but righted herself quickly.

"About time. I was wondering when you'd run for real." She threw at his retreating back.

I smiled as Ethan, and I sped up. A while later, she'd fallen back quite a way and he called back to her.

"Giving up, Bayne?" he laughed.

She pursed her lips at him. "I will not falter, and I will not fail!" she yelled back.

I laughed.

"Yoo-rah!" she yelled.

"Whoa, there soldier. Calm down," he chuckled.

She actually caught up to us during the leg of the trail and pulled ahead by the end of it.

"Ha! Pansies!" she called back over her shoulder.

Sweat had soaked her *cute* outfit. Her white T-shirt was almost transparent in the back and her sweats did little to hide the wobble in her legs. Her previously free-flowing hair had been pulled through the adjustment strap of the hat and was a tangled, wet mess.

"Cool down for the last bit, August, or you're going to regret it," I warned her.

"Aim high, Harper!" she replied as she sped up and pulled out of sight.

With August silent from exhaustion and Ethan using his breaths wisely to avoid being overly winded, I finally got the quiet I'd hoped for.

Of course, it wasn't filled with thoughts of work as I'd hoped. It was instead bombarded by images of Jarrett, sweet, incredible, manly Jarrett. Wondering if he would run with me like this or if I'd simply give up for lack of desire to leave the house. I could picture us curled up on the couch all day, or never getting out of bed for the weekend. Stop right there. I told myself. *No thinking of Jarrett and beds,* I scolded. I had to get as far away from that subject. Work. I needed to think of work. Engrave it into my thoughts to push him away.

I repeated anything that came to mind from a day's work. Being in the trees. Looking at the bark. Leaves. The sun peeking through the leaves. Jarrett's gorgeous eyes squinting in the light beneath the leaves.

"NO! No, no, no," I berated myself as I pushed ahead of Ethan around a curve where August leaned heaving against a tree.

Spotting me, she jumped up mumbling something about waiting for us before she rushed off out of sight again. I couldn't help but laugh and smile at her antics. I couldn't imagine a better friend.

I shook my head to throw the thought away and immediately tried to think of something distasteful. Something I hated. Black coffee. Bitter. Oysters. Raw. I frowned at the thought.

Daydreaming about a luscious brother, my skirt-chasing best friend, or interesting strangers in the forest was a hindrance to my work.

No matter how comfortable, unhinged, or intrigued they made me feel, I needed to ignore all of those feelings and concentrate on work.

"You know what?" August said between heaving breaths as I came upon her collapsed form at the end of the path, barely able to hold herself up on hands and knees. "You suck. You could have warned me," she panted exasperatedly, raising her hand at me and waving it weakly.

I looked at her with a trace of regret.

Her eyes darted past me, and she dropped into a push-up position, immediately forcing a few repetitions out.

"C'mon, Monroe! Be all that you can be…fifty!" she called out with a smile as she did her last push-up.

He held up his hands in defeat as she jumped up gracefully. "I won't work you until you cry, little girl. I know you're hurting deep down." He jogged to a stop.

"I'm just fine, kid. Looking forward to dinner." She grinned and patted her belly.

His smile faltered.

"You're paying for dessert too. And I am starving myself for the rest of the day to make room," she said smugly, licking her lips.

He nodded and threw his arms out. "Figures," he grumbled.

He never could seem to win when it came to August. She somehow always came out on top.

"I need a shower. Meet you at six?" I asked as I started to back away, pulling a grumbling Ethan along with me.

"See you back home," she said as she turned to jog to the Jeep.

I saw her legs wobble and give out for a moment and quickly turned away before she noticed me watching. I nudged Ethan and motioned towards her after she'd turned away.

"Watch," I murmured.

He did so as we made our way to the truck. She stopped twice to rub the muscles of her legs and once to "tie her shoe," which took entirely too long.

Ethan grinned as we opened our doors and slid inside before collapsing into the cushions.

"Never again," he said.

"What possessed us to do eight?" I asked.

"Teaching her a lesson." He pointed in her direction.

"Right." I turned to look at him and he met my gaze.

"It was worth it." He smirked.

"You two are awful." I shared the smile.

* * *

"…and a baked potato with everything on it," August finished as the waitress scratched down the orders.

"Alright. I'll have your orders out shortly." She smiled.

"Wait. We still need to order," I said.

The girl froze and glanced at August.

"Oh! I'll need a chocolate milkshake to wash that all down with too." She smiled devilishly.

"Did you want some of those entrees in to-go boxes?" the server asked timidly.

"Hell no. I'm starving." She grinned as she stared across the booth at Ethan's ashen face.

"Um, okay. What did you decide on then?" the waitress asked as she looked at me.

I rattled off my order and then kicked Ethan when he failed to respond at his turn.

"Ethan, honey, she wants your order," Ashley said with a little giggle as she nudged his shoulder. The girl Ethan had brought on our *double date*.

"I'm not your honey," he said before giving his simple order, still in shock at the amount this meal would cost him.

The girl slouched in her seat until the waitress walked away. I reached across the table and snagged the lemon from Ethan's water glass, dropping it into my own before stirring it briskly.

Ashley eyed me territorially and perked up in her seat.

"I was reading the other day about this cooking class they're having. It's learning stuff from around the world. I think I might sign up," she offered enthusiastically.

"Oh, you like to cook?" I smiled.

"Oh, who doesn't? It's so fun!" she crooned.

"Every girl should learn how to cook." Ethan nodded and shot a glance my way.

"Not everyone," I said purposefully.

"I think it makes sense," the girl smiled sweetly. "Someday when I decide to get married and have kids, I'll need to know how to cook, so I might as well learn now and perfect it," Ashley said.

"You're smarter than the average bear, aren't you, Ash?" Ethan turned to her and gave her an approving smile.

She beamed at the attention.

I felt like gagging.

"There's no rule that says marriage and kids means you have to cook. My mother didn't cook, and I turned out fine." I shrugged.

"Well, you're the obvious exception, Harper," Ethan said.

"Besides, Nell cooked for August, and look what it did to her," I said as my best friend lifted her glass to her mouth.

"What? Made me amazing? Sure did!" She smirked before taking a long drink.

Ashley laughed and then covered her mouth as if trying to hide her giggle.

I pondered her reaction for a minute. Did she think that was a burn of some sort? Should I have felt knocked down a peg? What was her angle?

I studied her. Nonchalantly leading her via questions and mentally noting each answer. Watched as she played coy and sweet for Ethan. Gagged as he ate it up encouragingly. She inched closer to him on the bench, and he scooted away as I smirked to myself. She offered up bites of her meal and tried to taste his multiple times. I felt an odd twinge of joy as he told her to leave his food alone.

So of course, I reached over and plucked food off his plate. And, as in every case before this, he didn't react to it at all.

I actually cheered in my head as a look of horror and hatred crossed her face. I couldn't hold back the smile I sent her way.

From that moment on, what started as a simple curiosity became an all-out war between us. She voiced the chill in the air to deaf ears. I got a single chill and Ethan dropped his jacket across the table and into my lap.

"What's this for?" I asked.

"You're cold. Put it on," he answered before taking a bite.

"I'm fine. Maybe Ashley could use it?" I smiled innocently.

"She should have brought a jacket. Now put it on," he said around the food in his mouth.

I held back the laugh. August did not.

"Wow, what a sweetheart, Ethan." She pulled a hearty swig of her milkshake.

"Never claimed to be." He shrugged.

"You are too," I said.

August glanced at me for a second with a strange look on her face.

"You don't count." Ethan smiled as the waitress set down new water with lemon in front of him.

He plucked the lemon from the edge of the glass.

"Oh, can I have that?" Ashley asked.

"Already spoken for," he said as he dropped it into my half-empty glass.

I smiled.

She glared.

"Hey, Ethan, I know we'd planned on going out after dinner to a movie but maybe we could rent something instead?" she asked with a low, sultry tone to her voice as her hand disappeared under the table.

He turned and smiled at her wolfishly.

"Yeah, we can do that," he said as he leaned over and whispered into her ear.

My stomach turned and I pushed my plate away.

"Can I have your rings, Lily?" August asked.

"Have at it. I'm done," I offered.

"You barely ate." Ethan eyed the food left on my plate.

"Not hungry I guess," I replied nonchalantly.

"You feel okay? You didn't eat any lunch today. You should be able to polish that off easily." Worry was lacing his tone.

I was a little shocked that he noticed so much about me. Suddenly, I realized he knew more than I thought he did.

"I'm fine," I responded flatly.

"We can head out if you want," he offered.

"The rest of us are still eating," August piped in.

"No need, Monroe. I'm just done eating," I assured him.

"I wouldn't mind going though if you wanted to leave, Ethan." Ashley smiled.

"I wouldn't mind finishing my food," he replied shortly.

"I thought maybe you were ready for dessert," she cooed.

"I'm ready for dessert. Ethan's buying," August sang happily as she waved down the waitress passing by.

After a quick order of two desserts, she took her leave, and Ethan bolted to the bathroom.

"Well, I hope he's learned his lesson," August said.

"What lesson is that?" I asked her.

"We'll see if he puts a meal on the line the next time he challenges me." She smiled triumphantly.

"You cost him a fortune tonight," I laughed.

"He lost a bet?" Ashley smiled as she asked.

"Oh yeah. He didn't think I could run eight miles," she bragged.

"Eight miles? Wow. Good for you." His plaything smiled sweetly.

"I work out, you know. I stay in pretty good shape," August boasted.

"Obviously, and you've got great taste too. I love that outfit." Ashley plumped up my best friend's already swollen ego.

"Isn't it though? See, Harper, not all the girls Ethan dates are idiots," she said, swatting me on the shoulder and then cringing at the muscle strain the simple movement caused.

My shoulders drooped and I gave her a scathing glance.

"Idiots, huh?" Ashley smiled.

"Generally," I laughed.

"Well, maybe he was making do with the trash until the right girl came along," she said with a snide undertone.

"Maybe," I voiced and held back the initial *then he's not done yet*, a remark that entered my mind.

She smirked as he came back to the table.

I excused myself to the bathroom as thoughts of wringing her little neck ran through my mind.

"What the hell is wrong with you, Harper?" I asked my reflection in the mirror.

Why in the name of all things science was I acting so annoyed with this girl? She's no different from any other conquest that Ethan Monroe has tried to conquer. She is as flighty and temporary as every other girl he goes after. Besides, even if she wasn't, it doesn't matter!

"This is Ethan!" I yelled at myself in the mirror. I took a few deep breaths and headed back out to the table.

"Why are you cutting that in half?" Ashley's voice carried back to me as I got closer.

"To share it," Ethan replied simply.

"Oh, that's so sweet, but I really didn't want anything." Her voice dripped with sugar-coated sweetness.

"It's not for you," he said as I arrived at the table to see him slide half of his cheesecake in front of my place.

I smirked and then mentally slapped myself for the reaction.

I still ate the dessert and damned if I didn't make a spectacle of its deliciousness. Her scowl, as wrong as it may be, brought me great joy.

13

Our Oasis

Ethan's blond hair was ragged, a different look for him.

"Your hair's getting long," I said as I reached over and ran my fingers through it.

"Yeah, I know. You think you could trim it for me?" he asked.

"I like it shaggy, very rugged, like a sexy mountain man or something." I smiled.

"Really?" he asked as he checked himself out in the rear-view mirror.

"Yeah, I'd hit that." I smirked.

"Calm down. I'm driving right now, you're going to have to wait." He flashed his crooked grin at me.

"Well, it's kind of a now or never deal. That's too bad." I nodded.

He turned the hazards on while slowly inching towards the shoulder. I playfully shoved at his face. "You wish."

"You're right." He gained speed again. "Not here. Not like this. We should wait till our wedding night."

"I don't think Ashley's going to want me at your wedding," I stated.

"Who?" he asked.

"Ashley? The girl you're dating," I reminded him.

A blank stare washed over his face as he shook his head in confusion.

"The girl. From yesterday. We ate food together." I spooned invisible food into my mouth.

"Her? Dating? Whoa. Slow down there. She's just a girl," he said.

"It's dating, Ethan. Not marriage," I soothed.

"Regardless, it's nothing. If she's going to get uppity about cheesecake, then she's not worth the time anyway," he said.

I'd certainly not intended to provoke her. Not before I saw the cheesecake anyway. But once he shared it with me… well, there was no stopping it then.

I did feel a little bad that he'd not had the night he'd planned. Instead, he got stuck with me and August.

"Yeah, sorry that we ruined your night."

"August is a force to be reckoned with. Makes me glad I was an only child." He smiled.

I gave him a strange look. "You're not though," I said.

"Drake and Margo don't count," he countered quickly.

"Why?" I asked.

"They were off at boarding school," he replied.

"So were you," I laughed.

"No, no. See I was in the states. At home. They were whisked away to France and Switzerland for amazing European adventures," he said.

"If I recall correctly, you broke down and begged your mother to let you stay in the states," I said with a smirk.

"If you believe that woman's side of the story over mine, we have some serious issues to resolve before the wedding," he said with a huff.

"You do know that she kept all those FaceTime calls from school, right?" I asked.

Coincidentally, Ethan grew up a short distance from me and attended boarding school in neighboring New Hampshire. Well, partially attended. He was asked to leave quietly before his fourteenth birthday following a botched blackmail plot. We did not have the same upbringing.

Ethan was the youngest of three children and the son of a real estate tycoon for a father and socialite for a mother. His family was drenched in two things— politics and wealth. His plan to aggravate his family by becoming a forest park ranger backfired. His mother proudly tells people of her son's *noble* work at her weekend equestrian club.

He turned to look at me quickly as his face grew pale.

I nodded slowly.

He hit the brakes and turned off on a side road. Screeching to a stop before twisting in his seat and facing me.

"All of them?" he asked lowly.

"Every single one," I said.

He dropped his head and shook it slowly. His hand came up to run through his hair as he sighed.

"Well, I guess that's it," he said sadly before turning back to the steering wheel and draping his arms over it.

"What?" I was confused.

"I can't marry you now, Harper," he said and then swore under his breath.

I actually felt stricken for a moment.

"What? Why?" I asked with a playful laugh. I closed my eyes the second the words left my mouth. Stupid!

"After that, why would you want to? I was hoping you'd never find out," he said sadly.

"I'll admit it was a little dramatic and maybe slightly crazy, but you were a kid. All kids do something stupid at one point," I reassured him. He was embarrassed his mother had shown me all the calls of his tween pleas to come home. He'd been a late bloomer and he was mortified to know I saw his awkward phase. I'd hate for him to discover I also found out he slept with an Optimus Prime action figure until he was eleven.

"Man, I thought that was a genius plan. Fun too. Expensive though. Those girls were not cheap," he reminisced.

"You paid them?" I said. I was appalled. He had grown so desperate to come home and escape his bullies that he concocted a plan to blackmail his headmaster— or at least make it appear that way.

"You saw me, Lily! I was hideous. And now you'll never be able to love me." He cringed.

I thought back for a second. Tried to picture the *hideous* teenage boy he seemed to envision.

"You were not hideous," I said.

He smiled softly at me. "So sweet. I'm going to miss you." He reached over and ran his thumb across my cheek.

"I'm not going anywhere and what exactly made you such a monster?" I swatted his hand away. I must have been out of my mind. I had always made a point to vehemently deny this marriage dream of his and now, 'I'm not going anywhere'?

"Ugh…I can't even…the eyebrow…coke bottle lenses…the tin grin… it hurts to even think about it," he said as he closed his eyes and scowled.

"So you went through a stage…" I began.

"A back brace, Lily! I wore orthotics!" he said angrily.

I barely withheld a laugh. "Yeah, leaving the brace on in the pictures was probably not your best decision," I said, scrunching up my nose.

"I was thirteen! Nobody had ever made me actually use my brain before. It was out of commission," he defended himself.

"You're lucky you just got kicked out. Blackmailing the headmaster? That should have gotten you arrested," I laughed.

"Well, it's the one time I was glad Mother worried about *what people would say*." He imitated her favorite line.

I smiled at him and reached over to rest my hand on his forearm. "I'm starving. Let's get to the lake."

"Agreed." He swung open his door.

I looked around and realized we were at the clearing we needed.

"C'mon, wifey. Let's have some dinner." Ethan smiled at me as he hopped out of the car.

I'd missed a perfect opportunity to finally rid him of the thought of our impending marriage.

"I can't marry you now, remember." I had seen his formative and vulnerable failures.

"Ah, you're not shallow and callous. You wouldn't hold those awkward years against me. That's why I love you." He kissed the crown of my head.

I groaned and swung open the back door in time to pull the cooler out of Ethan's curious reach.

"It's a ten-minute walk from here." I smiled.

He shook his head at me as he made his way around the car. I turned and started down the path towards the lake. The excitement was already starting as I thought about the evening ahead. I wasn't sure if it was the scenery, the company, or the combination of the two, but this was one of my favorite things to do.

We stumbled onto the private property a couple summers ago that housed the lake. Ethan agreed to keep an eye on the vacation home for the owner in exchange for us to have a place to go swimming without hordes of tourists. It was surrounded with the most amazing boulders. They appeared average by day, large and flat enough for a four-man tent to sit easily atop. They were rough to the touch around the edges but smooth along the face. A small part of me had hoped it would become our hideaway from the world. Of course, this was early in our friendship, a time when I was not privy to the playboy side of the man who would become one of my best friends.

"Babe, we need to come up here more often." He nodded as we arrived at the shore.

"When was the last time you were up here?" I asked.

"Same time as you were." He stepped ahead of me and leapt from rock to rock as he made his way to the top of a grouping of boulders.

"Really? You've never brought anyone else up here?" I was surprised.

"Of course not. This is ours." He set down the basket he'd carried and pulled out a large quilt.

I hadn't even thought of that. Why wouldn't he use this place? It's a perfect way to impress a girl. Why keep it between us?

"Did you really think I'd brought people here?" he asked without looking at me.

"I guess. I don't know why you wouldn't." I made my way up to him. He kept silent.

"It's really romantic. Secluded. Perfect girl bait." I smiled.

"I s'pose." He started unpacking the containers of food.

"You could get pretty wild actually. Nobody is around to hear a thing," I laughed.

He paused in his actions to look up at me. I couldn't move under his stare.

"You volunteering to get wild with me, Lily?" he asked lowly.

I swallowed and felt my cheeks go warm. I looked down quickly and tried to cover my reaction with a laugh as I set the cooler down at the edge of the blanket.

"Can't blame a guy for trying," he said after a second.

"Especially you, huh?"

"Yeah. Especially me," he replied with a weak laugh.

An uncomfortable silence enveloped us. The warmth of the air seemed suffocating as I avoided looking at him by glancing around the lake.

"Babe, seriously! Habanero beer! You do love me!" He grinned.

I smiled and looked down at him reaching into the cooler at my feet.

"Of course I do," I replied easily.

Because I did. I couldn't imagine my life without him in it. In fact, he'd been the reason behind more than a fair share of breakups in my world. Men did not like the thought of me having a male best friend. It was considerably worse that he was attractive and very involved in my life. More than once, they'd resorted to the ultimatum. Him or me. Well, that was an easy choice every time.

He popped open one of the beers and it hissed before he took long gulps. I couldn't help but smile. I liked that I could please him. It was nice to feel comfortable with him. I didn't have to guess about anything. I could list his favorites as if they were my own. I knew that dusk was his favorite time of day and that he loved when I wore green. I appreciated the fact that we knew everything about each other and was grateful that it didn't push us apart. It made us closer.

He ignored that I was overly analytical when it came to men. I didn't hate him for taking advantage of every girl he met. I was practical. He was a strange mix of dreamer and miser.

"I brought a surprise for you." He patted the spot beside him.

I smiled as I lowered myself to sit.

"Ta-da!" he said as he plucked a small jar of pickled onions from the basket.

I laughed. "Typical."

"What? You love these nasty things," he said, a little confused.

"I do. I was thinking how much of a weird match we are, and you just proved it. Thank you for bringing them." I leaned over and kissed him on the cheek.

"Weird match? I don't get it," he said.

"Never mind. So what else is on the menu today?" I asked as I tried to peek at the containers.

"Madam, today we have a wide variety of tempting delicacies." He imitated with a poor French accent.

I laughed as he proceeded to present each dish with a flourish of his hands.

We filled our stomachs and then sprawled out to let our food settle as we chatted.

"You feeling a little better?" he asked as he rolled onto his side and ran his fingers through my hair.

"How could I not be relaxed here?" I smiled as I turned to look at him.

His head was propped on his hand, and he gave me a warm grin.

"Good. I was getting really worried about you." He was serious now.

I rolled onto my side and mimicked his position.

"I'm fine." I shrugged with one shoulder.

"You're not. I don't know what's going on in that little chestnut head of yours, but it's something big," he said as he tapped my nose lightly.

"Just work." I laid my head down on my forearms.

"I've seen you stressed with work, Lily. This is something more." His brows furrowed.

I took a slow deep breath as Jarrett's face rushed through my mind. I wanted to tell him. I've been talking to Jarrett. After all these years we finally confessed our feelings for one another and shared a couple of blissful moments, but I kept my mouth shut.

"I knew this would happen." He rolled onto his back and closed his eyes.

"What?" I asked. Worried he could read my mind.

"He always does this. What happened this time?" he asked.

Memories flowed back and I warmed at the thought. "Nothing. Why do you think something happened?" I asked. I didn't want to tell him.

"I know you better than anyone, Harper. Something happened," he replied pointedly.

I shook my head to deny it.

"Did he finally get to you?" he asked quietly. He couldn't look at me.

"Who?" I pretended not to know.

"Jarrett. I know he's been vying for your attention. Did he finally break you down?" he asked.

"No." Why couldn't I tell him?

"Did you sleep with him?" he asked softly.

"Ethan, that's none of your damn business," I told him as I turned to look at him.

"Nah. I know. I knew you would eventually. You've always had a thing for him." He shrugged as he sat himself up.

"A little crush maybe. He's Augusts' brother for Christ's sake." I said, more to convince myself than him.

"You don't have to keep it from me, you know," he murmured as he looked at me.

I was shocked by the dullness in his eyes. Sadness fogged over them. I couldn't deny that it hurt to see it there, knowing that I was the cause of it. And all I wanted to do was make it go away.

"Ethan, don't start overthinking things." I smiled reassuringly.

The corner of his mouth turned up slightly.

"Besides, what I really need to know is if anyone is living around where we've been working right now." I hoped the change of subject would divert his attention.

"Not that I know of. Why do you ask?" His tone turned serious.

"Well, I've seen this guy a few times a couple of weeks ago. He was walking through the forest," I said aloud, before silently thanking the stranger I was using as a subject change.

"A hiker?" he asked skeptically.

"Not like any hiker I've ever seen. He certainly wasn't dressed for it." I remembered the black-haired man with the piercing blue eyes.

"A poacher possibly?" A bit of excitement laced the question.

"No, I doubt it. He didn't have a weapon or gear of any kind. He was just"— I paused— "strolling through the trees. That's why I thought maybe he lived in the area," I explained.

"There's a house up there, but it's one of those summer homes for investment-banker types," he said. "I think the guy hardly uses the place."

"Could you check for me? I don't know if we should be worried," I asked.

"Absolutely. I'll head up to his place first thing in the morning. You should have said something the first time you saw him, Lily. Who knows who this guy is?" he admonished as he got to his feet.

"Yeah, I know. I didn't think it was necessary until I saw him in town." I remembered the encounter in the park and goosebumps freckled my skin at the thought.

"You saw him in town too? Are you sure he wasn't following you?" he implored protectively.

"Oh, I'm sure." I rehashed the confrontation.

He frowned at me.

"Ethan, stop worrying," I laughed as I got to my feet.

"Can't do it." He shook his head with troubled eyes.

"Try. I'm fine. In fact, I'll be perfect if we can get a swim in before it gets too cold." I grabbed his hand to pull him toward the water.

"A private lake at dusk with an almost naked Lily? Do you think I'd honestly turn that down?" He smirked as he kicked off his shoes.

I laughed as I followed suit.

"Last one drives home?" he wagered.

"Deal." I peeled off my shorts and kicked them away before pulling my shirt over my head. I bit my lip as I looked down at my favorite bra.

"No time to be shy," Ethan laughed as he started walking backward toward the edge.

"Shy? As if. This happens to be my favorite bra," I plucked it off and dropped it on the rock before dashing to the edge and leaping off.

"Distractions are cheating!" he called as I dropped into the cool water.

I floated up slowly under the trail of bubbles above me. I laughed when I broke the surface.

"Distractions? You really should be immune by now," I called out to him as his head bobbed out of the water.

"Even the strongest of men couldn't be immune to you, my love." He began swimming in circles around me.

"And there's the sweetness I was talking about." I let my legs float up to the surface.

"Just honest. Nothing sweet about it." He dropped below.

How he couldn't see it I'd never understand. And why it was reserved solely for me would never make sense. As adamant as he was about marrying me, he knew it would never happen. We were both stuck in limbo.

"It's starting," he said as he came up beside me.

I dropped my legs to tread water and turned to the boulders at the edge. The moon had risen, and it was dark. The temperature had dropped enough for the rocks to be warmer than the air surrounding them.

I watched as the vapors rose from their invisible slumber, a glimmering, swirling mist reaching towards the night, as though the stars were born from the rock faces before rising to their midnight skies. Countless sparkles caught in the moonlight. Mesmerizing and beautiful, I watched intently. This was why Ethan and I came here. This was *our* oasis. Where wondrous emotions emerged. I barely noticed as an arm wrapped around my waist and gently towed me backward through the water. I vaguely realized that I'd come to a stop with my back against firm but smooth flesh and that my hair had been swept over my shoulder. My eyes fluttered closed as smooth lips grazed against the skin below my ear. Warning signs flashed through my mind, but something made me ignore them. This felt too good to relinquish. I leaned my head aside as the teasing of his lips trailed down my neck.

"You're supposed to stop me." His voice was deep and sounded thick.

"I don't want to." Mine was airy.

"Lily," he murmured.

My eyes shot open. This was Ethan.

"Stop." I forced the word from my throat.

"I don't want to." He used my words against me.

I tried to pull away from his arm tucked tightly around my waist. "I'm not one of them, Ethan," I whispered.

He sighed and let me go.

I pushed away from him and swam silently away.

"I'm tired of them," he murmured softly behind me.

I swallowed hard as I continued to the shore and pulled myself from the water.

Tired of them? What did that mean?

I started pulling my clothes on as he swam closer.

"Lily…" he began slowly.

"Ethan, don't worry about it," I said lightly. "I should know better." I forced a laugh.

"No, listen—" he began again.

"Really. Don't worry about it. It's no big deal. No harm, no foul." I pasted a smile on my face as I glanced at him. "I'm going to get stuff packed up."

I saw his shoulders droop in the moonlight as I made my way to clean up our things.

To the north, beyond a cluster of pines, I hesitated at what appeared to be someone walking. As the dark figure paused, I could see they were facing me. The person wasn't what drew my curiosity. It was the singular glowing rings encompassing their arms and thighs. A strange bioluminescence that one would see on the beaches of some night-blackened coast. They faded and disappeared for moments, as though they were slowly pacing between the trees in an aurora-like thrum. Glancing at Ethan, he seemed unaware of his presence. The man was silent as an autumn cemetery while he walked, before slipping under a low-hanging branch of a fir and vanishing altogether.

I pretended to sleep on the way back. Was his reaction based on jealousy? Why now? *Now* of all times, when I've just had something with Jarrett. Is it freaking mating season? Am I in heat? What's happening to me right now?

I felt sorry for the doleful look on Ethan's face that I spied from beneath my lashes on the drive home, and the urge to reach out crept into my chest.

14

So this is my fault?

Ever since Ethan had dropped me off at home, all I'd done was walk the entire length of the apartment. Wringing my hands together or throwing them out at my sides as I asked my questions to the empty surround. August was out for the night or probably at Mason's. I didn't care. My mind was going in circles, and she wasn't here to tell me what was a bad idea.

Fifteen minutes later I was storming up to the door of his townhouse. It was newer with a buffed black front door inlaid with a frosted pane of glass. I came here for movie nights when August was in heat…or at least that was how I thought of it sometimes when her and Mason were on again.

My fist was pounding before I even realized what was happening. His voice was muted through the heavy door.

"Who is it?" He was extremely annoyed.

"Ethan, open the fucking door," I demanded.

"Lily? What's wrong?" I could hear him quickly moving in my direction. I ignored the gratitude I felt at the worry lacing his voice.

"Why didn't you use your key?"

"I'll ask the questions!" I said as I pushed past him and strode into the expensive kitchen.

"What questions?" he asked as he locked the door behind me.

"What was that?" I flipped around to face him.

He looked around confused. "What?" He took a step closer to me.

"Don't come any closer. Just answer me," I said as I held out a hand to stop his advance.

He froze. "What are you talking about?" he said slowly.

"At the boulders." My face was void of emotion.

"Lily…I dropped you off two hours ago. You've been up this entire time?"

"You can't be super, sexy, blond Ethan…" I spoke brokenly. "Now all of sudden you're done with girls!" I blurted.

He opened his mouth but snapped it closed again as he sank onto the bar stool beside him. "What do you want from me, Harper?" His face was blanketed with defeat.

"I want an answer," I pushed.

"Answer to what? The fact that I couldn't stop myself? Maybe lost a little control? I don't have an answer for that. It happened. I'm sorry. It won't happen again," he rambled on quietly.

"Not that. What did you mean?" I asked, shaking away the pleasant feeling his words gave me.

"When?" He closed his eyes and rubbed his temples.

"*I'm tired of them,*" I repeated his words.

"You heard that?" he asked softly.

"What does it mean, Ethan?" I pushed for an answer.

He looked away from me for a moment and rose to his feet. "Nothing. It means nothing." He began to walk out of the room.

"Nothing? Really? Because it sounds to me like you're looking for someone new to add to your list of conquests, Ethan," I shouted.

"Of course you would think that." He laughed harshly.

I followed behind him. "What is that supposed to mean?"

"Lily Harper, always looking to count a guy out for one thing or another," he called over his shoulder in a sing-song voice.

My mouth dropped open in shock.

"He's too critical or too laid back. Not driven enough in his career or works too much. Too boring. Too immature." He spouted off excuses I'd used over the years.

"I have standards, Ethan. I won't settle," I yelled.

He turned to face me with a mixture of outrage and hurt. "Settle? Is that what you'd be doing if it was us? Settling?" He strode across the room and stopped a breath away from me.

I shook my head no but couldn't speak.

"How can you deny *this*?" His hands gripped my arms firmly.

I gulped.

"Why do you keep pushing it away?" His voice had gone softer, and his hands slid up to cup my face. "You've never even given me a chance."

I felt tears building behind my eyes. How wrong he was.

"I want a shot to prove myself, Lily," he whispered as his mouth covered mine.

I froze for a moment, unable to react under the conflicting emotions racking my mind.

I couldn't help myself as I leaned into the kiss. My lips parted against his despite my worries. And when he buried his fingers in my hair as his other hand slid down my spine, my arms went around his waist, my own hands pressing against his bare back, nails making soft crescents in the flesh along his spine.

He pulled away abruptly and tipped his face to the ceiling. "You need to go." He turned away from me as his hands went to his hips.

I turned to leave feeling suddenly rejected.

"Lily?" he said from behind me.

"Yeah?" My eyes moistened.

"Just think about it." It was softly requested before the padding of his feet against the floor told me he was walking away.

I took a deep breath as I let myself out.

He'd kissed me…and not like a *we're drunk* kiss. Like a kiss that had feeling. "Whoa." I dropped onto my bike softly. "Wow," I exhaled. I wanted to march back in there and do it again.

Pure habit forced my hands to turn the key and slip the helmet over my head. My eyes were able to watch but my mind was trying to find a path through the cluster of clouding emotions. My history with men was short. I'd never been that girl who needed a guy to keep her occupied. I wasn't prone to connections based on romanticized ideals of love. It needed to be right, not just feel right. But this… this was perfect. Felt amazing, unexpectedly and overwhelmingly flawless.

He could be ready. He could finally be done with the girls. It's the only thing that ever stood between us then. If only I could believe him. We would make a great life together.

Until he got bored or restless or some pretty girl crossed his path, caved to the carnal desires of his body, and ignored the commitment we'd made.

He's not a sure thing.

But he's always put me first, above any of them.

I argued with myself the entire route home and by the time I'd closed the door behind me, I'd lost sight of the facts and fear had taken over.

"No way," I said softly as I leaned against the door at my back. My head rested against the hardwood and my arms hung limply at my sides. "Fucking inconceivable!"

I flung myself through the apartment as I kicked my shoes off carelessly. Ripping my shirt over my head and dropping it to the floor as I went to the bathroom.

"What am I doing?" I asked myself as I twisted the faucet to full blast. "So stupid," I scolded myself.

I cupped my hands under the water and filled them to overflowing before splashing my face. I looked at myself in the mirror.

"Idiot," I cried as I pointed angrily at the girl in the glass. "He kissed me. And I kissed him back! Willingly! I liked it!" It echoed off the tile.

I'd kissed him as though he was…someone besides Ethan Monroe. Like he was…Jarrett.

"I'm such an idiot," I scolded myself.

I'm going to throw away a chance with Jarrett to be…what? A temporary resting place for Ethan's dick! No!

"What are the rules, Lily?" I asked myself in anger as I grabbed a towel from the rack. "Don't be dumb," I mumbled into the cotton.

And what do I do? I kiss Ethan! Want him to kiss me even!

"Ugh!" I growled into the emptiness. "This is not happening."

I dropped the towel on the vanity and rushed over to pick up my phone. The line on the other end was ringing before I had even registered dialing a number. I pulled the phone away from my ear to glance at the screen and then ended the call immediately.

"Not like this." I shook my head and collapsed back on the mattress behind me.

The phone vibrated in my hand, and I answered it knowingly. "I can't believe you answered. It's late."

"You answered, dimwit. Did you get kicked in the head?" August asked.

"Sorry, I thought it was someone else." I was oddly disappointed.

"Who else could it be? You have no other friends," she teased.

"What do you need?" I asked curtly.

"You want to hang out? Avery canceled. She ended up having to work tonight." A friend of hers who she used to work at a hotel with in college.

"Not tonight." I was frustrated.

"I'll be home in ten." She ignored me.

Maybe I should talk to August, but I knew what she would say. She had immediately warned me of the dangers of Ethan when I met him. *He's the type of guy fathers cock their shotguns for. A chronic Casanova would sooner get you in bed than care about what you're thinking.* She explained that her brothers, Grey and Logan, were the same and she could recognize the symptoms. She'd been right… up to tonight.

"What's wrong?" She was setting down her purse on the counter. "Why've you been crying?"

"Nothing. Just guys." I shrugged. "Ethan said some hurtful things tonight." I was being careful to omit the bigger sequence of events that had taken place earlier.

"Well, there's your problem right there." She rolled her eyes. "Ethan's my friend too, but the guy is completely selfish when it comes to women. I know that he's always sweet to you, Harper, but it's about time you see him for what he is. A shallow jerk. He knows nothing about dating, and he has no clue how to have a real girlfriend."

I scoffed. "He's not a jerk. And that's rich coming from you!" I could feel the anger boiling in my stomach. "What about you and Bobby?"

"I don't want to talk about hi—it," she corrected quickly, taken aback that I knew his name.

"Bobby?" I said the name aloud again. Suddenly remembering the boy from back home that had August in knots. A rare sight.

She turned sharply and gazed at me with a stern face.

"I saw you two at the barbecue and Jimmy said something about you two dating back in the day." I cut her with my words.

She closed her eyes. "I don't want to talk about it."

"Jimmy said he broke your heart. Why didn't you ever mention him?" I said it without thinking. She couldn't sit there and hate on Ethan when she too was being cavalier in her love life.

"Well, Dad has a big mouth sometimes and you don't know when to mind your own business," she lashed out.

I was momentarily speechless. August wasn't one to bite with her words.

"You should talk," I defended, hurt by her statement.

"What do you want, Lily? Do you want to hear all the gory details? How I chose this instead of him? That he didn't choose me?" There was frustration and pain in her voice.

"No, August, but after years of you pressing me towards and away from guy after guy, nagging at me for being choosy or picky or overthinking everything about them, for being cautious, I didn't expect you to get pissed at one measly inquiry into your own love life." I bounced to my feet as I spoke, and my hands clenched at my sides.

"You are too picky!" she yelled.

I shook my head and turned to leave.

"Where are you going?" she retorted.

"I'm going to head out." I began to leave the room.

"I'll come with you." Her shoes moved against the floor.

"I need a walk…alone." I threw a frail smile over my shoulder, and she nodded.

"I'll see you in the morning."

"Okay." I was at the door. I wanted to get out of there. I couldn't wrap my head around the day's events. I didn't have any desire to relive them. The amazing boulder experience, kissing Ethan, and fighting with *both* of my best friends.

"Shit. I need a drink." I automatically changed my path and headed directly to my preferred drinking hole.

15

A Chivalrous Ghost

I slammed the small glass back down on the wooden bar.

"Fill her up, Joe," I called to the other end of the counter.

"Lily, my name is Quinn. We had two classes together. I'm friends with August," he explained while walking down to my end of where I sat alone. "Maybe this should be your last one?" He turned, bent, and plucked another bottle from the shelf. "Bourbon's a little rough, don't you think?" he asked, eyeing me sideways allowing the liquid to pour through the silver spout into the tiny shot glass.

"Rough times call for rough liquor." I swung my head back and allowed the burning liquid to sear its way down my throat. "I kissed him, Joe."

"Quinn," he corrected me. Now leaning forward watching me, palms pressed to the resin-covered oak surface.

"Right." I pointed a wobbly finger at the man. "I kissed him."

"Who did you kiss?" he asked, uninterested.

I looked around the bar and saw I was alone but leaned in anyways. "My best friend"—my eyes glanced back and forth quickly— "Monroe," I whispered from behind half a hand.

"I see. That's a twist." He nodded, unsure of how to respond.

"And I liked it. I shouldn't like it," I groaned, pushing angry fists to both sides of my head, shaking it vigorously back and forth in hopes the moment would fade from my thoughts.

"How 'bout I call you a ride, Lily?" Quinn replied. "Everyone makes mistakes." He turned walking towards the antique-looking phone at the other end of the bar. "I'm sure by morning after you two have slept on it, you'll have kissed and made up." He stopped, "I didn't mean it like that." He looked back over his shoulder. "Sorry." He frowned.

I swatted a hand. "I'm going to walk!" I slipped off the barstool a little trying to make my exit. My jeans were still dirty from the boulders and my T-shirt was askew in my tipsy stupor.

"You sure, Lily?" he called, but I was already out the door.

My hand flitted back towards him. "Yes sir," I slurred.

I walked down the street angrily at first. Then in more of a zigzag pattern as the last shot caught up to me. "You cannot defeat me, sidewalk." I pointed down at the cement. "You will not make me fall," I shouted down at it.

I was completely aware that I was this girl right now. The girl that is shouting in the night, drunk, and alone. All I needed was a brown paper bag and the cops chastising me and the night would be perfect.

I began to whistle. I knew I was doing a poor job, but I couldn't help but try to erase my bitter mood with something slightly more upbeat. I sped up when I realized that my vision and judgment were becoming cloudy.

"Where do I live, Mr. Streetlight?" I looked up at the tall black metal pole. "Hmm, where do you suppose that is?" I tapped my chin, folding my other arm across my stomach and resting my elbow on it.

I looked around. Panic was nowhere to be found. I was becoming increasingly tired and tried hard to remember where I had left my cell phone. Other than the small wad of cash I had angrily stuffed in a pocket, I think I'd left it at home.

My mind was finding it difficult to comprehend my surroundings until I finally surrendered. "Fine, here looks good." I bowed to the street as though it were seemingly taunting me.

I bent, lifting a leg. I tugged the laces loose and ripped the boot from my left foot throwing it lazily over my shoulder.

"Dumb Ethan!" I shouted. "With his dumb good looks." I started to feel the anger in the pit of my stomach again.

"Be quiet, stomach!" I pointed a finger at my torso half bent over.

I pulled the other boot from my foot and chucked it straight out in front of me. I thought I could hear footsteps behind me, but I chose to ignore them. Serves Ethan right driving me to a drunken state down the street being stalked by a maybe murderer.

I pulled the long silver chain I kept tucked to my chest over my head. Getting it caught in my hair. Determined, I turned in circles following it trying to win the battle.

I draped it over the corner of a bench I scouted and deemed suitable for sleep.

"He smelled like cinnamon." I crawled onto the bench and lay face first down into the wooden planks. One arm draped awkwardly to the ground, the other firmly bent under my chest. "Yucky cinnamon," I grumbled.

I exhaled deeply and closed my eyes. That's when I felt it. A flash of warmth. My arms began to tingle. The sensation exploded into my chest and down my spine.

"Need to get home?" A smooth and deep voice spoke down to me.

I squinted, opening an eye up towards the street light. "Nope. This is my new home." I flipped over and turned my head into the wood. "My bench," I hummed, smiling.

"Wouldn't you prefer your bed?" the voice resonated again.

"Am I breaking the law, Officer?" I asked, still not caring that the situation had invited a visitor.

"Not law enforcement." He cleared his throat. "Just concerned that you're having a bad night and don't want to see you get into trouble," he finished, unsure.

"I feel warm. Tingly even." I turned my head towards the stranger and wiggled my toes. "Smells good. Like hot. Fire maybe?" I reasoned aloud.

"Alcohol poisoning. You had an awful lot of bourbon for such a small girl," the man explained.

"How do you know?" The first bite of panic hit my fingertips.

"I can smell it. I even think anyone eating at the diner down the street can smell you," he pointed out. The light was behind him masking his appearance. The only thing I could take in was his size. Massive. The muscles that fought against his cotton clothes could have won.

"You're a big fella." I smiled sideways. "Don't kill me. I'm important," I spoke, sitting up huffing out my chest.

The alcohol rushed to my head and before I knew it, I was slipping quickly forward.

A swift but soft hand swooped down and caught me by the waist. I felt a shock where the skin contacted.

"We sparked." I giggled, provoking a burp.

"That we did." I could hear the stranger's voice laced with a smile. His other arm followed, and he reached down gently helping me rise to my feet. "I picked up your shoes and necklace for you," he explained warmly. A hint of something underlying but the drinks wouldn't let me pinpoint it. Nervousness perhaps?

He helped me slip my shoes on when the attempts I made crashed and burned. Squatting on the ground graciously, he patiently guided me while I mumbled and groaned about how I wanted to go to bed.

When he stood up, the ounces of balance I had maintained fled. I was scooped up and over his shoulder in a fit of laughter before I could comprehend the act.

"Coffee should help." He started walking. "Unless you can tell me where you live now?" he asked politely.

"Guess!" I huffed through a thick smile, crossing my arms as I bobbed along. His arm strapped tightly around the lower half of my legs, bent over his shoulder at my waist.

"The hard way then," he spoke to himself.

"I wouldn't normally drink like this if it wasn't for *him*." I spoke the word with a tinge of spite.

"Who is *him*?" he mocked.

"My best friend." I paused. Oh, what the hell? Never going to see him again anyways. "He made me angry kiss him!" I spat.

"He *made* you?" he asked skeptically.

"Yep!" I nodded. "He was all like, 'I'm confused and want to be a grown-up,'" I uttered angrily. "Like after this many years you just *decide* you don't want to date everyone you see with your *giant* wandering eye," I explained animatedly with both hands flailing.

My arms were dangling, swinging loosely from side to side.

"Your backside is cute." I grinned back over my shoulder trying to catch sight of my stranger's face.

A deep laugh. "Thanks." He smiled.

We stood on the corner waiting for the light to change. I hummed sweetly and smiled when I looked down, noticing my necklace was firmly grasped in his large fingers.

"Should I be scared that you're going to kill me?" I asked, seemingly unaware of possible danger.

"Hardly. Not unless a murderer crosses my path and overpowers me," he explained matter-of-factly.

"Good. August would be lost without me." I paused. "I carry her pretty much."

"August an important month for you?" he asked casually.

"My other best friend. Her name is August," I explained then coughed. "She makes sure I know I'm alive…daily," I added in a slur. "Why am I not afraid of you?" I asked suddenly.

"Why do I care if you get hurt?" he replied.

"I don't know," I spoke slowly, attempting to ponder while drunk. "I bet it's because you don't want to befriend me and then try and make me fall in love with you," I added bitterly, dredging up Ethan.

"I hope not. This is"— his step hesitated— "out of character for me," he added a little more grimly.

We came to a halt. I looked up to see a large brick building behind me. "I don't live here, Mr. Stranger," I instructed.

"I know." He started pulling me forward and with the utmost care sat me gently on the ground. "I need a clearer head for you to point us in the right direction."

I closed my eyes tight, waiting for him to drop me while maneuvering my body until my toes graced the pavement. I popped my eyes open to find them staring directly into the piercing blue irises of a recognizable stranger.

My mouth hung agape for a moment before I inhaled sharply and called all too loudly. "You're him!" A finger rushed to point in his face.

"Who's him?" he asked, slightly scared and a little more than confused.

"The man I grabbed all crazy at the park." I demonstrated by shoving at his arm. "The guy from the woods," I spoke, toning down my volume. "This is perfect," I groaned sarcastically and still inebriated.

"That was you?" His stare was instantaneously firm. "Woods?" he asked. Obviously, the second half of what I said was soaking in.

"Yep!" I nodded my head vigorously, smiling. Crossing my arms in some triumph that I had found him again.

He placed two heavy hands on my shoulders and sat me next to the door of the diner on the oversized sill. "Sit still," he instructed with a firm finger. Before I could reply he had disappeared inside.

I blew at my bangs that were scattered about the front of my face from the all too amusing ride. My feet held fast to the ground. My hands gripping my knees waiting for him to return. My conscious thinking mind repeating, *Don't let him get away. Make sure and find out who he is*. I grinned knowing my blood was beginning to filter out the alcohol a little. Not by much but enough to allow sane thoughts to cross.

The door swung open, and a large coffee cup was handed to me. "Drink up." He tipped it towards my hand.

I took it willingly and watched tilting it towards my lips as he strode in front of me and then came to sit next to me on the stoop.

"I prefer a bench," I muttered from behind the lid.

"I need to ask you something serious, Lily," he replied.

"How did you know my name was Lily?" I asked, looking at him awkwardly. "You are stalking me!" I called.

"You told me in the park. *I'm just Lily*. Now focus." He turned his torso towards me while I started staring straight ahead. Why couldn't I have been of sound mind when I'd seen him? This is some demented version of karma.

"Lily, did you tell anyone about seeing me in the forest?" he asked.

I stared at him. Lost in the depths of his glaring blue eyes. His jaw was thick and the smells emanating from him were defying all odds. He smelled delicious. My hands were slowly becoming infatuated with a want to touch him. "No," I replied in a small voice, not wanting to make him angry. I looked down while taking another sip.

"No one?" he asked, noticing his effect and coating his voice with a softer tone.

I looked up smiling. "Nobody."

"Do you live there?" he asked.

"No, I work there," I answered eagerly, wanting to please him. "I thought that you were..." I couldn't find a word to fill the void.

"I know what you mean." He leaned back in his perfect posture and looked around curiously trying to find a word.

"Magnetic," I whispered. A hint of soberness was taking over my vocals.

"Agreed." Running a hand through the thick hair his scent was driven towards me. I automatically leaned in. "This is so strange." I ached at the look of confusion tightly placed across his lips.

"I live up and over the hill there," I pointed. "I can walk from here."

"I would prefer you didn't," he told me firmly. "Allow me." He stood and reached down, helping me up. I didn't know what to say so I sucked on the coffee to avoid contact.

My mind began to cloud, and sleep pinched every muscle. I vaguely recalled walking up the steps and into my apartment. Did I even close the door?

I awoke somewhere around four a.m. Ethan had called numerous times but I didn't answer. The image of the stranger who sent my mind spinning replayed.

"Your necklace, Lilian." He placed it gently over my head. I followed and I lay on my bed, eyes already closed. My shoes kicked to the floor. "Sleep well." He smiled and was gone.

I didn't sleep until his presence was absent from my nerves. A grave sadness hit my heart, another chance encounter, and still no name.

16

Surprise

I stood in the shower far too long. I didn't care if it was the weekend. I would stay here all day if I could. I wanted to wipe all hints of bourbon from my skin, and I didn't want to face Ethan. I wanted to understand why a perfect stranger that I crossed paths with occasionally would suffocate my thoughts in a five-second encounter.

I walked into the living room, staring aimlessly. I looked at my cell phone and noticed that August had called numerous times, probably to see if I was up for a hike when she left earlier this morning. I was avoiding both my best friends. What had everything come down to?

I had lost my mind. I was drawn to a stranger, in love with a brother, and crushing on my best friend. This was ridiculous. I collapsed onto my couch and did the first thing I hadn't done in a long time.

I cried. The tears flowed and I did little to sniff them away. I hated the way the handsome stranger made me feel whenever he was near. I hated that I missed Jarrett so painfully when I wasn't with him that I mulled over it for weeks. That I had underlying feelings for my best friend, and they surfaced after one spiteful kiss when I worked so hard to push them away.

Flashes of them all flooded my mind. I cried harder. I wanted Ethan to kiss my temple better. Wanted Jarrett to steal me away to some place in that sensual way he does. And wanted the mysterious stranger with the black hair to come back into my life, asking his probing questions, not hinting anymore at his identity than our previous rendezvous.

I wiped my tears on my forearm and sniffled, glancing down at my phone. Swiping open my photos, I began scrolling. Jarrett grinned proudly as he held up a large fish in his net he had caught when I was visiting. That photo right beside a picture Ethan had taken of him and me at a brewery the weekend before we left. My face held a look of amusement. Below those were the photos I had taken of the mysterious clearing with the petrified charred trees. I clicked one and enlarged it before swiping to the last one I hurriedly snapped before leaving that morning.

What the...

Spreading my index and thumb, I zoomed to the far-right corner of the photo. My breath caught in my throat. It was *him*. The mysterious man with the out- of- place white shirt and icy blue eyes. He was beyond the tree line and staring directly at me.

The curious stranger that I kept bumping into. I swiped through the rest of the photos, and he was in none of them. What was happening?

A knock on the door.

"Go away," I grumbled.

They repeated.

"Ugh." I pulled myself up from the couch and stomped towards the door, doing nothing to hide the fact I'd been crying. If it were Ethan, I had every intention of slapping him. If it were August forgetting her keys again, I would crush her in the weight of my bawling hug.

"I'm not in the mood today. I had a terrible—" I stopped cold looking up.

"Sorry I didn't answer when you called." I couldn't believe it. Jarrett was standing at my door alone. "Why are you crying?" His eyes were immediately concerned.

I stood speechless. Emotions crammed my throat, and I scrunched up my face. Tears flowed wildly down my cheeks.

"Oh, Lily." He dropped his pack on the wooden deck and stepped into the doorway. Pulling me into him, holding my head, he took my face burying my puffy eyes into his chest. Kisses spilling from his lips into my hair.

"Did someone hurt you?" He pulled my face back to look into my eyes.

All I could manage was to shake my head no.

"Say something!" He shook me gently.

"I missed you," I croaked.

He leaned back and laughed. "I couldn't bear it any longer! I had to come see you." He kissed my cheeks. Leaning back sliding his pack through the door and kicking it shut with a heel. He stood smiling at me.

My brain kicked to life. "You're here," I breathed.

"I'm here." He grinned.

"Oh my God, you're here!" My eyes got wide. "My hair, apartment, and outfit look like shit!" I yelped.

"You look beautiful. I love what you're wearing. It's you. And your apartment. I'm just happy there's no one within ten miles to interrupt." He grinned.

"Except your sister." Crap. What if August came home asking what happened last night? "Does she know you're here?" I turned to look for my phone.

"Hell yes. It was her idea. I mean I was nervous because I thought she was exaggerating about how you missed me the way I missed you but I'm glad for once she wasn't embellishing." He stepped towards me.

"No Baynes?" I eyed him. My tear-stained cheeks dried at the turn of events.

"Nobody. Just me." He put a hand to his chest.

"Nobody," I repeated slowly in a whisper.

Instinct won over any other rationality in my brain. I closed the gap and wrapped my arms around his neck pulling him down and kissing him with everything I had been wishing for, for the last few weeks. He lifted me from the floor and echoed my actions.

"I didn't think my heart could miss someone this much," he breathed into my hair, his smell rushing into my lungs.

"I know." I closed my eyes, pressing into him. My mind caught up to the moment. "Ahem," I chirped.

"Sorry. I just… it's so good to see you." He grinned. "So can I have the tour?" He nodded towards the rest of the apartment, picking up his backpack and placing it over one shoulder.

He was as large as Ethan was, crowding the room with his presence. I beamed completely unaware of anything previous to the moment he had been at my door.

"Well." I shrugged looking up at him feeling tiny. "This is it. August and I moved in last fall. It's a lot bigger than our old place on Wabash."

"You sleep on this bench here?" He nudged the wood with his knee.

I giggled. "No." My mind was racing. I couldn't accept that he was here, in my apartment, standing next to me, and there wasn't a single Bayne brother to interrupt.

"I showed you mine." He looked down at me, happiness gracing all corners of his face.

"Fair enough. Follow me." I started walking towards my bedroom, pointing out the rooms on the way. "Living room, kitchen, spare bathroom, August's bedroom…and this"— I inhaled anxiously— "is my room." I sounded like a nervous teenager.

"It's wonderful." He sat down on the edge of my bed and pulled me forward by my hips. A candid Jarrett. A Jarrett that wasn't going to be stopped. My face turned sultry. He pulled me forward forcing me to topple onto him. Our lips were inches apart. I stopped, rolling over next to him onto my back.

"I love it." He pulled in a deep breath. "It smells like you." I smiled at the compliment.

"That's what I thought about your cabin." I propped myself onto my side holding my head up with a flat palm. "Even when you weren't there, it was like you were." I smiled.

"Could you be any more adorable, Lily Bear?" He did the same, popping up beside me.

"Why Lily Bear?" I asked scooting closer to be near him.

"I think fishing with guns cemented that one for us."

"I'm never gonna live that one down, am I?" I cocked my head sideways.

"I thought it was cute." He grinned. "Hence, Lily Bear." He kissed the tip of my nose. I closed my eyes, and he softly brushed his lips across my lids.

"It makes me sound like I'm twelve," I spoke quietly.

"It's adorable like you." He lay back, interlocking his fingers behind his head looking at the ceiling. "I remember when you hopped out of Dad's truck the first time August brought you home and I thought, 'Wow, how can something so small make you feel this big?'" He smiled, closing his eyes. He disappeared momentarily into his thoughts. "I knew that I would never have a chance with such a beautiful girl." His face was saddened. "But I couldn't wait anymore. I knew I had to have you. When you kissed me back a few weeks ago it was like—" he moaned and it took everything in me not to tear his clothes from his skin— "my dreams were becoming a reality. I was so easily bored with so many girls, none of them were anything compared to what I held you at."

"I'm lame," I chimed in softly.

He shot back onto his side quickly and leaned close enough that we were pressed together again. "But you're not," he whispered. "I love that you're blind to the fact that you don't need to try to break hearts." He stared intensely.

The thought dawned on me. "Do any of your brothers know you're here?"

"Nope, just sister, Mom, and Dad. We took safety precautions to make sure we would have no followers." His hand came up to rest on my side.

So warm.

The conversation halted when the connection became obvious. I leaned in and kissed him and this time, I meant it, meant it as I had in the middle of that steam-filled street in Washington. Like I wanted it to be with Ethan but knew that it couldn't be. Like I didn't care if I was caught up in feelings. Jarrett was everything I wanted to be with.

I missed him in the wake of his absence. I longed for him when his face burst into my memories. I dreaded what would happen if we weren't able to see each other again.

My hands went wild, yanking up the gray thermal shirt he was wearing. My fingers fumbling around the silver buttons fastening his jeans. His left hand that was resting on my side trailed underneath the thin prison of cotton I wore and pulled at my spine. His other hand held my face gently as he pulled me to rest near him. Our lips, kisses, and tongues never losing the connection.

"Oh crap. Please don't be *doing* my brother! Nobody needs to see that." August bumped into the half-closed door. "I brought breakfast!" I jumped and in my haste slipped from the top of him and dropped to the floor. August was standing in my doorway. One hand over her eyes shielding her and the other holding up a giant paper bag resonating with delicious scents from what I could tell was my favorite breakfast spot.

"Nope. Not now anyway." Jarrett stood up and helped me to my feet adjusting his jeans. "You can open your eyes." He smiled wide.

"Are you sure it's safe? I don't want to break up the lover's reunion." She spread her fingers.

"I'm going to push you." Her eyes opened immediately.

"So how long will you be staying? Should I get the spare room made up?" I attempted to change the subject from her obvious interruption.

"No room. Just painted! Redecorating and all and using that room for storage." She briskly walked back down the hallway.

"Really?" I followed her out into the living room.

"Yep. I guess he will have to stay in your room!" She wouldn't turn to face me and continued to pull the food from the bag and spread it across the bar countertop.

I looked over at Jarrett who was standing on the edge of the room. He was staring down at the carpet and both hands were tucked tightly in his pockets. I couldn't resist. "So I get to keep you?" I started to smile. "How long?" I couldn't have said it quickly enough.

"My flight leaves tomorrow night." He grinned wide, the elation apparent across his face.

He glided over to me, "You don't mind, do you, Lily? Because if it's too much I can stay at a hotel."

"No!" I snapped my mouth closed. "I mean, no. That's silly. Of course, you can stay here. I have a big bed. I mean, room. Bedroom."

"Smooth, Harper." August was gnawing at a breakfast burrito.

"Shut up!" I shot. "Of course, I will harbor a handsome young man when he is turned away from family."

"Or because we've earned our alone time after years of crushes?" He raised his brows at me.

"Cheers to that!" She raised a burrito.

17

My Grotto

I frantically pulled shirts from the hangers, pausing to hold on to my shoulders before tossing it to my floor.

"Okay, so he's in my apartment. I wasn't prepared for this. Lily, what do you wear?"

I hadn't done laundry in days and couldn't find anything close to appropriate. I shut my phone off in haste to avoid Ethan. I couldn't imagine dealing with him now. He would be livid to find out the man that turns me inside out came to surprise me. Or would he be? I didn't have time to ponder the emotional roller coaster that was my best friend right now.

"Are you hiding from me?" Jarrett's velvety voice whispered to my back.

I jumped. "Sorry. I was…" I bit my lower lip timidly.

"You were?" he asked, amused.

"Okay, I was trying to find something else to wear," I surrendered.

He looked confused. "What for?"

"Because I wanted to look nice"— I stared at the floor, slightly embarrassed— "for you."

"Lily," he breathed, closing the space between us. "You are the most beautiful woman I have ever known." He stopped, abashed.

"What's wrong?" I was apprehensive of his sudden change in demeanor.

"I've never been able to say that out loud to you. Felt good," he murmured, tucking my hair behind my ear.

"Six years is a long time to crush on someone. It's a lot to live up to." I walked around him to sit on the end of my bed anxiously.

"So Bennett told you that, huh?" He leaned up against my vanity. "So then why don't we go slowly?"

"I'm not worth that many years."

"Hell yes, you are." His posture became more assertive. He grabbed both sides of my face cradling my cheeks lightly. "Lily, I would never waste my time pining after someone that wasn't worth it."

"Pining?"

"Well, yeah. I look forward to you coming. I often try to find excuses to come here and every time I get near you. All I want is you." He grinned.

I blushed hard. "You do?"

"Promise." He stood up. "Well. My sister is faking busy in an effort to push us together and I have never fully been able to appreciate this side of the Rockies. What are we doing today?" His hands on his hips.

My face scrunched up in thought. A grin spread through my cheeks. "Can I take you somewhere?"

"Do you have to ask?" he replied.

* * *

"Are you doing alright?" I looked at him concerned that the hike was becoming too much.

"What are you trying to say? I do log for a living, Lily. As hard as it is to believe, it can be a little physical sometimes." He stepped over a log and around me.

"I mean, I guess if that's what helps you sleep at night." We stepped around trees and giggled, the conversation never dying.

"Favorite season?" he asked inquisitively.

"Spring probably," I called over my shoulder, getting excited at the sound my ears were tuned into. I looked straight ahead and could see the willows coming into view.

"Why?" he asked, catching up to me.

"Because it's when the world lights up and everything comes alive again. I love it." I stopped in my reverie.

"Every word to pass your lips is one more reason I'm glad I'm with you." He grinned, turning away. I caught myself eyeing him suspiciously. "Coming?"

"Yeah, you're *with* me?" I caught up walking beside him again.

"I'm picky. I'm not going to spend my time with just anyone if it's not the right person," he spoke softly.

"Right person, huh?" I turned the questions onto him now.

"Sure, someone who can handle my deep darks." He looked away, hiding whatever expression occupied his face.

"Oh crap. I don't want to know. Do you butcher things?" I called, frustrated. "I knew that you were too perfect."

"No!" he laughed. "Nothing to worry about. Too perfect, huh?"

I shoved at his face and crept forward. My fingertips gently swept the strands of the willow's hair, gracing the forest floor, aside. "This is my place." I turned around quickly. "If you tell August you will die."

"Never." He held a hand to his chest sweetly.

"I come here when I need a place that's all me. You're the first person other than me to come here." I grabbed the ropes I had in my backpack and started quickly tying knots.

"Lily." He stood motionless. "This is extraordinary."

"I know." I breathed, kneeling next to him.

"Where does it go?" He leaned over the edge of the opening, guarded by the giant trunks.

"The waterfall? It sweeps sideways underground." I turned to him and started tying the heavy ropes around him. "Let's go."

When our feet were pressed to the mossy floor that surrounded the recessed grotto I couldn't help but smile at the expression Jarrett wore on his face. "You like it?" I peeked at him.

"Love it," he breathed, pausing to take in the cavern.

We were about twenty feet down into the ground with a large opening being heavily guarded by various trees and willows. The small river came rushing over the edge and crashed into the floor falling sideways and dipping into a large opening. Steam rose from small hot springs that weren't more than a foot in diameter, overflowing and spilling calmly into each other.

"I know. I was hoping that you would." I took his hand when he stepped from the ropes and pulled him into the sunlight near a wall that was moss-covered boulders. Massive roots wrapped wildly around them from the giant trees above. Holding them in place, a green cage.

"This is unreal." His other hand reached up towards the rocks and his fingertips gently brushed across their faces. "This whole place looks like something only people could dream of." He turned his head towards me quickly. "I never want to leave." He smiled softly.

"I feel that way sometimes too." I looked up towards the sky allowing the sunlight to wash my face, relaxing me.

He was lying on his side hand propped up like he had been this morning. I lay beside him on my stomach, my legs crossed and swinging lightly back and forth. My arms crossed in front of me on the ground, my face sideways using them as a makeshift pillow, the steam swirling around us tickling our skin every so often.

"If you could go into space, would you?" I asked.

"Not sure. I don't know. I never wanted to be an astronaut as a kid." His eyes pulled together with the slightest hint of thought. "So what about you? Is it my turn yet?" He raised his brows.

"Yes, sorry, I was being selfish. It's just that most nights we're both so tired after work, we don't have time for this much conversation. Go." I grinned, blushing that I had monopolized the conversation.

"Can I ask you *anything*?" He sat up leaning back on both palms.

I nodded, smiling nervously.

"How old were you when your dad died?" His face grew still.

I inhaled slowly. "Five. Next?"

"Sorry, I know it's probably sensitive. Mom always said if we wanted to know that we would need to ask you ourselves. That pretty much put a stop to anybody asking." He laughed at the inside joke. I didn't.

I rolled onto my back and bent my knees, folding my arms behind my head. The wind blew the willows' protective fingers lightly around the hidden opening. The shadows cast across my face. "Next," I whispered, closing my eyes.

"Okay." He waited. I could hear him shifting, changing position. "What about your mom? I've never heard you mention her ever."

Something inside my chest sparked and shifted. Instantaneously becoming stronger. I bolted upright. "Did you feel that?"

"What?" He stared worried at my change.

"That!" I looked down pushing a hard palm into my chest below my collarbone. "That *push*?"

"No. What are you talking about, Lily?" He leaned in, staring down at where I was pressing my hand while lifting one of his.

My chest felt like a stake was shoved through the side my heart occupied with a chain tied to the end and was painfully pulling on it. "There! Again!" I clawed at the ribs occupying the left side.

"Maybe we should get you to the hospital. It could be your heart." Terror was cupping his eyes.

"No." I placed a calm hand on his knee. "It doesn't hurt. Not like that anyway." I inhaled.

"Are you sure?" He was scared that I was playing down my symptoms.

"Promise. Must have sat up too quickly." I smiled trying to reassure him. All of a sudden, I wanted to get out of there. Run through the woods quickly to the south, a magnetic drive that was practically tearing at my nerves, and muscles.

I looked up staring in the direction my chest was pulling me towards. An invisible path that wasn't apparent to my company. I downplayed the symptom and did what I could to assess them without worrying him.

It wasn't painful in the physical sense. Like I missed someone that had just left and knew I wouldn't see for a while. The feeling that you get when you want to grab their hand and pull them back towards you. A *missing* pain you suffer occasionally.

I leaned back pretending to relax. It took everything I had not to step away from him. He settled into his comfortable position again. Eyeing me for several uneasy minutes until the conversation drifted back to what it was before. He didn't ask any more prying personal questions that I definitely didn't want to answer.

The pull slowly started to dissipate. The ache evaporated from behind my bones when a warm spark flared hard in my lungs. I closed my eyes, controlling it as best I could when they shot open suddenly. I looked up exhaling and my irises locked on him.

The man with soot-like hair and blue eyes, standing to the south of the opening hiding halfway behind a tree. The suave fellow who fed me coffee and tucked my drunk ass into bed. He wore a green T-shirt that stretched thin across his broad shoulders and loose jeans. He was camouflaged well. And he was staring directly at me. I bit my breath, hiding it in my throat.

I wanted to climb up to him and find out why he followed us here to my place, but I wasn't scared. Jarrett hadn't noticed at all and continued talking. I stared for several minutes until he smiled and stepped backward out of sight.

What had he been doing here? Maybe Ethan was right and he was stalking me. My mind raced through the realm of possibilities for a realistic answer. Who was this man?

* * *

Dusk had spread across the horizon, and it took everything in my legs to push me back to the truck. Jarrett noticed my fatigue when we stepped onto the blacktop again.

"Tired?" He eyed me smiling.

"Long day." I tried to smile in reply. It had been more than he'd known. The *pulling* would come and go periodically. I had seen the blue-eyed man two more times watching. No fear accompanied the sight of his luminous face. Jarrett not noticing. After hours of his absence, Jarrett decided we should finally leave, and I crawled from the hole exhausted. I walked laughing and playing, poking at Jarrett and running quickly from his reach when I looked back adjusting my backpack. The stranger was there again. Smiling.

His disappearance brought the exhaustion again. Adrenaline surging at his presence and draining in his truancy. I started crawling weakly behind the wheel. I can hardly recall Jarrett gently pushing me into the passenger seat and taking over. The ride was short, and I lightly dreamt while leaning into the warmth of his shoulder.

He plucked me from the truck and carefully carried me to the door. Pulling my shoes from my feet and tugging my jeans from my hips when we reached my bedroom. I smiled at his actions and promises of being a gentleman. He pulled his shirt off and over his head tossing it to the floor and saturating my bed with his smell. I curled into his chest and smiled when his arms wrapped around me with ease. He pulled the comforter over me warmly and kissed my head softly until I drifted.

"I've missed you, Lily," he breathed so quietly I was sure I wasn't meant to hear it.

I didn't reply. Only closed my eyes and felt pained when I realized I missed the strange ghost with the black hair that wandered in and out of my life.

18

Midnight Dinner and a Broken Heart

I was lying in my bed, the comforter spread wildly about the mattress. The bed sheets were tangled around my legs, appearing as a ribbon of ivory. My arms were casually strewn to my sides. "Okay, how about food?" I scrunched up my face. "And Nell's cooking doesn't count!" I pointed to the bathroom door that was open and arched my back for emphasis.

"I could eat meat, breakfast, lunch, dinner, and midnight dinner," his voice echoed from the tiled room.

"Midnight dinner?" I called. "Is that a real thing?"

"Um, yes," he mumbled, spitting out the minty foam hindering his speech. "Everyone gets hungry at midnight. It's human nature. You don't?"

"Not generally I usually sleep around that time." I giggled. "I like cookies. Like a lot. I could probably eat those at midnight."

"You just can't appreciate midnight dinners!" He tossed up a brassy hand. "Ignorance. My turn! Favorite…sound? I'd like to see you find an answer for that one, *Miss Everything*." He leaned through the door frame, shirtless, only wearing a pair of white boxers. He pulled the toothbrush out of his mouth and pointed it at me doubtingly.

"I love the sound the leaves make in the summer up in the mountains. I won!" I grinned, kicking my feet excitedly.

The faucet ran for a moment and then he was standing at the door yet again. His elbow above his head bent against the frame. "An answer for everything!" He reached down and snatched up some jeans from the top of his duffle. A vibrating buzz beat against the nightstand. One leg in and the other balancing on the carpet. "Can you get that?"

"Hello?" I giggled into the receiver watching him tip as he grabbed for the end of my bed.

"Knew it!" *Click.*

I held the phone out. "They hung up. That was weird."

"What did they say?" he asked.

"'Knew it'?" I stared at the phone, head cocked sideways.

"Crap!" Before he barely finished the word the phone was vibrating again. He took it from my hands. "I'm sick in the hospital. Go away!" He imitated my voice the best that he could and hung up quickly. He stood staring at the phone, waiting for it to do something.

It rang again and he sent the call to voicemail. My phone began to buzz to my right. I started to reach for it.

"No!" He leapt across the bed and landed on both knees pinning my hips. I stared at him shocked. "I mean, no," he repeated it more softly. "Let me handle this. They've figured it out."

His phone pulsed again, and I still didn't understand what was happening.

"Yes?" he answered with a breezy voice. "Don't know what you're talking about." His lips tight while he gently shook his head back and forth. "Nope, not following." He was kneeling over the top of me. Reaching down to pick and play with the buttons on my overly worn bright pink top that fell to mid-thigh. I was caged in the sheets and giggled as he began to walk two of his fingers across my stomach towards my side. "You can't hear anyone," he spoke into the phone sarcastically and shushed me with a dense smile growing across his face.

"Who are you talking to?" I caustically played innocent.

"Traitor." He covered the mouthpiece with one hand. He hit speakerphone. "Why would I be with Lily? Don't you think that you would have noticed that I'd left with luggage?"

"Mom probably smuggled you out. She's been against us since the beginning!" Grey replied, his voice smoldering slightly. Several grunts of approval sounded in the background.

Jarrett reached to my side quickly and started to creep under my shirt. I smiled approvingly but before I knew what was happening a firm hand was tickling me abruptly.

I involuntarily crowed with laughter. The phone had fallen to the bedspread, and he continued to tickle while shushing me with the opposing hand.

"Can't. Breathe," I attempted and the sheets tightened.

"He's killing her!" Logan belted. I must have been on speakerphone. A roar of voices flooded the room. "Lily, do you still have that taser we sent you for your birthday?"

"It was a cattle prod…" I half chuckled.

"Hold him off. We're on our way!" Grey shouted.

"I tried to talk them out of the taser," he muttered, covering the mouthpiece.

"We heard that. You've been usurped! We're now the oldest!" Logan declared to his twin.

"I'll stay here with Lily," Jarrett taunted them.

"Don't come home, Jarrett. You're no longer welcome at the homestead," Grey said hotly, while hums of approval seconded it in the background.

They hung up. "What they fail to realize is I've always been Mom's favorite. Besides, I'm the only one who knows where the keys to the backhoe are after that summer they decided to do some *light excavating* when they wanted a pool. We had to replace the entire septic system that July and you don't forget that smell."

"Wasn't that the summer that August and I went to Ethan's family vineyard in Napa? Ethan had to physically carry her out of the private cellar when it was time to go home." I grinned.

"You and Ethan are close, huh?" he asked casually.

"He's always been there for when I needed him." I shrugged.

With no hint of his intentions, he reached around and brought me closer, his tongue trailing the side of my throat. Inevitably, I let out a small moan of approval. His hand that had been tickling my side earlier now reached up under my shirt gripping the side it had teased. The other held the back of my neck.

The kiss didn't end. He growled into my hair. My tongue ran nomadic. Flowing across his lower lip. I stopped thinking and only felt. Felt his lips trailing my neck, shoulder, and lips. Felt the *want* that screamed from my hormones. I found myself unbuckling his jeans using a free foot to push them away from his body. I yanked at the boxers that compulsively gripped his hip bones.

In the fire brewing volcanically between our bodies, so much so, I was sure combustion would result. I arched my back, as my body hummed in wait. Biting my lip so hard my nerves started to shake. Haste had sent my shirt sliding down the bedroom wall a moment earlier from a flick of his wrist. My chest was bare, his boxers fighting against my fingertips. My skin screamed at me, begging for the beginning.

The kisses didn't cease as he lowered himself below my collarbone. His left hand clutched my back, the other cupping a breast as his tongue browsed my skin, goosebumps contagiously gathering.

The ache grew between my thighs, and I reached a hand down the front of his boxers. I rhythmically began to stroke his shaft. It pulsed thick with blood, and he let out a low groan of pleasure.

Then I felt it. An ache in my chest. A pain that cleared all thoughts, my eyes rolled back at the present moment while my mouth formed the words. "Jarrett?" I pulled my hand away.

"Lily." His voice was low.

"Slow." I exhaled the thought.

"I'll go slowly." He nodded.

I pressed a hand to his shoulder.

"No. We're taking it slow." The ache was making me more aware.

He pulled back, sitting on his haunches, breathing irregularly. He scooted off the bed. "Right." The look in his eyes begged differently.

"I'm sorry," I apologized, furrowing my brows.

"Never say you're sorry." He laughed a breathy laugh, walking around the edge of the bed and leaning over to kiss me sweetly on the head.

He walked away.

"Where are you going?" I asked him, worried.

"To take a shower," he called backward.

"But you already took one."

"Yeah but this one is going to be cold!" He grinned.

* * *

"So why trees?" he asked before sucking on his straw across the table from me.

"It's going to sound weird but…there's a familiarity about them." I chewed on the pieces of lettuce mildly.

"Like home?" His eyes squinted in curiosity.

"More than that." I took a deep breath. "Like when I'm walking through the woods I feel like I'm right. Like I'm meant to be among this old group of friends." I could feel the smile warming my lips. "As a kid, I would hide in the woods when I was upset. I would dream about them. When I came to Colorado, there was this driving impulse to be near them." I looked at the window longingly. "Like I'm never close enough. They are one of the oldest living things that occupy the earth. Some are thousands of years old. Standing as still giants in quiet masses."

"Do you ever stop being so different? For even a minute? I wish I could appreciate something half as much as you appreciate most things." His face grew glum.

"Not true! I hate tapioca pudding." I puckered up my nose in disgust.

"A lot of people hate tapioca pudding," he lulled.

"Okay," I scrunched up my face in thought, "I don't like authoritative figures in large groups. Creeps me out. I don't know how to explain it, but the best I can do is sum it up with I feel threatened or something." I pondered the honest statement.

"Nope, still flawless. Everyone has irrational fears." He shrugged.

I rolled my eyes. "Whatever." I laughed and leaned over the table kissing him. "You're too kind." I looked around the restaurant as I took my last bite. "So do you think we should ambush August and say hi? I feel bad that you came to see her and I'm completely stealing away all your time for myself." My shoulders dropped.

"You honestly think I flew all the way here to spend the weekend with my sister I saw a month ago? Hardly, Lily. Accept it. I came to see you." He grinned and washed down his final bite of food with a drink from his glass. "I want to spend every minute of it with my girl."

My face flushed red. "Your girl?" I interjected weakly.

He stood reaching down for my hand to help me up. "Yes, Lily. I chose you." He kissed my cheek and began walking. "And I want to take my girl and enjoy the day."

* * *

"Honestly, I can truly say this is lame," I pouted from the top of my counter. I was sitting cross-legged.

"I know, Lily. I think so too, but until we can figure this out more, we're just going to endure the painful suffering." Jarrett caressed my jaw, sweetly kissing me.

"This is all August's fault," I whimpered.

"How? For my flight being on time?" His fingers were playing with my hair as he spoke.

"No, because she was being all responsible and was on time for once." I shrugged, crossing my arms. "She can't show up for an important day of work on time but nope! Here to get her brother on the dot." I blew at the hair that fell in front of my eyes. "I'm going to make her work her ass off tomorrow," I spitefully finished.

He leaned back and let out a hearty laugh. "Not her fault. Be grateful she put us together."

"I guess." I bristled with animosity. Someone had to be the enemy, so I chose her.

The horn honked outside. I peeked around him and pulled his hands in hugging him. "No, I want to keep you. You're my favorite Bayne." I smiled, pressing my face into his shoulder.

"Okay! That's it." He reached around me quickly, swinging me over his shoulder. "I'm taking you with me!"

The fit of giggles was constant as he reached down grabbing his pack and kicking through the front door. It was dark out, but his pace didn't slow when he jogged easily down the stairs calling down to the open windows of August's Jeep.

"I'm taking her with August. I'll miss her too much otherwise!" He tossed the bag into the back through the open window. August laughed at the antics outside her passenger door.

He set me down and seriousness grabbed hold of him. "I'm really going to miss you, Lily." His eyes saddened.

"I know. This stinks," I mumbled weakly.

The window on the door rolled up for some privacy. His face still held the remnants of a smile.

"I'll come back as soon as I can," he whispered, wrapping his arms around me.

"Hurry." Tears streaked my cheeks lightly.

"You're my girl. I'll do my damndest." He kissed my cheeks and then finally swept me inches from the ground for the breathless kiss that would stain my memories for days after.

All too soon the Jeep was turning the corner and I waved, smiling through the wetness.

"So, is this why you didn't answer my calls the last few days?" Ethan's dark voice called slowly between vehicles.

I hadn't seen him. He must have parked down the street.

"Great. I'm happy for you two." His eyes were pained.

My gaze followed the length of his arm as he tossed a bunch of grocery store daisies to the asphalt in front of him. Sadness enveloped me as I realized he'd come to apologize, and I'd been too wrapped up in Jarrett to notice him.

"For nearly two days I sat taunted by what I did to you and you're off flirting with some jerk that picks and chooses when to get some." My heart pinched at the damage his words caused.

"Ethan," I whispered as the tears ambled past my eyelashes again.

"No, don't *Ethan* me, Lily!" He walked angrily pointing a finger. "I...I..." His shoulders dropped. "I have to go."

He was gone before the knot in my throat would clear enough for me to speak. I shouldn't have felt guilty, but I did.

19

Time to Hit the Range Again

He's being irrational. There wasn't anything when he asked. Not really. I wanted it to be something and maybe it's turned into something now, but I wasn't lying before. He shouldn't be mad, and it's his fault anyway! If he hadn't been lurking in the shadows spying on me, I would have told him about it.

Eventually.

I sighed.

"Stop that!" I scolded myself aloud.

Entirely too much sighing lately.

I should be ecstatic about my life. I have the chance to have the relationship I've always wanted, with a man who is for lack of a better word, perfection. My friends keep my life interesting. There is a brand-new mystery to be solved with this stranger who bobs and weaves through my life.

Not that I necessarily need another man around.

Jarrett and his inebriating…everything made me feel like the future would have all that I'd wanted. Ethan, aside from this bout of misplaced anger, was easily the greatest best friend the world could have dropped into my life.

"What am I even doing?" I shoved my gear into random pockets and dropped down from my perch.

"I don't need them," I said forcefully as I unhooked my tether and hung it over my shoulder. Straightening out my jacket and brushing off my jeans as I scanned the area expecting him to surface in the distance. The transient stranger. I hadn't been taking notes, but it seemed he was due for an appearance. It had been long enough since the last one.

Not that I had really thought about it. He had crossed my mind a time or two but that didn't make it anything. He was a curiosity.

That's what they all were to some degree.

Wants.

I craved Jarrett. To have him compliment me and make me blush. To make the world melt away when he's near me. I wanted him to kiss me and make me forget about everything else.

And I yearned for Ethan. For him to motivate me. Calming my racing heart with a hand on my knee when I was upset. I want him to be completely adorable in the way that he worries and prepares to avoid my coming to harm.

The stranger, for whatever reason, was wanted too. I liked when he showed up in my forest and how he walked into my life. Even at the waterfall or walking me home, at random quiet moments when he would invade my thoughts.

I shouldn't feel bad or be made to feel bad—for any of it.

And that's just that. I won't apologize for allowing myself to pursue each and every possibility put in front of me. I don't have to answer to anyone but me.

The internal conversation continued as I trekked through the underbrush en route to where August should be waiting. The closer I got, the more appreciative I was of my best girlfriend.

I could hear her singing. Her voice bounced from trunk to trunk before reaching my ears. Enjoyment and happiness are evident with each word. Enough to make me smile at her obvious bliss.

August was belting out the Lyrics to *Sugar, We're Going Down* by *Fall Out Boy* as I stepped out from the trees.

I chuckled as I watched her dancing around, rifle in hand. Feigning a shot at some invisible foe.

"Ah, shit," I said softly as I saw the fluttering of butterfly wings over her shoulder.

It happened in an instant. August saw them out of the corner of her eye and jumped what seemed a mile off the ground, flailing her arms at them as she screeched.

"Mother hell! Back off, bastards!" she yelled as she flipped around and pointed the barrel at them as if that alone would halt the vicious attack she perceived.

I stepped into the clearing and opened my mouth to calm her. She looked straight at me, her eyes already wide, and fired. I ducked away from the trajectory of the bird shot that would follow and froze when the gun fired.

"August!" I yelled as I dropped to my knees.

"Ah, shit!" she said as she rushed over to me and knelt beside me.

I cursed, vehemently and repeatedly.

The bird shot left tiny paths through the muscle on my bicep that sent a searing pain through my entire arm and shoulder area.

"Shit, August. You shot me!" I said as I clenched my teeth and pressed my left hand over the wounds in my arm.

"Mother hell! Ah, shit!" August said, wringing her hands together before throwing them in the air and letting out a disgusted sigh. "Fucking bear would have won this fight!"

"A bear? Really? I look nothing like a bear," I said as my forehead wrinkled.

"Blame the winged bitches! There was a whole flock of them a second before I saw you. Their nasty little wings in my face!" she said, wiggling her fingers in front of her. "Dusted me. I'm sure of it! Blinded me, really. All I saw was this big brown thing in the shadows. Fired and missed apparently. Time to hit the range again."

"You're pissed that you didn't kill the bear? Which is *me* by the way! Oh my God, Ethan was right!" I said as I groaned at the burning sting the pellets had made.

"Quit your whining! Hell, I barely grazed you! I'd be lucky to take down a rabbit at that distance. And Ethan is never right." She waved an irritated index finger at me.

"Hey, I'm actively bleeding." I removed my palm and gave an incredulous chuckle.

"It's seeping and your fault! Come barreling out of the brush like that! What else would you expect me to do? You looked like a bear! I was defending myself!" she yelled.

"You would have heard a fucking bear! It would have been larger and snarling," I laughed at her ridiculous excuse.

"It's snarling at me now," she muttered under her breath.

"Um, because you fucking shot me," I responded in a snarky tone.

"Watch your language," she scowled. "You were poked with metal from a distance."

"I was shot over a pair of monarchs." I never thought butterflies would be the wildlife that would get me out here.

"There were more than two I'll have you know," she said with a frown.

"That is not the issue!" I shot with a glare as a pull started to radiate through my chest. It was the same feeling at the waterfall.

"I know! The issue is that I missed it! I could have been bear food, Lily!" she gushed as she knelt and unzipped our first aid kit.

"August! That's not the issue." I shook my head.

"How is it not? You'll survive a flesh wound, Lily! I could have been fucking eaten! You don't survive being eaten!" She tore open a gauze pad.

I dropped my head back and broke into a laugh of disbelief.

"You're fucking with me, right? You can't be serious," I said with a roll of my eyes.

"Of course I'm serious! Don't you see how those winged devils are evil? They did this! They bombarded me! Brought the whole clan along to play this little game!" She haphazardly swabbed the wounds with antiseptic.

"Two butterflies, August! Not a flock. Not a clan. And abso-fuckinglutely not a plethora," I spat through gritted teeth.

"You're delirious with pain. You obviously don't remember clearly," she declared.

"I wouldn't say delirious," I challenged, half laughing.

"I would! You've been swearing up a storm today." She gave me an admonishing look.

I was speechless after that. August, the girl whose proficiency in the profane would turn a sailor's stomach in disgust, had scolded me for *my* language right now. I must be delirious.

"Still hurt?" she asked as she poked at the flesh beside the entry wounds.

"It doesn't tickle, August." I straightened out my bandage.

She shrugged. "Whiner," she uttered under her breath.

"Can you help me get up?" I held a hand out to her.

"Ew. You're all bloody." She stood as she spoke and turned to leave.

"Where are you going?" I couldn't believe that she'd just go.

"I'm going to get the sat phone from Grizzly. Ethan is going to strangle me. He's finally going to have a reason to be all paranoid and a real instance where he'll surely blame me for you being hurt. Great." She turned as she lamented her situation.

I sighed. "It was an accident."

"Accident? Like that will matter! He likes you better than me, Lily! I'll never live this down." She faded out of sight.

"Well, this has been a fun day." I dropped my head to the ground.

"She's an interesting woman," a voice murmured from the shadows.

I turned toward the sound. The voice was familiar to me, soothing, resonating so deeply that it startled me. "Interesting, yeah, and extremely thoughtless right now," I responded.

"Some people deal with stress that way." He knelt beside me, and his hand covered my wrist. The jolt was there again but less jarring. Less shocking. More comforting.

I lifted my hand away from the wound before he even asked.

"And then there's August." I looked at the bloody mess on my shirt.

"It doesn't look too deep." He took my arm gently in his hand and examined it closely.

"What are you doing here?" I couldn't help but question, as sudden desensitization blanketed my arm. I no longer felt the burning sting from the bullet's paths. I vaguely referenced my knowledge of shock and its symptoms. I wasn't cold. I wasn't lightheaded. Seemingly fine. Must be adrenaline I decided.

"I was in the area." He glanced at me as his lips turned up in a smile.

"You seem to be in the area a lot." I returned the smirk playfully.

"I go where I feel the need to be."

"Well, elusive stranger with no name, I think you're stalking me." I smiled as I said it. Curious about his name and his odd appearances, but not concerned.

"I have a name." He chuckled as he pulled the first aid kit from my bag and grabbed a bundle of gauze.

"And what is it?" I couldn't turn my eyes away from him and the numbness had flooded through my entire arm and shoulder.

"Elijah," he answered and then turned sharply away, looking off into the trees further into the forest.

"Eli." It sounded right for him and tasted sweet on my tongue as I repeated it.

He smiled softly as I said it. "I have to go." It was hesitant as it left his lips, as though he were reluctant to leave.

"You're going to leave me here too?" It inadvertently sounded sad.

"August will be back in a moment, and she's correct. It's a flesh wound."

Leaves rustled from her return and I knew that she was merely a moment away.

"I know but I'm still mad at her."

He laughed as he stood to leave. "It will pass." He turned to walk away.

"Lily, Ethan's on his way." She was breaking through to the clearing when I glanced at her quickly and then back to Eli.

He was gone. There was no goodbye or even the ruffling of a leaf. He'd disappeared into the shadows.

"Eli?" I called out softly.

"Oh, great, you've gone into shock. How will I be punished for that, do you suppose?" She knelt and felt my forehead.

I pulled away from her hand.

"I'm not in shock," I assured her.

"Then who were you talking to? Because nobody was there except you," she questioned.

Do I tell her about the stranger? No. Definitely not. I wasn't even sure who— or what— he was.

"Nobody. How long until he gets here?" I changed the subject.

"Not long. He was close so we're supposed to head to the road." She clenched my hand in hers as she helped me to my feet. I cringed at the movement. The pain had returned when Eli had gone.

Eli. I liked saying the name. Even if it was only in my mind.

As we moved purposefully through the sparse stance of trees, we could hear his truck tires screeching as they closed in on us.

20

Netting, Nightlights, and a Cursed Parking Lot

"Sir, calm down!" The nurse's hands pulsed.

"This is my wife! The hell I'll calm down!" Ethan roared.

"I said I was sorry, Ethan." August choked on weak tears while they were loading me onto the gurney from Ethan's truck. I hate hospitals but I obliged in the hope that I could avoid the commotion stirring around me.

The officers jotted on their papers continuously consulting with each other. It took a lot to convince them this was all a result of an accidental discharge.

He turned on her with a savage force. "Leave!" The ire bled through his vocals in a way that I could never place with him.

"Ethan, I didn't see her." The words hindered from racking sobs.

"That's the thing, August Bayne. You never see anyone but yourself!" he spoke savagely towards her. The oxygen mask prohibited my ability to halt the asperity he was feeling. I raised a hand in hopes to help.

"Don't move, Lily. I don't want you to do further damage." His words twisted back to tender towards me. I was able to catch the malevolence brewing in his view when he turned to face August again.

"What more do you want me to say, Ethan?" August tried to avert the fan of fire about to hit.

"Shut up, you stupid bitch!" Ethan leaned down over her, a rage taking over his posture.

August's lower lip quivered as she tried to stop the tears that pricked at her tiny, pale lids. She staggered backward, wounded by the callous words, and turned away jogging towards her Jeep after her best friend's angry outburst.

All officials took witness to his volatile state and stood still. My mind shut off as a cold streak of liquid crossed into my vein from the IV port and I closed my eyes to it, making sure to whisper, "Don't fight."

* * *

Ethan and August were adamant about remaining in separate rooms at all times. One would leave before the other arrived or excuse themselves if a collision of timing occurred.

"You should really say you're sorry. That was too much, Ethan," I spoke from my bed, winded by the drugs that coursed through me.

He wouldn't respond and August's mood had dimmed as well. They both refused to speak to each other and apparently were starting to feel the same way about me.

Ethan wasn't quite ready to forgive me for Jarrett while August was hurt so much her demeanor lessened and she felt little need to carry on a conversation.

"Okay. Well, call if you need something." Ethan was walking towards the front door after stopping in to check on me.

"Yeah," I mumbled. This was more miserable than the time August flipped Grizzly over and knocked me out cold.

"The day after tomorrow if you're feeling better I would like to take you somewhere."

"Where?" I strained my voice at the change in direction, but it was too late and he was already out the door. I yanked the pillow over my head and screamed. I hated everything right now.

I missed happy Ethan. The shameless flirt I knew in the beginning.

* * *

I leaned away from the creepy guy that was seated next to me at the bar. His breath was rank with beer, and he kept making comments about the color of my cheeks looking like Snow White's when she was sleeping.

August had promised me a night of fun and forgetfulness after another one of her epic fights with Mason. Something about him kissing a girl when they were supposed to be taking time to reflect on their feelings for one another. She was *reflecting,* alright. Right onto some brown-eyed guy that looked like an eerie version of Mason from an alternate reality.

"Maybe I could wake *you* up with a kiss?" the guy slurred, while spitting through his teeth onto my shoulder.

I tried not to cringe.

"I'm here with my boyfriend," I lied in hopes the guy would back off and leave me alone.

"Well, I don't see him anywhere right now."

"He's right here," a gorgeous hazel-eyed blond laid an arm around my shoulder. "Hey, beautiful."

"Hi." I blushed nervously at my hero. It was Ethan Monroe, the sinfully handsome guy who pulled my car out of the ditch over the winter.

The sleazy fella backed off with a roll of his eyes and turned to walk away.

"Hope I wasn't being presumptuous. You looked like you could use a little rescuing there." He moved to sit beside me. "So, it looks like your best friend and my friend are dating." He glanced over to August who was giggling shamelessly at the faux Mason. "*Were* dating."

"On and off. I think we've begun an *off* phase."

"And you? Do you have a boyfriend?" A small smirk was playing across his lips.

"Why do you want to know?"

"Why do I want to know if the beautiful brunette has a boyfriend? Do you really have to ask?"

I let out a small laugh and turned away.

"Go out with me." He said it more as a statement.

"I don't even know you." I scrunched up my shoulders nervously.

"You're right. We should build our friendship first. Then once we're best friends, we can date." He licked his lower lip before a cocky smile took hold.

"How do you know we're going to be best friends?"

"I'm frequently promoted to best friend status. So it's decided. I will see you Saturday for a very friendly lunch, Harper. You like tacos? I know a great food truck."

"Harper?"

"Friends aren't on a first name basis. Those are couple's goals. I'll pick you up at eleven." He grinned as he strode away.

"Whatever you say, *Monroe*." I rolled my eyes and watched his shoulders shake as he laughed.

* * *

I had spent the last forty-eight hours laid up on my good side, planning my assault. I was going to confront him. I'd had enough of my friends pitting me against one another. I had deduced that Ethan was acting this way because he could sense that Jarrett and I were closer than he wanted us to be. I'd always been available and for the first time I wasn't.

"You know, I think you're a big prick. You kissed me and all of sudden assumed that my world has changed. Where was *this* Ethan years ago?" I questioned as I breathlessly stepped behind him. The sun was setting fast through the trees making it very difficult for me to see where I was going but I persisted.

He walked quietly ahead of me, not so much that he wouldn't be able to hear me but enough to pretend he didn't. I rolled my eyes and continued to talk.

"I'm sick of this. It's been a week and you guys are pretending to not even know each other! I am not going to be your glue. It was an accident! And it's really nice that I got shot and that's when you decided you wanted to talk to me again, and still, you have yet to tell me what the hell that kiss was about!" I huffed. I inhaled to kick start my next rant when I stopped. Staring ahead at what he'd done.

"Ethan…" I breathed his name. "What did you do?"

"Remember how you said that you wish you could lay up there some afternoons without all the gear?" He was looking at it.

"So you rigged this up? This must have taken you—"

"Weeks. Yeah." I looked to catch a bashful way about his eyes.

Fine black netting was strung between four large trees a couple dozen feet above the forest floor, like a large hammock. A handful of small white solar lanterns were kicking on as the dusky sun was lowering. They were hanging lightly from a few limbs. So small one would think they were large stars if you were quickly glancing up.

"I don't think I can climb up there." I swallowed hard.

"I know. I made an easy ladder. Normally, I would let you climb but being as you're currently on the injured list I thought ahead. Ladies first." He waved a hand upwards at the ladder bowing slightly.

I slowly crawled towards the middle and found a comfortable position to witness what I deemed impossible.

"So are you still mad?" I glanced over after nearly a half hour of silence. The forest had gone dark.

"I was never mad at you, Lily. You should know me better than that." His eyes glazed over with sadness. "I was hurt. I was thinking to myself. Finally! Maybe I didn't screw it up and maybe I still would have a chance." Closing his eyes, he continued, "Lily, when I'm with you, it's like my appetite is suppressed. I feel like I'm where I'm supposed to be. Then I saw you and Jarrett and my heart tore up, knowing I'd been too late." He scooted closer to me.

"Ethan, you're down and out and need some new girl." I looked over at him.

His lips pulled into a tight line and his hands balled into fists at his sides. He inhaled sharply through his nose as he tilted his head back.

"You're going through a lull. The blond from the restaurant that huffed about cheesecake was lame. You'll find the right one."

He leaned back and yelled, slamming his fists against the net and pulling himself to my side. "Don't you get it, Lilian? I want you! *Your* green eyes staring at me. *Your* pale skin reflecting the moonlight in *my* bed at night. *Your* small hands reaching for mine." His voice evened out and gently grabbed my hand, running his thumbs along the inside of my palms. "Your lips. Your smell in *my* lungs, not his." His face was pained.

"Ethan." The way I said it ached out loud.

"Don't say it. I can't hear you tell me it's him. The way you two were laughing the other night…" He stopped, and I peeked to see why.

"I wanted it to be me." He pulled me into him. "I want you, Lilian Harper, more than anything else."

"You're being melodramatic," I whispered. His face twisted in pain, the pale white lanterns casting shadows across his jaw.

"No, I'm not. You're my girl, the girl that makes my chest twist. Makes me feel like I swallowed caged moths."

I scrunched up my nose disgusted.

"The girl that I instill with adorable giggles. Like"— his face was serious— "yours."

I didn't know how to respond. I was sure that my mind had lost control of everything cognitive. Had I died after the gunshot and this was my mind coping? I didn't feel like I was lying next to Ethan. He'd changed somehow.

"Did this spark because of Jarrett and me? You know if I wasn't seeing him and it wasn't so serious I would believe that you wouldn't care so much." I drew lines up and down his fingers.

His face grew tense. "Dammit, Lily! Don't you get it?" He grasped my sides pulling me at him, yet still aware of the wound and the need to be tender. "I'm…" He gritted his teeth.

It hit me fast. I didn't want him to say it. I knew where this was going. I was lying if there hadn't been times over the years that the girls to appear around me didn't evoke jealousy from my gut.

Lilian Harper, stop blowing this! Jarrett was a million miles away and Ethan was here. Lying next to me on an oversized hammock amidst the moonlit trees gushing feelings about you. Looking sexy in torn-up blue jeans.

"I'm sorry, Ethan, but the idea of you sleeping with all those women…" I sighed. "I'm not looking for a steamy night between the sheets."

"I didn't."

"You didn't what?" I looked at him, confused.

"I haven't slept with anyone since I met you," he whispered, looking down. "Believe me. I tried. I wanted to! But it was you I wanted in my bed." His face was sad.

I didn't think. I was stunned.

I grabbed him by his jaw, letting my fingertips graze over the rough stubble. Sucking in the smell that sometimes sent my mind on tangents when he would crawl into bed with me on hot summer nights.

I pushed my whole body into his and hitched my left leg up over his hip. He pulled at my thigh instinctually and I was closer. His kiss was like fire. He was sweet yet passionate. His hips pulsed towards mine.

My fingers reached up over his shoulders and twisted into the loose waves of his blond hair. His lashes brushed across my cheekbones. His tongue tasted sweet. He let out a moan.

"Lily, I have wanted you since day one," he spoke between breaths.

I pulled his face towards mine and kissed him again. His massive hands pulled at my shirt.

Kissing Ethan was different from Jarrett. Jarrett sent me into a hypnotized trance that pushed me to mimic all his wants and all my underlying needs. Jarrett had a rough rumble about him. He growled and Ethan moaned. He was sweet and gentle. He pushed into what I wanted. It made it hard to stop.

I forced him away with my hands at his chest, gasping. "Ethan this is…" My eyes searching the leaves for an answer.

"Perfect?" He grinned.

"I was thinking *weird*." I bit the inside of my lower lip.

His face fell. I didn't want to hurt his feelings, but I had to be honest.

"I *do* want to kiss you again." I tried eagerly to regain control of my erratic breathing. I looked around hoping an answer would show itself.

"Lily." He cupped my face gently. "This doesn't have to be hard. Stop overthinking everything. Let me ask you something." He lay back while pulling me up to rest on his chest. "Was that not a spectacular kiss?"

"It was." I nodded lightly.

"And did you not crave something more for every second of it?" He started to draw rings around the bones of my spine like he always did.

"Yes, I did." He was right. Everything in me felt tangled now more than ever because this felt so right, too. Ethan was my best friend and Jarrett was my best friend's brother.

It dawned on me. "We can't tell August!" I blurted.

He leaned down and kissed my shoulder. "Harper. Stop. You'll give yourself a hemorrhage. Stop panicking." He kissed my temple like he always did.

I leaned up on his chest and smiled. "Fine. I'm being carefree, Lily."

He kissed me again.

* * *

The whole way home we laughed and flirted. It wasn't like Jarrett. We already knew each other and our lives. It was easier. The nervousness wasn't evident.

"I checked into the private residence up in the park. Guy hasn't been back in three years. Just keeps it up enough to get by. People come to take care of it I guess. So I'm really a little worried about your stalker." He was holding my hand across the console lazily as his other gripped the top of the steering wheel.

"Don't know who he was. I haven't seen him since or any signs of him so I'm not too concerned," I lied.

"Probably just a ghost." His statement rang truer than he knew.

"You're seriously going to walk me to my door?" I eyed him.

"I'd tuck you in if you let me." He grinned. He was standing on the pavement, and I was two steps above him, only able to see eye level.

"So how many times do you suppose I get to kiss you?" he asked, twisting his toe in the gravel.

"Why?" I cocked my head sideways.

"That's a *whenever I feel like* if I heard one!" He wrapped his arms around me wildly and his lungs shredded with laughter. He tilted me back, dipping me romantically kissing me yet again. He snarled into my neck.

"My Lily. Forever! Knew I'd marry you." He laughed into my hair and kissed me again. I obliged willfully. I had never seen him this happy.

His sweet hazel eyes were bright with happiness, and I smiled at him.

"What the hell?" a shrill voice called as the sound of metal hit the ground. "Lily, you're making out with Ethan?" August yelled.

I looked to see her standing back in shock where she was frozen and had dropped her keys. Her eyes were spilling angry tears brightening her turquoise irises that were filling with enraged terror.

"You're cheating on my brother with Ethan? Ethan! Ew!" She spit at the sound of his name. "This man slut?"

"August, let me say something." I was quickly walking towards her, determined to rectify the situation.

"That's why you were so pissed at me!" She pointed a shaky finger at Ethan standing at the foot of the steps. "Because I almost killed your girlfriend. While my brother has been practically giving himself ulcers worried about her and not being able to be here!"

She turned to me now. "You're screwing around with this shit bag?" she shouted.

"August," I attempted a quiet rebuttal, tears racing down my cheeks.

"No. Stay away from my brother!" She walked away leaving the get-well card she had dropped alongside her keys. "We are not friends anymore."

She was gone and I was running up the stairs wiping at my cheeks. I was really beginning to hate this damn parking lot.

21

Going Under

It didn't take me long to know that I had to talk to her. I grabbed my truck keys.

"Ethan, you don't get it. August is my best friend!" I shoved money into my pockets.

"She's shallow, Lily." He rolled his eyes leaning against the door frame.

"No, Ethan." I came to stand in front of him. "She's not," I exhaled. "She just isn't mushy. Without her, my days suck. She keeps me laughing in my worst moods. Like a little sunshine. She's been there too. If you want to maintain your grudge with her, fine, but I'm done being in the middle." I leaned up and kissed his cheek as usual, "I'll call you later, Ethan." I didn't turn back to see his reaction.

* * *

She was livid. I went down to the Boiler and found her sitting on a leather stool at the end of the bar. Quinn was behind the counter.

"So are you with him now?" She was twirling a bottle cap in her

218

hands. "I should call Jarrett… unless you're going to tell him?" She turned slightly.

"August! I don't know!" I huffed in frustration.

"Lily, are you serious right now? This is my brother! He feels something for you. He asks about you constantly. Don't string him along," she sneered.

It hurt the way she spoke about his feelings for me. I ran my fingers through my hair. Anger and annoyance seeped through every pore. I knew that I'd felt something for Jarrett. Hell, he was a dream for any girl. The hair, his eyes, that laugh, those lips. Just the idea of him made me warm. Injecting dreamy thoughts into my head. Enticing me to get lost on a tangent of memories and possibilities.

"I'm not trying to. There's other stuff going on right now," I said with a sigh. "I care about your brother, okay? I want to be with him."

"You're both so beautiful though. And you're supposed to marry him and be my sister," she said dispiritedly.

In true August form, her impulsiveness outweighs her rationality. He's a Pacific Northwest boy who grew up with plans of taking over the family business and having kids of his own. I couldn't even keep my beta fish, Elmwood, alive in the seventh grade! The focus of my career is on Colorado, and he's in Washington State. How would that even work? Could that even work? And what if it didn't? August and I would never be the same, and I'd be forced to say goodbye to the Baynes forever.

"August, I am not going to marry your brother, dammit! He lives states away from me and I told you— I have other priorities than locking lips with some guy's guy logger from the backwoods!" I said defensively in a heated rush. Immediately, I stopped. Too far. I thought. Way too far. I was angry, not ready to feel the things I was feeling.

She froze. "What the hell is that supposed to mean?" she asked with a mask of hurt across her face, and fiery anger lapping at her irises.

"What's wrong with his occupation?"

"Hey, I didn't mean it like that. I was just saying—" I began before she interrupted.

"Saying what, Lily? That he isn't enough for you? Not enough to keep a scientific, grant-receiving brainiac like you interested? That's fucking bullshit!" she screeched as her arms flew out beside her. "So you're saying I'm not good enough to walk beside you either! We're all shitting on the same pot here, Lily!" she finished as she turned away from me.

I shivered in the wave of icy hatred that radiated from her cold shoulder. August was a brilliant scientist. Beautiful and quick-witted. She could beat most people in any subject. I hated that she thought I felt less of her.

"August, you're being ridiculous. I was saying that Jarrett isn't someone I would naturally fall for." I paused before testing the turbulent emotional waters again. "Jarrett is wonderful," I said when she didn't reply. "I do like him. A lot. But...I..." I couldn't find my voice.

"But you think he's a project. Someone whose odds don't work in your favor. Illogical?" she said lowly as she flipped around to face me, eyes overflowing with venomous scorn. "Dammit, Lily! Give up on this rationality bullshit! Sorry, he's not a scholar with riches beyond all else. Not all of us could have Daddy leave us a lump sum after settlement. *Our* father didn't get himself killed," she said harshly. Hate spitting my way like an erupting geyser.

A thick lump caught in my throat, and I stood frozen. Mouth hung agape. August had never directed her hatred at me with such vehemence. Shock and hurt pulled tears to my eyes, drowning them in the moisture brimming over the bottom of my lashes. I turned away.

"Dammit, Lily. I'm sorry," she said, realizing that she'd crossed a very dangerous line. "I fucked up. That was low. It's just..." She hesitated.

"Jarrett's falling for you. I can't watch him suffer like that," she finished as she caught her lower lip between her teeth.

I trembled as the anger rushed from my center.

"My father was brilliant. An amazing human being," I said as I turned slowly back and stalked towards her. "You could never live up to someone that great," I spat, narrowing my eyes as I stopped in front of her. "Bitch," I seethed, and I ignored the hurt that flashed into her eyes.

I turned without another word. Disbelieving that she'd dared touch the subject. Walking away and not turning back as I wiped furiously at the wetness on my cheeks. I pushed through the crowd without a second thought.

* * *

I marched through the woods angrily, unable to forget. I didn't want to go back home and risk facing her. I thought a walk would help, but I found myself stomping along the trail more than relaxing.

She'd attacked my dad. My father! I spoke of him so rarely that she knew little about the man. Did she honestly think she had a right to mention him? Especially in such a hurtful way! I hated this! Tears stained my cheeks. Sniffling as I cried. Trying in vain to calm my ragged breathing. Hoping a cough would obscure the emotional outburst. A feeble attempt to hide the weakness I felt at the moment.

I get it. She was mad and felt I betrayed her brother. But she betrayed me. Best friends should rise above and be better than this.

"I knew I shouldn't have gotten involved with her brother!" I growled skyward.

Jarrett meant something to me. I just didn't know what yet. I hadn't even thought of the things she spouted out. I hadn't attempted to digest the possibilities of our relationship. I didn't want to! Maybe that's why I'd become so heated so quickly. She made me think of things I had no desire to think about. Things I wanted to forget. Made me ponder a choice I was not prepared to make.

Jarrett? Ethan?

Let's not forget the elusive Eli. A stranger, who was stalking me through the forest and appearing in my neighborhood randomly. Like that isn't creepy! And what was with that feeling? The pain in my chest below my collarbone when he was around. Like I couldn't get close enough to him. Like I wanted him there! I felt like I knew him. The same feeling when you recognize someone and can't quite place where they're from. The thought of it all fueled more tears.

How do you explain something you don't comprehend yourself? How would anyone understand? A person I wanted to see. To talk to. To touch.

I walked blindly through the forest. Debating the urge to turn and call my best friend. My heart told me to go back. Hug her and apologize until I couldn't breathe. But I didn't. The hateful words replayed in my head and my legs wouldn't let me stop.

And then, there it was. I could see the trees breathing with the rush of the river. A river I'd found while working and neglected to share with August, the same river I had taken Jarrett to. I'd followed it and discovered how it dropped off into the large cavern. I decided then and there that it would be my place. My *away* place.

White moonlight refracted off the water cascading over the edge. I wasn't afraid of the night in the woods. It was a beauty that horror movies smeared. A different life that couldn't be witnessed in the presence of daylight.

My retreat was hidden by willows and tall conifers. The willows with their weeping branches, tendrils flowing like fingers reaching down to the ground. Guarding the hidden sanctuary they surrounded. The large boulders built into a crescent around its edges crowding down the sides. I approached slowly. The tears, still apparent, but dissipating with the sight of my place. I could feel my breathing become even as it opened up to me. Reaching out with its serenity and calming the rapid beat of my heart as it anticipated the haven I approached.

My toes broke over the brink. I peered down and smiled through the remaining tears. The water fell away over the edge. Bewitching and hypnotic. I didn't register my body's movements. Preparing the equipment I needed to rappel over the edge. I turned and hitched the rope around the nearest anchor before swinging wide over the ledge.

I sighed in relief as I felt the mist kiss my skin. It was warm and it glittered in the night's rays. Anger was not plausible here. Not in this place. My feet buried into the ground, and I released the rope's clip from my belt. I stumbled toward the falls.

The rushing river crashed into the big empty cavern and jutted off to the right before disappearing under the floor and out of the room. I could smell the moss. I couldn't follow the river once I'd descended here. The current was too strong in the main flow of the waters. The rocks surrounding it became dangerously slippery and could easily crumble with my minimal weight. It allowed a smaller off chute that spilled over the banks, filling small pools to overflowing. Its captivating bluish-green waters were like nothing ever seen before. Shallow reservoirs of warmth reflecting the filtered light breaking in from above, steam rising from their faces.

I lowered myself to the ground beside it. Gaze transfixed on the current and its lack of effect on the rocks. Sniffling, I reached around my neck and removed the ever-present silver chain, always hanging close to me, against the skin hidden under every shirt. It was simple, at the bottom hung a key. The key to a typewriter. One my dad had given to me. A lone question mark graced its face.

I sighed heavily.

"Why did she have to go there?" I pleaded. "What is happening with my life right now?"

I was overwhelmed. August and her anger. Jarrett and his rough allure. Ethan and his 'best friend' ways that had turned into sweet longing. Eli and his strange appearances in my life. So many things jarring my peacefulness. I hated the discord.

I didn't know what I wanted. Half of me loved the man from Washington and could see myself with a future laid out ahead of me. The other half loved the protective and wildly charming man here at my side in Colorado. Maybe August was right. Maybe this was all wrong.

The rock cracked and fell away suddenly from where my feet were resting, startling me. My eyes flew open, and I jumped at the sound. Pulling my legs back towards me, I pushed away from the edge as I tried to catch my breath. Gathering my senses after the shock, I realized the loss of the chain.

"Shit!" I said as I searched the ground beside me, dragging my fingers through the matted grass.

"Shit. Shit. Shit!" I chanted as I scanned the area.

A sparkle caught my eye.

"Crap," I said slowly as I spotted the gleam of the silver necklace reflecting through the midnight blue tides.

Inching cautiously closer, I reached down for the chain. An unwarranted pain radiated through my chest, centered below my collarbone. As I reached for the key, the tide rushed in front of me. Faster than imaginable, before my mind caught up with the threat, the waters reached out. Their white-tipped fingers wrapping around me and easily engulfing my distracted search. Their force was instantly suffocating. I turned in the swirling waters.

"Oh no!" I yelled.

This was bad. Very bad.

"Help!" I shouted as my body hitched down and then shot up violently, "Someone! Help!" I cried.

I was not the worst of swimmers, but my pack was still glued to my back and my boots were an unnecessary weight, my toned arms could not compensate for their presence.

Head bobbing rapidly in the wicked current. My mind was erratically pleading. Loved ones flashing in front of me. I begged them for help.

"Jarrett!" I screamed irrationally as my head broke the surface. Instinct did not care that he would not hear my call.

"August!" I cried out as freshwater bombarded and choked my lungs.

A gurgled cry could be heard as blackness seeped in.

* * *

There I was. Oversized helmet slipping in front of my eyes with each bump the road threw our way. The wind muted. My arms fatigued from gripping his torso too tightly. A grin painted on my small face. My mom had begged him not to take me on his motorcycle.

"She's too little, William!"

All I could feel was happiness though. Hear…music? Was that music? It grew louder.

You know that saying, *You look, but it's already too late*? It never rang truer.

I felt my dad twist as the motorcycle propelled forward.

"I love you, Lily." He smiled softly. "Watch out. He's coming!"

His face was pained as he let go with an unknowable force.

Then his hands were around my small body. Too fast for my young mind to register or think to resist. He lifted me from the seat and flung me away to the ditch in the same instant that a squad car collided with him. Its sirens screamed their deafening music.

My dad never walked away from the wreck, but I miraculously was unscathed. Do you know what it's like for people to tell you that you're a miracle in the wake of your parent dying? It doesn't make you feel good. Or when they say how lucky you are. Luck doesn't feel lucky unless those around you share it. Like holding a winning lottery ticket after someone you loved just died of a heart attack. It feels wrong to celebrate something like that.

I asked my mom when I was twelve what my dad had meant…his dying words. She broke down crying and told me that panic made people say funny things.

When I was nine I was convinced he was warning me of someone, and I had night terrors for months. My little kid brain was sure that I was going to die.

When I was a teenager, I persuaded myself that my dad was trying to tell me something. Maybe in his final moments, a revelation came to him, and I should keep my eyes open for this *him*.

Now at twenty-five, I chalked it up to him warning me that the police officer pursuing the stolen car, barreling down that county road, was going to hit us.

* * *

Moonlight impaled the water around me, growing dimmer by the second. The edges of my vision blurred. Here it was. The place that was my serenity would become my demise.

Fear paralyzed me slowly, stealing away my ability to scream. I struggled against it and fought as valiantly as possible against the current. But deep down, I knew I'd lose this battle. Death would win. I tried frantically to unbuckle my pack from the waist and kick off my boots, but my efforts were useless.

"Ethan?" I whispered as my face broke the surface briefly.

Gasping desperately for my last breath of air, I was violently pulled under. Kicking with every scrap of energy that my body possessed. Knowing it was futile. Fingers clawing at the liquid helplessly. Holding my breath and refusing defeat. Squeezing my eyes closed against the burning. Lungs nearing their explosive end.

I would never tell Jarrett I miss him painfully when we were apart or that Ethan made me whole again when I was broken up. Or the stranger. The ghostly Eli that was quickly becoming *something*, ebbing at constant curiosity.

My body went limp. My chest was aflame and exhaling. Bubbles rising as one last plea escaped my lips.

Sorry. I mouthed silently.

Darkness engulfed me.

Death had prevailed.

22

Lily 1. Death 0.

I felt them. The warm, inviting hands of the reaper. They wrapped around me in a sweet caress. A vice-like grip pulling me upwards. I relaxed in their hold. Knowing that it was over. I would not have to feel the searing pain that held my chest captive for long.

How long does it take for them to erase the pain? My mind pondered as my stomach fluttered in fear.

I told myself to be open and accepting. I felt still. Frozen. There was no hope of fighting this even if my arms and legs weren't limp. My lungs compressed.

Why is this happening? My mind begged in silent wonder. Panic hit suddenly. Would I get my typewriter key back? *Could I at least have that?* I thought.

I tasted the cold on my lips. Felt the pressure in my chest again. And again. My hands felt empty. Darkness surrounded me.

Where is the light they spoke of? The path my mind would guide me down. The hand that would usher me?

Pain wracked my chest. I wanted it to stop. To beg for the end. Plead for mercy and a swift passage, to those I'd lost to my dad. I thought softly. How long would it be until I saw him?

There was a hollow echo. "Lily, come on, dammit!" It whispered hauntingly before trailing away as light filtered into my eyes.

It's not working!

Light.

I could see light!

Like stars dotting my pupils through the darkness.

"Why?" the voice cried fiercely. Angrily.

Air infiltrated my broken lungs. A breath was forced down my throat. It was not the vile, acrid taste I'd expected. Instead, it was like honey. Addicting. I didn't want this to end. Until I felt the cracking stab. As though someone had twisted a knife into my side.

My eyes fluttered.

"Stay *here* with *me!*" the haunting voice said.

Suddenly, I could feel the sharp stab of rocks jutting into my back with each shallow breath. This was not what I'd expected at all. A small, illogical part of me had always wanted the peace they'd foretold. The colors. The promised tunnel. The happy reunion with the dearly departed. This was not it. My hope had been fruitless. Their claims against my misguided lack of faith, all lies. This was the proof. This was the science of the afterlife. Pain.

Claustrophobic emptiness, condemned to relive the pain for all eternity. Nerves electrified all the bodies' processes still in full swing. How long would it take? Would I feel all this until the very end? Until the last molecular cell halts its purpose. Would I have to endure it all?

Probably.

Super! I thought sarcastically.

A compressed force thrust down onto my rib cage yet again, tearing a breath from my lungs. I felt a sudden crack in my left side.

No more. I screamed into the recess of my mind. I could not persevere through death with such immense pain radiating throughout my body. I forced my eyes open. Moonlight and shadows blinded me all at once. How odd? Was that the answer? Open your eyes and accept. Simply that was the key to crossing into the afterlife.

A figure came into view. My eyes adjusted weakly. As they cleared, focusing on the silhouette in front of me, they widened with shock, and all at once, I understood everything.

"You," I breathed.

"Me," he replied breathlessly, wiping his mouth.

"This is death?" I asked in confusion.

"No," he replied exasperated.

"There was nothingness," I replied.

"You were"—he paused, hesitant to say the words— "lost for several moments, but I got a hold of you," he finished distantly.

"I'm beginning to think you really are stalking me," I managed. "Maybe I shouldn't mind. You did step in." I paused. "Thanks for that. My pack and such were weighing me down. I think I was drowning." My explanation sounded lame. "Obviously." I gestured towards him. "You were there." I nodded to the hot water behind me.

Pain flashed across his face and was quickly replaced with frustrated anger. "It felt wrong to allow it to happen," he said as he pushed a heavy hand through his dark hair.

With a sigh, he sat back and let his head fall. Tilting his face to the sky, he was bathed in moonlight. The beauty stole my breath.

I groaned and looked away. "Ah, shit," I said as my hand went to my left side. "I feel like I can't catch my breath."

"I'm sorry. I broke three ribs while I revived you," he said through closed eyes.

I rolled mine at his standoffish responses and cold demeanor.

"Keep your apologies. Shouldn't you be running off by now? Leaving me all mysteriously?" I snapped in frustration. My anger fed by pain. "That is your thing, right?" I asked through gritted teeth.

He brought his eyes to meet my annoyed gaze.

"Your ankle is sprained as well," he said, gesturing at the injury I'd yet to feel.

"Not the first time. I am perfectly capable of handling myself," I said, annoyed.

He blinked at me repeatedly as if unable to comprehend my irritation.

"How did you find me anyway? Unless you really were following me?" I asked, amused.

"I did no such thing. Not that you could stop me." He shrugged.

"Oh, really? Well, Eli with no last name who can't seem to say much…" I began.

"I felt your need for help. I heard you through the trees…I live nearby…" He trailed off in wonder as his face looked to the sky again.

"You *felt* my need?" I asked in disbelief.

He glanced in my direction and then closed his eyes again slowly. "Yes. Felt." He sighed.

"That's impossible," I said.

"I agree," he scoffed.

"Fabulous," I said softly.

He let out a slow breath as if to concur.

"I don't understand any of this. Who are you, Eli, and what is this?" I asked softly.

Lying on my back, I took short breaths to avoid as much pain as possible. The pain would distract me, and right now my curiosity needed satisfaction. I peered over at him. His shirt pulled low and askew. His collarbone and shoulder peeking from below. His jeans dusted with burnt soot. His careless attire did nothing to mask the overwhelming facade. Models on the elite runways would sell their souls to the devil for a chance to resemble this man. High cheekbones. Pale red lips. Flawless jawline. Ink-like hair that tiptoed on wavy. His eyes were the hardest for me to accept. No human on earth could have a pair of perfectly blue eyes. It was unnatural in an entirely unnerving manner.

His scent rose from him, tugging at some primal part of me, and I bathed in the delightful shivers that coursed through my body.

A cough erupted from me rocking my body and eliciting an involuntary groan. I pinched my eyes shut and clenched my fists against the ground, willing my lungs to shy away from the broken bones as my nails bit into my palms.

He was at my side. "Calm down and slow your breath, Lily," he commanded.

I bit my lip as I forced compliance from my body.

"I need to get you to a doctor. Those ribs need wrapping," he said gently.

I opened my eyes to see pain in *his*.

"Answer my question and I'll go without a fight," I soothed.

He could not conceal the slight grin that momentarily graced his lips. "Are you always this difficult?" he questioned.

"This is nothing," I said sarcastically.

Relief washed over his face. I liked that. I wanted to see that again. Many times over. Along with a multitude of other emotions. I wanted to *cause* them.

Dread struck me.

"My necklace!" I yelped. "No. My dad gave it to me," I said as tears pricked behind my lids.

His hand drifted into my line of sight. A delicate silver chain dangled from his pinky.

"Thank you! How did you...? Thank you so much!" I gushed in elation as I reached for it.

"You need medical attention." He seemed hesitant to continue as he gently laid the necklace around my shoulders.

"Okay, I can do that," I said assuredly as I tried to sit up. "Shit," I said softly, realizing that I would not be able to do this on my own. "Could you give me hand?" I asked with a pained expression as I looked to where I'd last seen him.

He was no longer there. He'd moved to my feet and was gently slipping them through the intricate rope knots he'd already created. He rigged my legs up and slid in behind me, careful to lift me.

In spite of his gentle hands, my ribs were aflame with spasms. Stealing away the precious puffs of breath before they reached my lungs. Breaking down the last bit of resolve I had to maintain some independence.

He whispered into my ear in such a calming manner. "Lily. Close your eyes and concentrate on nothing but your breathing. We cannot run the risk of puncturing anything out here. I've crossed the line far too much already," he said firmly.

His voice was rough, as though the mere thought of it both confused and pained him. I felt no need to question as the volatile pain assaulted my nerves.

"Breathe," he repeated quietly.

It was working. Whatever this command was made the pain recede. So much so that I felt sleepy in his arms. I felt movement push through me.

"Thank you," I said softly, surprising myself with the words. "Eli?" I whispered sluggishly.

"What?" he asked delicately.

"Why do I know you?" I asked.

"I don't know," he replied.

"Just know, ya know?" I replied dreamily.

"Just know?" he asked with a pause before he sighed. "I feel the same. I understand," he said quietly.

"Exactly," I said brokenly as I turned my face further into him. My cheek resting on his chest. Warmth and comfort surrounding me.

"Mmm. You smell good," I mumbled.

"Really?" he said with amusement.

"Yes. I like it," I said matter-of-factly.

He chuckled.

"You chuckle at me a lot," I stated.

"You amuse me a lot," he responded.

"Is that all I do?" I asked softly as I tilted my head to look up at him with hazy eyes.

I watched the contour of his throat expand and retract as he swallowed slowly.

"You intrigue me also. Confuse me. *Tempt* me," he said as though admission of such things were difficult.

"You're curious about me," I said as he set my feet on the forest floor above the cavernous retreat we'd left.

"Here." He gently let go of me. "I'll help you to the road near your vehicle so we can call for help." He began mindlessly undoing the knots he'd tied.

I felt a shift as he moved. The tingling warmth that had overwhelmed me by the waterfall, had begun to ebb from my toes and fingertips.

"I rode the bike," I replied lazily.

"Bike?" he questioned.

"Of course," I said. The fuzzy warmth was making it difficult to focus on my coherency.

He shook his head slightly as he stared at me.

"What?" I asked with a blank look.

He smiled but said nothing as he continued to watch me.

"Are you checking me out right now?" I asked suddenly. "That's rude!" I finished with a snort. "I think I might have a boyfriend. Maybe two. I can't be sure." I grimaced.

He laughed. Not a soft, throaty chuckle, but a forceful laugh.

"You have the worst timing, Eli," I said as I readjusted my stance with a cringe.

"How so?" he asked as he tossed the rope aside and stood up in front of me. He reached out to offer a hand of support.

I swatted it away weakly, "I can manage," I said as my independent streak reared its ugly head.

I bit my cheek to hold back the whimper of pain pushing through my throat. One hand went to my ribs as I put all of my weight on my good foot.

"Let me help," he said.

"Why?" I asked as I turned to head down the path I'd used before. Water dripped from my clothes and squished in my boots. I felt like a drowned cat.

"It's needed." He watched me limp slowly away.

"You only think so." I continued my slow and admittedly painful trek.

"You don't agree?" he asked as he was suddenly beside me.

"No." I disregarded the limp in my step, the searing bolts of agony in my ribs, and the trivial bits of oxygen entering my lungs.

"So willful," he muttered from beside me.

I gave him a sidelong glance as the water surrounding my feet gurgled loudly.

"That was my boots," I mumbled.

He smiled.

"I'd tell you to go away but you're pretty easy on the eyes." And honestly, I was glad I wasn't alone at this moment.

"Easy on the eyes?" He looked amused.

"Don't get a big head about it." I turned away.

"You think I'm attractive." It wasn't a question.

"Please don't be one of those guys," I groaned.

As he opened his mouth to respond, a root jutted out in front of me. Catching my toe under it, I lurched forward. His arms were around me, pulling me safely upright.

"Do you still believe my help is unnecessary?" he asked with a shining grin.

I gave him a sarcastic sneer and didn't answer. The pain overwhelmed me for the moment. I took slow, calming breaths, to will it away.

He moved back to my side and rested a hand at the small of my back while offering the other for me to hold.

I hesitated.

He sighed. "It won't kill you to rely on someone else for a little while," he said.

"It might," I mumbled. I longed for my best friends to be here helping, then shook my head to clear away the thoughts. "But I won't let it," I said softly as I settled my hand in his.

He smiled and nodded as his fingers tentatively engulfed mine.

I tried to concentrate on staying steady. Regulating my breaths. Ignoring the aches. His closeness made that almost impossible. I couldn't stop myself from glancing at him. The natural feel of our fingers as they entwined. The steady stimulation of the nerves in my back as his thumb pressed against the wet cotton of my shirt. His all-encompassing magnetism urged my body to drift his way. The unwavering timber of his voice falling on my alert ears.

"Why the bike?" he asked.

"It's practical," I answered between pained inhales.

"You're an experienced rider?" He looked at me with true interest.

I laughed for a second despite the pain it caused. "Well, I'm not an idiot. I wouldn't drive it if I didn't know what I was doing," I half smiled.

"You don't strike me as reckless."

"How could I?" I turned to him suddenly. "You know nothing about me." I cringed from the sudden movement I'd made.

"I know more than I should," he replied quietly.

"That's what happens when you stalk someone," I scolded.

"Lily." He admonished me with his tone.

"I'm not complaining!" I said defensively.

He sighed. "This should not be happening," he said as his shoulders slumped.

"This? What *this* are you talking about?" I asked.

"All of this," he said as he pulled his hand from mine to motion between us.

"What exactly *is* this Eli?" I asked.

He took in a slow breath and then furrowed his brow.

"This is…everything," he said as we came upon the clearing I'd left the bike parked in.

"That doesn't even make sense," I chided.

"Not in the least," he agreed.

As we came to the motorcycle, I rested against it. He stepped away and ran a hand through his hair.

"You do that when you're nervous—run your hand through your hair. What did you mean? Everything?" I prodded.

"I'll push the bike down to the road." He ignored my question.

"Not until you answer me," I replied.

"I can't answer you," he responded firmly.

"It's not difficult!" I said heatedly.

"It is for me!" His voice rose.

"Sorry, it's so painful to even speak to me!" I huffed in frustration.

"Painful?" he questioned.

"I see it in your eyes, Eli. The tone of your voice. You can't stand this. I keep running into you and it's like I am the biggest inconvenience. Why do you bother talking to me at all?" I asked without thought.

"It's not pain that you're seeing." He hesitated. "It's hard to explain."

"Obviously, you don't want to explain or you would do it." I was rapidly becoming agitated by his reluctance to answer anything.

"What I should do is walk away and leave you to your life, and yet here I am. What I'm doing now is trying to understand why." He too was frustrated.

"You're looking for answers." I understood. I was doing the same.

"To questions I didn't even know existed." His voice was low.

I nodded.

"If I can help, I'd be glad to." I meant it. I didn't want to see him struggle. If I could help, I would.

"You can help by getting to the hospital and letting them take care of you." His frustration had faded, and concern had taken over.

I merely nodded as I gingerly turned, taking small, measured breaths as I carefully inched my leg over the bike.

"When I have my answers, so shall you." It sounded like a promise.

And he didn't strike me as a man who ever broke a promise.

23

Bench Therapy

I couldn't explain my last few days. I hadn't spoken of the incident to Ethan for fear he would contact the police about my stalker and then chastise me for doing something as stupid as running into the forest in the middle of the night. Which it was.

August was speaking to me on a needed basis. She offered a mild apology that came off as short and irritable. Words beyond that were minimal at best.

The hospital called her after my all too wet experience since she was my emergency contact. I couldn't have been more embarrassed when it was the same ER staff who had witnessed my ridiculous scene previously. The fact that Eli chose to evade me only made it appear much more awkward.

Standing in the hospital entrance, crimped over alone, arm wrapped from a gunshot wound, and favoring an obviously sprained ankle.

I didn't want to go to work and be around August. She left me to walk to the site one morning, and another time she left Grizzly for me to ride after she already made the hike on foot.

I feared any electronic devices that could further connect me to Jarrett or Ethan. I was terrified to take a walk because whenever

I meandered, the ghostly Eli would grace me. I stuck tight to my apartment. Getting out of bed had become a chore. It had been over a week, and I still hadn't devised a plan to confront any of them.

I hopped out of my truck and reached in to grab my pack.

"I know you're avoiding me," Ethan's disheartened vocals quietly spoke to my back.

I stopped. I wasn't sure I was ready to look at him. "Ethan, I'm just a little confused right now." I stepped back to catch the pain in his face.

He looked terrible. His wavy blond cowlicks were misshapen and skewed. The pink around his lids had been replaced with black circles. His face had a gaunt pull and overall he appeared slumped and thin.

"Ethan, are you okay?" I was terrified at his unkempt appearance. "You're a mess."

"I wanted to talk to you. I wasn't sure how long I should have waited to bring it up." His eyes drooped and he swayed leaning into my truck for support. "I'm not sleeping. It's weird not being around you." He scrunched up his eyes in pain.

Following me towards my apartment, I let him in. Heavily dragging his feet to the living room but he didn't sit. I slipped my pack off slowly and met him in the middle flipping on a switch he failed to catch.

"I know, Monroe. I need time to figure this out for myself." His jaw was thick with whiskers that he rubbed anxiously, the look in his eyes despondent.

"Lily, I don't think you understand what you do to me." His eyes started to gloss over. "I *need* you. You're my little addiction." He smiled a small smile and it quickly evaporated.

"Ethan, I want something here." I motioned between us while debating whether I truly meant my own words. "I just can't be sure what that *something* is?" I turned the statement into a question of doubt.

"Lilian." He never called me that. His stance was still. He was huge in my living room, and I felt further dwarfed by his sadness. His hands were limp at his sides and his eyes were dull. He was wearing torn jeans and an old T-shirt that he usually saved for work days.

"Don't say anything. I know what you're going to say." He looked up at my interruption. "You're going to tell me you made a grave mistake and let your hormones get the best of you. Let your itching need to conquer defeat you. I'm not mad at you." I felt sad admitting it all out loud. "I'm mad at myself for allowing me to believe it."

"I'm in love with you," he whispered.

I stood there, unmoving, swallowing hard. The emotions racing through my head were too much.

"I have to go."

"Lilian, I just told you—" He tried to reiterate.

My hand flew up. "Ethan, don't say something you can't unsay."

"Lily, I mean it." His hands balled into his chest, "I don't want to unsay it. I need you to know that I love—"

"Stop!" I interjected. I turned and jogged away. "I can't be here!" I wanted to cry but it didn't feel right. To scream but that didn't fit either. I was confused. All I knew was that I needed out.

* * *

I shuffled my feet along the sidewalk. No destination in my future. I had waited to hear this from Ethan for so long. I worked so hard to push it away. Accept that it would never be. But now he shows up in the late hours of the day and confesses the love he's been harboring for me all this time after a real chance at something with someone else.

I was angry at first, only to be confused in the end. I cared so deeply about both of them and wanted to be near both of them. They were everything the other wasn't yet still the entire situation felt *off*.

I sighed and blew my bangs from my face. Why did I always get my hair cut this way? They were always in my face! I stood, angrily trying to push them away from my eyes, when it spilled over, and I started swishing my hair about heatedly

My stance was rigid, my fists clenched at my hips. "I'm fighting with my hair."

"Yes and it's funny," a glassy, low voice responded.

I blew my hair away and quickly squashed the rest aside hastily. Blushing that there had been a witness to my event. My mouth was tight and my eyes wide. Sitting on the bench I had attempted to sleep on in a drunken stupor was Eli. Oil- black hair and eyes built solely for piercing purposes.

"I see you have recovered from your misfortunes well." He smiled a soft, sarcastic smirk.

"Yeah, thanks for the help with the gunshot. I didn't have a chance to say anything the other night." I noticed he was wearing casual sandals matching his khakis. A bold navy-blue button-up appeared to be well pressed. "And thanks for the water rescue. I probably would have died without you there." I looked in time to witness the heaviness behind his eyes.

"Something bothering you?" I questioned.

He smiled.

"I'm a great listener, you know. I have to be. August is my friend." I walked over to him nonchalantly. I paused and took a deep breath then pushed a hand to his chest.

"Lay down," I instructed firmly.

He seemed about to say something but closed his mouth and lay back looking slightly confused. The road was vacant, and the sun was all but gone. Street lights illuminating our encounter.

I turned, spotting a large blue mailbox, and tried my best to swiftly climb atop. I spun to face him and crossed my legs.

"Okay." I elongated the word. "Welcome to therapy." I placed an invisible pair of glasses on the bridge of my nose. "So tell me…Eli, is it?" A matching invisible notepad and pen graced my palms. "What troubles you?"

He laughed. It was seductive and captivating. My heart burned and I wanted more…so much more. An easy stranger with no baggage.

"Well, I suppose my"— he stopped, looking around—"brothers?" He questioned the usage of the term. "They're not pleased with my decision-making."

"I see. Uh-hm." I nodded pretending to jot notes and tap my chin.

"They feel my loyalties are swaying." A small flash of anger crossed his brow.

"Loyalties? Can you tell me more about *that*?" I pointed with my fake pen.

He smiled. "I look after a large number of people. It's my job. It's important and nothing can ever take away from that. Where I'm from its first— above family, friends, or anything else." His eyes dropped.

"Why do they think you aren't loyal anymore?" I started asking real questions. My therapy jokes dissipating.

"Because I've been interested in one particular person." He propped up on an elbow, "I find her to be an interesting rarity." His stare drilled into mine. The pull on my chest grew.

"Was that your boyfriend in the woods the other afternoon?" he asked sitting up, his stare intense.

"No," I whispered, my exterior growing shy.

"You don't like him?" He pushed for a better answer.

"Why were you in the woods that day? Or any other day for that matter?" I wanted answers too.

"I live there. I told you that the other night," he was short. "Who are you?" he narrowed his eyes.

I slid off the mailbox slowly. "Lily. Who are you?" I was barely speaking above a whisper.

He stood and began looking around. Checking for someone?

I was feet away from him, his smell a thick glow. His skin was so flawless I speculated if I touched him, his image would waiver like a dream. My frame leaned into him. Every nerve *wanted* him. Nothing like Ethan or Jarrett's *want*. This was dense, something I could feel. A tangible draw.

"Do you feel the pull?" Seriousness dripped from his every word.

"Yes," I breathed.

"Have you ever felt this before?" he continued despite my weakness for him.

"No." I shut my eyes and breathed through my mouth trying to remain aware. "I feel it all the time but when I'm around you it feels physical." I tried to speak clearly.

"Me too." He looked down at the pavement thick with thought. "It's frowned upon to speak to you. Not specifically *you* but the law prohibits anything among your type." His words flowed past his lips before he could retract them.

"My type?" I cocked my head sideways.

He stood like a statue before finally answering.

"Humans," he said calmly.

"Who are you?" My eyes were wide.

"My name is Elijah. It's late, Lily. Go home." I blinked slowly and when the dark blur subsided. He was gone. Not even a footstep echoed from the pavement surrounding me.

24

A Clairvoyant Invitation

I was hunched over on the floor at the foot of my hotel bed. Life had taken a dramatic turn for the unexpected. I didn't want to face anyone and now I was slightly scared on top of everything. I booked a place to avoid August…well, to avoid everyone actually, but mostly…some *man* was stalking me and calling me a *human*. Bottom line: this was weird shit.

My laptop was on the floor in front of me and I had typed all symptoms of psychological killers in the search engines. I was being stalked by a man who apparently was well-kept, intelligent, articulate, and alluring in every sense of the word. I refused to be either the girl strangled in the forest or the crazy woman filing a false police report.

I sat back against the bed and interlaced my fingers stretching them over my head and cracking my knuckles. I was being unrealistic. This man had officially saved me on three occasions. He could have killed me when I was drunk. When I was helplessly wounded from a bullet or even when I had been drowning.

He's not a killer. So now what do I have? A good-smelling, well-dressed man that is not a killer? Great.

"Square one," I grumbled aloud.

I couldn't tell Ethan because he would go ballistic. Jarrett would probably be endearing and understandably charming. August would ask if he's hot. I would get angry at everyone.

I made it clear to the receptionist at the front desk that I was not available should any calls come no matter how emergent. Unless a death had occurred, I was not to be contacted. I needed to think. I needed to give my brain time to breathe.

I would need to ask Eli questions. However, that presented problems itself. The name he had given me posed no solutions to any of my searches. Not even a residential one. I was frustrated and the lack of answers was beginning to make me angry.

It had been two days and I had even gone as far as sneaking into the ranger station to look up information about the residence that was on the park property but to no avail.

I picked up my cell phone and quickly paged down to a certain number, ignoring all the missed alerts on my phone from the various three that were tormenting me recently. My thumb hovered over the call button hesitantly for a moment before I pressed it.

It rang so long I almost hung up. "Lilian?"

My throat went dry at the sound of the voice on the other end.

"Are you going to speak?" she asked pointedly.

"Hello, Mother." I broke the silence.

"You don't sound well." I could hear her heels clicking on the granite of the museum floor.

"Working?" I posed, annoyed that she knew by the sounds of my voice.

"A curator never sleeps Lilian." Her breathing was even. I could picture her thick hair pulled into a low tight bun. Her face tired using a light blush as a disguise. Black fitted jacket and pencil skirt. Her pointy heels she always wore when someone important was meeting her.

"I know this is a bad time for you, so I'll get straight to the point." I inhaled deeply. "I was thinking about dad the other night." The clicking of her heels stopped abruptly.

"What for?" she spoke briskly.

The anger leaked through the dam. "I can't think about my father?"

The other end of the line was silent.

"When he had told me to *watch for him*. What do you think he meant?" I asked curiously. "Men?"

"Lilian, I have a client ten feet in front of me. If you have a point, make it," she spoke curtly.

"I've met someone." I hung up the phone.

* * *

I twisted in the sheets while I slipped deeper into sleep. I could see his eyes and they matched mine perfectly. His hair highlighted the same streaks of gold in the sun. I could feel the anger bubbling that he wasn't wearing his helmet, but the ride overwhelmed me and I involuntarily grinned.

"Lilian, I'm worried that I won't have much more time to talk to you," he spoke as he slowly crept along the road while I held on carefully. "You're very special to me. More than you could ever understand. But not everyone sees you that way. Always be skeptical but never fearful…"

"Daddy, I'm smart. You saw it in my eyes, remember?" I chimed.

His throaty laugh rang in my heart. "Listen, my sweetheart, they will come and try to take us away. I'm worried that it will be sooner than later. Should they break through your outer circle, remember not to be reckless. You can out think whomever you please."

"Who?" I piped in.

"Sweetie…" His words of wisdom stopped cold. I looked up to gather what he was looking at, but I was too small and could only capture a glimpse. A man standing on the street corner well- dressed, smiling straight at me, smoky blue eyes that protruded with wisdom, his skin flawless like that of a dream. When I saw him, there was music.

"Lily, I love you." My father's warm touch gathered around my sides, and he flung me away in an instant, "watch for him."

The words replayed over and over again. The words no person besides me had heard.

I screamed, my eyes snapping open, bed sheets soaked with the terror of my sweat. I had had the dream a million nights. But this time a tiny line connected the next dot.

Who was the man on the street corner?

* * *

Three soft knocks rapped at my door. The feeling in my chest shifted. I didn't want to, but I knew I had to. I exhaled hard, slightly irritated that someone at the front desk was interrupting. I caught the numbers on the clock. It was eleven. Super.

Cracking my neck and dragging my heels across the carpet down the long hall towards the door. A suite seemed a bit much, but I was angry and wanted to hatefully splurge.

I touched the lock, and a spark caught my fingertip. I stopped, slowly pulling the door back and my breath caught in my throat.

"It's not too late, I hope." His sinfully sweet voice spoke from the muted hallway.

"How did you find me?" I asked, peeking from behind the chain of the door.

"Were you trying to hide? I came to ask you something." Eli's stare was intense. "If it's too much I can come back at another time."

"No," I whispered. I wasn't angry that he was there, simply stunned.

"I was curious if you would like to accompany me to dinner? " He paused, and the tiniest hint of nervousness was apparent in the corners of his eyes. "Tomorrow at 8:00, perhaps?"

I stood unblinking. His leer was intimidating. I was barely able to answer from the dryness in my mouth.

"Um…" I hesitated, at the unexpected man that had found me here. "Saturday," I spoke softly. "I could do Saturday."

"Okay. Saturday at eight. I'm looking forward to it. I will meet you here." He beamed at the acceptance.

"Can we do nine?" I asked at the last minute.

A warm smile graced his cheeks, "Saturday at nine it is." He handed me a black envelope. "Sleep well." He was gliding down the hallway and around the corner before I could say anything else.

I closed the door slowly and carefully walked back into the room holding the invitation as though at any moment it would open up and stab me.

I stopped at the foot of my bed and lowered carefully while I opened it. The invitation itself was elaborate. It smelled like spices my mind couldn't pinpoint. A soft smile held firm on my lips. As I opened it, my breath let out slowly at the delicate swirls that had been painted on, metallic silver over the eggplant purple textured parchment.

Lilian Harper

My name in perfect calligraphy, a silver ribbon bound the invitation closed, long in length it cascaded nearly a foot once freed from the black envelope.

I pulled it away and let it fall to the floor. The corners bloomed outwards like a flower and the smile on my face grew wider.

Elijah Ward so kindly requests the presence of Lilian Harper
on the eve...

I drew in a sharp breath, my hands covering my mouth, eyes wide. There, at the bottom of the beautifully handmade invitation, among the elegant silver lilies read:

...of Saturday @ nine o'clock p.m.
for dinner.

The time that I'd suggested. Standing still I whispered aloud. "Who are you?"

25

Awakening

I stood pacing back and forth in front of the bed. I shook out my hands to try and stop the trembles. I wasn't nervous for the fact that I was going on a date with a total stranger but for the fact that it felt completely right.

I looked at myself in the mirror one more time. A simple white, cotton dress, my typewriter key my only accessory, my hair spilling in wild chocolaty waves around my shoulders. I chose ballerina slippers with a small, knitted flower embellishing the toes. I turned to showcase the dangerously low cut on the back, the adjustable part of my necklace dangling between my shoulders.

"Don't look at the clock. It will drive you crazy," I said as I looked at the clock one final time. Or at least that was what I was telling myself. He would be here any moment.

I sat down on the edge of the bed, standing immediately, my body rigid, unable to find a comfortable position anywhere. The phone rang and I jumped, yelping with the movement.

"Hello?" I answered shakily.

"Ms. Harper, this is the front desk. You have a guest waiting for you in the lobby," she spoke breathlessly. Apparently, she too noticed Eli's

251

presence.

"Thank you. I'll be right down." I hung up without saying goodbye. Any sense I had, left with the click of the phone call. "He's here!" I smiled wide. "He's here. Crap."

My heart paused when I saw him standing there. I looked over to see several women watching him from the hotel bar and glanced away quickly when they noticed I was surveying them. He wore black pants and a charcoal dress shirt that was untucked. Sleeves rolled as usual at the forearms.

His jaw tight, excited perhaps? His hands casually placed in his pockets.

I walked towards him slowly, reminding myself not to sound ignorant. "Sharp." I smiled lightly.

"Yes, I suppose I clean up nice. I feel special," he said, looking me up and down.

"Because?"

"You wore a dress." He smiled.

"I wore a dress. I s'pose I clean up nice as well." I smiled.

"We should get going. It'll be getting dark, and I have something planned." He turned and began walking from the lobby.

I quickly looked back in time to catch the women that were twisting, following after me with their eyes, a bit of jealousy tugging at their expressions.

The shock wasn't gone long when I walked outside to where Eli was holding the passenger door open.

"You drive this?" I asked, my mouth hanging ajar in shock.

"Sometimes," he spoke, smiling, one hand on the door while the other still lounged in his pocket.

"I didn't think that they made these commercially," I stammered through my look of astonishment.

"They don't."

I slipped into the black leather seat. Small white and blue lights illuminated every button and number. The sound of the engine was a mere purr from inside. The door gently closed automatically, and I observed him walking around the front end of the vehicle, passing the bright chrome grill the setting sun reflected onto his dark clothes. His walk was smooth and casual.

He elapsed gently into the driver's seat and swiftly shifted the car, gliding forward and driving from the lot. Not without several pairs of eyes following first though.

"Are you nervous?" he posed, keeping his eyes forward on the road.

"No," I quietly responded while mine were cast downward. I felt eminently shy. I could feel my skin rise in excitement, calling out to him.

Conversation was minimal as we climbed into the mountains and through the thick of the trees. Heading towards an area I was unfamiliar with.

"This area doesn't allow visitors." I nodded towards a sign.

"I'm not visiting. Live here, remember?" He smiled a refined smile.

The car slowed, easing to the edge of the road. An untraveled piece of pavement I knew rarely from my knowledge of the region. The sun's final rays peeking through the leaves that were swaying in the mountain breeze, as he opened my door I inhaled deeply through my nose breathing out through my mouth slowly as I stood.

He smiled. "Sound of the leaves?"

"Yeah," I whispered, taken aback slightly that he had been able to pinpoint it so exactly. "How did you—?"

"Me too." And I was shocked when he did the same.

Closing the door behind me I looked up to take in my surroundings. Large wooden pillars lined the road expanding their reach far, held together by the power lines connecting them. Vintage streetlights jutted out sparingly beginning to flicker on. My hair blew around me.

He smiled as he took my hand and said, "Your hair smells remarkable."

I couldn't reply, only revel in the motion of our hands connected as he led me into the woods.

"If you would like, so your clothes don't get dirty I could help you." He sounded hesitant but firm. As though he wanted to but knew he shouldn't.

"Capable." I put up a palm in reassurance. I maneuvered behind him easily, careful not to snag my dress or dirty my shoes. When he finally stopped he turned and was smiling wide at my lavish attempts to work my way around a downed log.

"Please?" he asked for the hundredth time.

My lips were tight, and determination grew deep around my eyes. I jumped lightly grabbing a low-hanging branch and swung forward landing on the balls of my feet.

"Impressive." He smirked. He walked over to place my hand in his yet again. The warmth sent another jolt through my chest, and I was mesmerized. He stopped, turning to me.

"Stand right here. Don't move." He was gone. No sound, no heavy movement of the leaves.

I waited, arms at my side looking in circles for where he had disappeared to. Starting to get worried, I realized the all too real possibility that I could be having a mental break and hallucinating the entire situation. I could be in a dress out in an unfamiliar forest when it was getting dark…alone.

A shiver trailed down my spine. I blinked into the shrinking sunset and slowed my breath. I wasn't afraid of the woods, but the unknown. I opened my mouth to call his name when all of a sudden a flash of shining fabric cascaded from above. I blinked and stood unmoving. A wide ribbon of deep crimson satin dangled, gently swaying in the breeze.

I looked up. "It's a lift. There's a loop at the bottom to sit in," he called down to me. I stared as a look of astonishment pinched my cheeks. In the highest limbs of the three largest trees, Eli was standing on a wooden platform suspended, carefully built around their cores. A circle cut through the wall-less floor off to one side, his smiling face gleaming through.

"How did you get up there?" I called, looking around for his route.

"Irrelevant. Step in." He smiled, his white teeth illuminating a glow across his face.

"Pushy," I mumbled, reaching out and spreading the sheer-glossy fabric.

"Be nice," he called.

Gliding upwards lightly while slowly spinning in delicate circles I was careless of the possibility that I could plummet to the forest floor. Yet I was surprised at the absence of swaying or tugging, an elegant swing that I found myself leaning back and smiling in, basking in the setting rays of the golden sun. Holding on carefully I let my other arm cut through the warm summer air as I traveled skyward.

The sound of the leaves breathing into my ear drums, the breeze kissing my skin, and the sun exhaling at the end of the day.

"I know you're adamant about the absence of my help, but if I could… I'm sure you haven't mastered flying quite yet." While one hand firmly grasped the satin the other reached around and so gently, I couldn't feel his caress, pulled me safely to stand beside him.

"That was unbelievable." I grinned. "I could feel it all. You know how you can hear when you're down there." I pointed through the hole to the ground nearly a hundred feet down. "But up here…"

"You're in the heart of it?" he posed.

I stopped. Staring at him and I nodded slowly. It was unreal how he put words to the feelings I couldn't.

"I love it. That's why I built this." He motioned.

There, amidst the highest thick of branches placed between three towering trees was an expansive wooden platform. It's only walls, the thick leaves filtering in the light, guarding the two of us from the world's view. Limbs draped overhead reaching towards each other coming up shy in the center. An opening led to the most beautiful view of the sky.

"Good job," I stumbled through the compliment.

He chuckled at my embarrassment. "Thank you. It's calming when I miss home but need to think."

"I know what you mean." I did? I guess I did. I went to the waterfall when all other efforts failed or immersed myself in work when I didn't want to face reality.

A large cushion took up an entire side of the hideaway. Massive, soft throw pillows accentuated every inch, and a large blanket was strewn across the makeshift bed. I drew in a deep breath when I looked at the limbs and realized the dozens of white pillared candles of different heights hanging lightly, placed in silver trays, protected from the winds reach behind glass enclosures.

"Go sit before dinner gets chilly." He motioned while placing a hand on the small of my back. My vertebrae vibrated from the touch. My lungs purred involuntarily.

I slipped off my shoes and slid towards the middle watching while he reached behind a corner where I was unable to see.

A rounded white dinner plate occupied both hands. Kneeling, he placed one in front of me and another where he would sit. Rising again he brought back two large wine glasses sloshing with a breathy aroma of bloody-red wine. My mouth watered.

"I hope I got it right." He motioned at the plate with his wine glass before he pulled a thick sip.

I stared in disbelief. "It's marinated lamb." If I had a favorite, this was it. I looked from the plate to his face as he smiled lightly. "My dad used to make this for me. He used to tell me that I was never too young to learn mature tastes. He would drink red wine and sneak me sips or pour some in my ice water, blushing it pink so I could be like him."

"I knew you would like this." He took a bite of his.

"You missed one thing though—"

"Ah, I almost forgot!" he jumped to his feet, still chewing. Coming back with a white linen cloth wrapped loosely around a large lump. "Sourdough bread." He smiled and unfolded it gently, steam rising from the loaf.

"How did you know this?" I asked, taking a bite. "It's the same. No one knew that about my dad. I'm sure if you even asked my mother she would have repressed the memory enough to have forgotten it." It tasted the same, the smell of the fresh bread, and the thick caress of the wine.

"I wanted to make you smile. Success." He motioned with his fork before taking another bite.

I ate slowly, watching his movements, mannerisms, and mild attempts at conversation.

"Ask your questions, Lily." He started gathering the empty dishes. Standing he disappeared and re-emerged with a sliver of red velvet cake atop a copper platter that had been garnished with red daylilies.

"I love red velvet cake! Question one: are you stalking me?" I asked, admiring momentarily before taking a bite of the rich homemade dessert.

"No." He smiled crookedly.

"How do you know things?" I hesitated, unsure if I should ask. "The invitation? There was no way that you could have known the time."

"Yes or no," he replied after swallowing.

"Yes or no what?" I carefully chewed while I mulled.

"Yes or no questions. It's our first date. I need to appear mysterious."

He winked.

"You are! You have to be the most mysterious man I've ever met, so much so that I honestly am starting to question whether or not you're real. If it wasn't for the fact that every time you touch me I get a jolt I would start to think I'm hallucinating," I blurted.

"Is that a yes or a no?" he pondered, raising a brow in question.

"Okay." I tapped my chin. I would play by his rules, he didn't know that Lily Harper could be inquisitive. "Do you always walk through the forest in khakis and a button-up? Don't you own jeans?" I cocked my head sideways.

A laugh echoed in his chest. "yes."

"To question one or two?" My brows furrowed.

"You decide." His arms crossed as he leaned back waiting for the next question.

"So difficult," I huffed. Pondering my next move, as though we were amidst a game of chess. "Do the police find you a person of interest?"

"Not that I don't know about." Another laugh.

"Right." I smacked my lips together in thought. I pondered for a moment before cutting to the chase. "What did you mean when I saw you last time, that you weren't human?"

He maintained a light demeanor. "No."

I huffed hard. "'Kay, the hard way then. Can you fly?" I shot him a curious eye.

"You can't?" He smiled looking up.

"Well, I don't mean like that. Like a superhero or something." He said nothing and continued to smile politely. "Fine. So the invitation, my father's dinner… can you read minds or something?" I paused hoping for a better answer.

"No and…*or something*."

My eyes grew wide. "So you can do something then?"

"Intuition." He tapped his temple lightly with the tip of his index finger.

I rolled my eyes and carefully calculated my next question. Searching the leaves for a direction, it hit me. "Got it!" I yelped a little too loudly. "I mean, I thought of another one," I spoke more calmly, embarrassed at my outburst. "You said that you live in the forest, but when I checked the area the only residence is currently unoccupied at this time." I crossed my arms at my sure triumph.

"Did I forget to notify them that I was back? I suppose it's been three years." He rubbed his jaw in thought. "Maybe I should ask you. Are you a person of interest to the authorities?" he mocked calmly.

"I didn't think about that." My shoulders dropped slightly.

"You're doing beautifully," he nudged.

"Will your brothers be mad if they find out that you're out with me?"

His face grew solemn, and his lips parted slightly unsure of how to answer. "Yes."

I hadn't expected that. "How come?" I leaned in. Now that I was getting somewhere. Doing my best to ignore the fact that his *pull* was sweeping my mind irrationally sideways. "Are you in a cult family or something? Do they only let you talk to certain people that will join them? How do you feel about comets?" I started blurting everything coming to my mind.

"I think that's enough for one night, Lily Harper."

I couldn't hide the disappointment that had washed over my face, and it was apparent that he had noticed as well. Leaning in he whispered through a wide smile. "Comets are captivating when witnessed through a telescope. However, you eclipse the pull they create with a simple smile."

I stared. That had to be the best compliment bar none, and I'm not just saying for myself. I meant for anyone. It made him that much more desirable.

He paid no mind to my shock and continued to twist around the petals of a daylily he had plucked from the empty copper plate.

"Thank you," I whispered. I wasn't quite sure where to go from there.

He smiled. "Can I ask *you* a question?" He watched his hands play. I nodded.

"Why the name 'Lily'? A delicate name for such a fiery soul," he spoke, staring at the deep red petals staining his fingertips.

"My mother's favorite flower. I liked it until my dad died and then my distaste for her only fueled disgust. I would change it if..." I trailed off.

"Underneath everything, beauty exists." He laid the woven petals of what was the day lily in my palm. "People often forget to take in the larger frame of things. Look deeper. See beauty...like I see you."

I drew in a sharp breath. He had spun the petals of the day lily and twisted them to appear as a rose.

"You..." In awe, I swallowed to mask the tears that brimmed in my eyes. I lied. *That* was the best compliment ever and it wasn't even spoken. "Eli." I smiled looking up at him. "Where did you come from?"

He looked down and away. A question perhaps, he was hoping that I wouldn't have asked.

"It's late." His head leaned quickly to the right. Had he heard something? I looked in the direction he was staring. The leaves swayed lightly and although the sun had almost completely diminished the forest floor appeared empty. When his body relaxed mine did as well.

He stood and reached down for my hand. This time it was less suggestive and appeared more forceful.

"Is something wrong?" I was concerned about the change in his demeanor.

"No." He was being short. "It's best that we leave."

"Okay," I said, unsure.

We walked over to the opening in the floor, and he let go of my hand as he reached up and anchored the satin to a sturdy branch overhead knotting it tightly. He wrapped it around his forearm and grabbed a handful. Without pausing he quickly leaned over and reached around my waist pulling me to his side.

So swiftly he stepped from the platform, and I buried my head into the crook of his collar bone, we plunged to the forest floor. A swooshing sound as we cut through the trees. My feet gently graced the dirt and I exhaled.

"Whoa. A little warning would have been nice." I tugged at the bottom of my dress.

"You didn't have time to be scared. We should really be going." He turned and casually walked back in the direction we had come.

I wiped the shocked expression off my face and followed quietly. I wasn't sure what I should say or do, so I kept my lips in a tight line. Less aware of the dirt that I was getting on my dress and more aware that this man was wildly mysterious.

I could see the faint gleam of the expensive car coming into view through the waving leaves. I had fallen somewhat behind and tried to hurry to catch up to him as he stood on the pavement at the hood of the car waiting for me.

I wasn't sure what look was occupying his eyes, but a deep thought seemed to capture most of his attention. Distant perhaps?

"Dinner was nice," I spoke quietly as I came to stand in front of him.

He was thinking seriously before his lips parted, "Lily…"

I leaned in, nodding slowly.

He bit his lower lip and for the first time appeared slightly human. An odd phrase to place on him but this was a rare occurrence during our chance encounters. Not speaking, he stared intensely past me.

When his irises finally met mine I was forced to hold my breath as I watched his pupils dilate.

"I have to do this." He exhaled.

Suddenly, his hands reached up and unlike Jarrett's command or Ethan's weakness, this was new. His palms paused in midair, as though he was unsure of whether or not he should continue. Sun barely exhaled over the horizon, and the indigo skies were ablaze with the burning of endless stars, well-spaced streetlights illuminated our presence alone here.

I couldn't hear the sound of the leaves. My breathing muted the world. The *pull* in my chest was screaming like a freight train towards him. My eyes watched as his hands hesitated and reached up cradling my face gently.

His palms were massive, caressing my entire head. I felt small compared to his size. His wide chest, thick legs, and arms surrounded my body. My breathing didn't feel nervous or erratic as I had felt before, but ready. My stare was serious, knowing and wanting, I licked my lips in wait.

He watched for my reaction and surrendered. Leaning in he found my lips with his.

My chest exploded violently, the *pull's* power erupting. His tongue tasted hot. His skin was sweeter than anything my mind could conjure. I closed my eyes and breathed as my hands reached toward him pulling him close to me like nothing I *ever* wanted in a thousand lifetimes.

When we were near, my nerves buzzed but while we were kissing it was like I could feel his nerves too. I was excited. Like we were one person melded together.

A humming in the background was growing louder. I could hear it in the corner of my mind but paid no attention until the buzzing built to a massive climax and a snap burst so loudly we were jolted apart while panting. We witnessed just in time as all the streetlights blasted into a shower of white sparks up and down the pavement to both sides of us.

I was instantly aware of everything. I stared at him, bending over and grabbing my knee caps, my lungs begging for oxygen. I looked up at him, mouth agape in sheer awe and seriousness.

"What…the hell…was that?" I spoke between deep breaths.

A loud rustle in the forest behind us disrupted my train of thought. I followed his eyes backward, seeing nothing.

"We have to go." His eyes were wide.

I followed him as he opened the door to my side of the car and got in quietly. I didn't say anything.

He got in and pulled away without speaking, glancing lightly back hiding the glare he was forcing down on the trees.

I didn't need to ask what he was feeling, because like I had felt his nerves, and tasted his heartbeat drumming during our kiss, I could now feel *his* fear along with the *pull* in my chest.

26

A Fight Among Brothers

I felt damaged as I sat curled on the tub floor keeping my knees close to my chest, my arms wound tightly, holding my limbs. I hadn't slept calmly in days. The water of the shower drenched me. My hair dripping down my face, small streams running over my eyelashes. I couldn't tell the tears from the water anymore. I breathed hard through my mouth. A spray of mist blew outward with my breath.

I checked out of the hotel that night and came straight home. I replayed the words he spoke in a rush when we arrived back.

"Get out, Lily." I sensed the danger and anger behind his vocals. What had startled him so badly in the trees? Especially to provoke this type of reaction.

"Wait. Will you tell me what that was back there?" I pleaded with my eyes.

"A mistake." His jaw clenched as he stared ahead through the windshield. I ignored the looks that the ostentatious vehicle was drawing from passersby.

"But it was more than that, Eli. I felt something. And I don't mean emotionally. I felt *you*." I squeezed my eyes tightly shut trying to recapture the feeling. So intense they felt like I hadn't been human myself. "I could feel your lungs in my chest as though they were my own." I caught the twitch of his eyes as his hands began to tremble.

"Leave, Lily!" he yelled.

I sat back quickly, hurt by his anger that pinched my heart. Turning, I left without another word, making sure to never look back as I scaled the steps towards my room. Even when I felt his pain he put on me with his words and how he regretted it.

* * *

I leaned forward and shut off the water. Pulling the towel that was damply dangling from my curtain rod, casting it over my soaked skin. I hadn't been to work for three days, not wanting to leave. I couldn't begin to convey the void of feelings. Every emotion I encountered now seemed muted compared to what I had felt when I was near him, not even mentioning when we were kissing.

I pulled on the jeans I wore the last two days. I didn't care what August would say. I shut my phone off three days ago and kept the door to my room locked. I was really surprised that Ethan hadn't appeared at my step in some ridiculous panic, but I was sure that he wasn't communicating with August and hadn't caught wind of the fact that I hadn't shown up for work yet this week.

It stung more knowing that August hadn't knocked on my bedroom door. Was she really that bitter? It seemed childish in comparison. I wanted to talk to her so desperately but didn't feel that I could.

Not bothering with drying my hair, damp dreads would suffice. I caught a glimpse of my sullen face in the mirror. Dark swollen circles masked my eyes. My posture was tired, but my mind was awake. I grimaced at the thought of what his absence had done. As though it seemed I'd lost my mind.

Collapsing onto my bed the tears never stopped. My insides felt broken. Pandora's Box was opened, a bombarding flood of emotions I couldn't get back. I replayed moments from the night and was sure that I hadn't done anything wrong.

"Why you, Eli? What did you do? Who are you? Ugh!" I grunted and grabbed the pillow groaning into it.

A loud pounding on the door erupted, cutting into my reverie. It didn't stop, not pausing only to become louder.

I took my time opening it. Bracing myself, if it were Ethan he would eventually use his key or perhaps break a window, I thought smugly to myself.

"Okay, so you're alive, dammit." August was standing in the hallway. "Charlotte called my mom and said you called her a week ago all pissed and having some dad flashback shit. I wanted to give you space, I was pissed at you and shit for being a cheater behind my brother's back." She stood with anger radiating from her cold stance.

My mother called Nell? Great.

Arms crossed, tapping her foot irritably, "I couldn't leave you alone though when you didn't show up again this morning by the clearing for work." The glimmer of worry tugged at the corners of her eyes. Then as though she was noticing me for the first time, her hands dropped to her sides and all anger receded. "What the hell's the matter? You look like crap."

"Something's wrong with my chest," I blurted it out involuntarily. "I mean…I'm messed up right now," I stared out the door hoping Eli would appear.

"Is it about your dad?" she asked, becoming more and more concerned.

I held my breath. I wanted to scream no. Wanted to tear out this ache in my chest. To bleed the truth to her. Tell her that some ghost I had sporadically been talking to isn't human. And when we kissed…I closed my eyes…when we kissed it was like a mortar had gone off in my chest and we synced. I could *feel* him under my skin. Nothing was a comparison.

"Yeah…my dad." I sighed.

She stood for a moment, "I'm sorry, Lily. I don't know what happened but if you want to talk, forget about stupid boys, and we can talk." She reached out for a hug.

I automatically drew back.

"Harper? Are you alright?" I didn't feel alright. He hadn't called, shown up, or even made an appearance during any of the walks I took trying to provoke him.

I shook my head no.

"How about you come to work today and we can try and figure out what we can do? Maybe take off this weekend?" she offered.

My attention sparked momentarily. "I'll get my things."

I closed the door.

* * *

I didn't tighten my safety harness. I left my gun locked in its case back on the four-wheeler. August packed lunch but I assured her repeatedly that I wasn't hungry. I dropped my notes halfway up the hindering climb and didn't bother to go back. I wanted to hide. The rushing breeze felt amazing, breathing life back into me.

Losing track of time, I wasn't sure what hour it was. Midday perhaps? August didn't come to check on me for lunch, so I think she understood I still needed to be alone. I quietly sat, complacent among the limbs, not working but watching as small birds came dangerously close.

That's when I heard it.

I leaned forward slowly. At first, I thought that I was imagining things. But then clearly it happened again.

Voices. Men's voices.

Intuition held my tongue, forcing me not to call out.

They were loud. Yelling even. I turned and began to climb downwards. Was it Ethan? I paused. If it had been, I discovered I wanted to see him. To cry into his massive warm arms and exhale all my woes. But I knew that was no more after what he had said to me that night in my living room. We were broken, our friendship tainted.

I held onto trees as I stepped lightly towards the sounds. They were angry, infuriated. I still couldn't hear clearly what the argument was, but it was apparent there was one. I continued hiding as they grew in booming volume. I glanced over my shoulder making sure August wasn't rushing up beside me, sure she was still far away. I continued.

"The laws have been broken!" A violent voice ripped past the bark. I peeked around the trunk I was camouflaged behind.

"Your words bleed lies!" Another heated voice tore past me.

My bangs fell in front of my eyes, and I hastily swept them back. I could clearly see two men in the light of the afternoon facing my direction. They were in front of someone just out of sight with his back to me.

Their size was formidable, their voices punishing, yet a calm stance in the way they held their ground. Standing side by side the man with hair as red as flames wildly strewn about kept his arms up using them animatedly as he spoke. His eyes were a chartreuse green, his anger did nothing to mask their beauty. His jaw was narrow and shoulders broad, clothes that designers dreamt up caressing the muscles.

The other with sandy chocolate hair, warm brown eyes, and olive brown skin. He was barefoot, wearing cut-off jeans with tattered hems below the knee. A black button-up polo pulled taught across his back. A thick neck erupting from the collar. His arms remained crossed and when he yelled it seemed to come across with a hint of regret.

"You lured an innocent human being into something forbidden! From your own region, brother!" the brown-haired man spoke lowly, hurt evident in his lecture.

"You betrayed your brothers!" The flame-haired man was hostile with his anger. Running a heavy hand through his hair while pointing at the person being chastised that I couldn't see. He walked in circles, and I gave a small gasp when I fully gathered his immense size. He gritted his teeth and spat sideways when his back was turned to me. "The foolish jeopardy of your people is unworthy. You must relinquish your watch." I tasted the hot hate he spoke, and my stomach turned.

An outburst blew from the victim, and he stepped into view. I gasped instantly, clutching my hand over my mouth. "You tell me to step back from here!" It was Eli, beautifully breathtaking. His skin dazzled in the daylight. I was caught in the sight of him so deeply I almost oversaw the fight taking place in front of me.

"Lucian!" Eli looked at him gesturing angrily with his fists. "My protection for my humans will never wane!"

The tanned man said nothing, anguish was apparent across his face.

"Don't look to Lucian to fix your mistakes, Elijah! This is absolute finality. You overstepped. Do not make me take them from you!" the other interjected.

A bellowing roar ripped from Eli, and he screamed at the man. "Zacarius, you are out of line! I will call the others down on you."

"Do not threaten me!" Zacarius shot back. He paused, a look of darkness crossed his brow. "They all know. Why do you think we're here? Perhaps this could be avoided."

"In what way?" Lucian spoke, seemingly surprised.

"I cut her down." A sick smile overtook Zacarius' face.

Eli's head shot up. "I'll kill you first."

Lucian grew white and Zacarius staggered back before the anger exploded.

Zacarius bounded towards Eli in two small steps, and I gripped the bark with fingertips so hard they were white.

Eli was quick and grabbed Zacarius, gripping his shoulders he took the impossibly large man with the red hair and threw him into the trunk of one of the many trees surrounding them, my mouth wide as I watched the tree buckle. The force he impacted was unrealistic. Zacarius stood again and leapt onto Eli pinning him to the ground with a knee. Eli grabbed his neck, flipping him to the ground like a rag doll. The forest floor gave way leaving behind a massive dent. Eli stood, quickly bounding towards Zacarius, ready to attack again.

Lucian grabbed at the men. "Stop this! Before it's too—" His face shot skyward, watching something cutting him off while the men ignored his commands.

I followed his line of vision and squinted. Two large dark blurs plummeted towards us. My feet were frozen to the ground. I blinked regrettably, missing their approach. The leaves blew viciously, and the trees creaked. I held the timber when a thundering sound crashed into the dirt.

My eyes were wide at what was now standing in front of me. Two more massive men. My frame shook trying to comprehend what I'd seen. They had fallen from the sky, and with force, yet landed on their feet. They had dented the earth so terribly that when they advanced they were forced to leap upwards first from the craters they created. Moving so fast now that they were indistinct, the fighting was improbable. Trees buckling, bodies smashing into the surrounding landscape, yelling so loud it was sure to be heard for great distances. Fighting I had never witnessed, violent roars and guttural hatred fueling their movements.

Clarity dawned and I knew it wasn't human. This force was unnatural. I was terrified. The tremors rocked my hands. I swallowed in an attempt to clear my throat. How were these men his brothers? They looked nothing alike; the only similarity was their great stature and magnificent beauty.

I had forgotten my need for hiding. When Eli reached at a blond-haired man from behind and wrenched him angrily backward, flinging him towards me, he crashed into the dirt to my side, and I screamed in horror. It was drowned in the pool of surrounding uproar and clashes.

I looked up clinging to my tree in desperation as the ground rumbled and boomed below my feet. Shaking so hard my knees and hips begged to give. Eli looked up and his face grew soft, and he raised a gentle hand. He saw me.

Using all my mustering strength I backed away from his stares and turned to run, unwilling to watch for another moment. I tripped and fell and crawled to my feet into another run until I couldn't breathe, and I didn't stop running until I could only hear muted thunder behind me.

I ran past my harness tangled at the base of the tree I'd been working in. I stepped sideways and fell scrambling behind a massive tree. Forcing my back to the trunk and heaving so hard trying not to suffocate the limits I'd pushed my body to. I closed my eyes and cried through the wracking coughs my throat produced. I was fighting the sensation not to vomit.

"What the fuck was that?" I spoke through chattering teeth from the exhausted shaking. "Not alright." I stopped, realizing the deafening barrage of growls had ceased.

My jaw snapped shut and I breathed hard through my nose. Maintaining silence, I listened. Nothing. Not even the sound of voices echoing back towards me. Wagering my possibilities I poked my head back towards where I had come from.

"There you are!"

I screamed.

"Lily, I'm sorry." Eli's palms were up. "I had no idea you were here. I was angry at them for being so close."

Standing, I realized that I couldn't move. "Stay away from me!" I yelled, trying to grasp a firm tone.

His face was sympathetic. "I didn't want to scare you. My brothers can be intimidating, especially when they're passionate about something." He stepped a careful foot in my direction.

"No!" I pointed at his foot with my eyes and began backing away. The shaking gave hints of minimal balance. I didn't pay attention and my foot caught a root rising above the dirt. I hit the ground hard.

"Lily, I am sorry. Don't panic. I won't hurt you. They don't understand." His face was overwhelmed with sadness. "I don't understand." He sighed. "Please let me help you." He tried to slowly approach.

"Those men were your brothers?" I panted.

"Yes...but—"

"That was not human. Nobody can fight like that!" I interrupted.

He tried again to step closer.

Horrifying terror drenched me. I screamed again. "Stay away from me!" I started hyperventilating.

"Lily, calm down. You're going to pass out," he proceeded. "Let me explain."

"They want to kill me?" My eyes were awash with salty tears. "They don't even know me. For kissing you?" I inhaled. "It's not fair. Because I wanted *you*?"

"I want you too." His warm smile was sorrowful as he pushed a hand within inches of my reach.

"Don't kill me, please. Just get away from me!" I shrieked. I tried to stand unsuccessfully.

I finally lost. I couldn't fight the terror anymore and I began to collapse, my erratic breathing past the brink. I cascaded towards the ground. Before I landed, the light faded, and blackness took over.

27

Into the Garden

I awoke carefully leaning against the trunk of a tree. It was still daylight. A lump caught in my throat and tears started to bite at the edges of my eyes. What had I witnessed? I instantly felt guilty for telling him to leave, but I was scared.

My chin pulled to my chest painfully and my hand reached into the left side of my pack and pulled out what I felt was well deserved at this moment. A delicately silver engraved flask that had black leather wrapped warmly around its curves, burned with fragile swirling designs, I untwisted the cap and pulled a hardy swallow. My father always kept his whiskey filled, so I inherently did the same. I always liked the taste. Many would say a man's drink, but I didn't care.

I looked around and knew I was alone. Taking another deep swig I tilted my chin to the sky and the tears ran from the corners of my eyes dripping past my temples freely.

I blinked and sighed heavily. "I'm going crazy." I coughed back a sarcastic laugh. I was obviously losing my mind.

Another drink. The warmth burned through my throat.

"These feelings are stupid." I shrugged and continued. "What the hell is happening?" I began to realize that my crowd-less speech was meant for someone.

"You frightened me. I thought you were stalking me at one point." Now I felt regret that I hadn't given him a chance to explain.

The numbness in my chest started to recede and I attributed it to finally letting out what I had cramped up inside me for so many weeks, the days had begun to blend together. A hurt was slowly replacing the adrenaline surge I had felt earlier, and I inhaled sharply through gritted teeth. The *want* to see his face seeped into my thoughts. I closed my eyes and drifted.

"I guess I just thought…" Surrender pushed past my words. "I don't know. Maybe I thought there was a reason I kept running into you," I shook my head back and forth frustrated at myself.

I downed the rest of the flask instantly regretting that I hadn't eaten or drank anything today. I dug the heels of my boots into the dirt and let my head loll against the tree before I passed out.

***

I awoke in my bed nearly three days ago with August's voice spouting happily from the kitchen. Apparently, she had found me slumped over Grizzly in a state of unconsciousness. I had a feeling Eli had something to do with that. The doctors attributed it to exhaustion. I slept for twenty-one hours straight according to them.

I had decided not to tell anyone anything. To give them any reason to believe I had gone mad. Jarrett called and left a message to call if I needed him. I didn't reply. Ethan came but there was hurt in his stance, which I only caught for a moment before he excused himself. Disheveled did nothing to describe his unkempt appearance.

I decided to take some time from work and rest. A sabbatical. I couldn't find the words to divulge the fear soaking in my head from that day. I couldn't understand what was more painful, the hateful words I drove towards Eli or the fact that I regretted them so painfully.

He hadn't been there when I woke up. He wasn't around when I was alone, nor did he show up when I looked for him. Whispering into the night walks I took when my caregivers were deep in their dreams.

The doctor was probably right. I was exhausted, and my mind was tricking me. Perhaps, August wasn't real, and she was my Tyler Durden. That brought another wave of tears. My mind was completely unfair to have dreamt of the romance of a candlelit treetop dinner.

I understood the power of the subconscious. Our minds could truly be our worst enemies.

* * *

I could feel my body drifting towards the dreams. The dreams I hated, the dreams I loved, a place where I could see them again. It was only seconds.

"Maybe we should speak with him?" Lucian pleaded with the man, looking from one to another. "He'll return. We just need to give him more time." His smooth voice was overly persuading. "He grew attached to her. He needs time to mourn the ending of their relationship. His loyalties to us are still there."

"I'm sorry, Lucian. I know that Elijah holds a place for you, but unfortunately, the brothers have made a decision. This is final." A heavy hand from the man I couldn't clearly see came to rest atop one of Lucian's slumped shoulders.

"This is wrong! Going against one of our own without his knowledge?" His voice was growing in strength. "He's our brother. We love him."

"Lucian." The man's voice was soft, and he turned so that I could focus. His misty gray eyes came into view, and I sighed heavily at his beauty. Although slightly older, his face still had a youthful draw to it. Hair cut short jutting in bristled directions. The only hints of age were barely the crow's feet crimping the edges of his tired eyes, a man who looked to hold many secrets and timeless woes.

The images of the dream blurred and came back into view. It was the two of them standing face to face.

"Aurelius, I don't want to go against him," Lucian said, defeated.

"The time has come." Aurelius looked less thoughtful and more forceful. "To show Elijah the strength of our love." He stepped back and allowed his heels to reach out of the realm of my vision, leaning slowly, his arms directly outwards as he fell over the edge of this unseen room similar to a jumper on a bridge. "We will end this for him, Lucian." And with a simple twist of his head, his entire body followed the direction of his pouring fall.

I watched as his lips went taut. Nostrils flaring as his eyes clouded painfully in thought, sadness basking his face in shadows.

I watched as he too stepped forward, and we began to free fall.

Lucian's face transformed from one, canvassing compassion, to one of complete resolve. Void of any other choice. His brow held no furrow of thought, his eyes bright with anger, and his lips tight as they slipped over his teeth. A feral cry began. Neither pain nor fear laced its guttural timber. Pure conviction drenched my ears as I watched the being of sadness from moments before contorting into a creature of menace. The roar escaping him grew stronger as he fell, and my heartbeat stopped altogether.

* * *

"They're coming." My eyes flew open as the words fell from my lips.

I bolted upright from where I'd slept against the cool forest floor. I'd been coming here for the last week in hopes I would see Eli and be able to talk to him. My breath was erratic and sweat beaded at my temples. My hand rose to swipe at a moist train on my cheek. Looking at my fingertips, I wondered why I'd cried. And as my thumb brushed over the wetness, I listened to the forest. In the distance ahead of me, birds screeched, a call of warning to all that could hear. Something had spooked them. I scanned the horizon, looking for answers, but was only greeted with a darkening shadow of the swarm heading toward me. I scooted back against the tree standing close by. I slid up against the bark until I was steady on my feet, eyes never leaving the throng of birds ahead. The wailing grew louder, and the flurry of their flapping wings reached my ears.

"So many…" Realizing the looming blackness was indeed a large flock.

As the crows rushed at me, breaking to swerve around the tree that held me upright, I watched them. Looking left and to the right, and then up. My mouth opened in awe. My shoulders turned as I followed their path with my eyes. Until suddenly they were gone, allowing light to filter softly through the trees, permitting the normally subdued songs of the forest to return.

Except…they didn't.

There was no gentle rustle as the leaves shivered in the light breeze. No creaking branches as a squirrel leapt among them. Not a single errant bird calling from any direction. Not even the muted buzz of pestering insects.

There was nothing.

Nothing but silence.

A sense of alarm warmed my stomach.

"Impossible." The forest was motionless.

A powerful quake shook the ground beneath my feet. A familiar sound rumbled in the distance. A warm suffocating gust of air surrounded me, causing the hair on my cheek to graze the skin.

Run! The voice of some archaic and crucial instinct sounded in my mind.

I listened simultaneously, breaking into a sprint.

What was I running from? And even if there was something to escape, I was injured. I was still healing from broken ribs and a weakened ankle. There would be no winning this race.

And still, I ran, blindly through the trees, eyes darting to and fro. Hoping for…something. Something I couldn't even begin to define or explain, or even understand.

My rampant thoughts halted as I slid to a stop at the sudden appearance of people in front of me, and erratic breathing forcing the walls of my chest to heave as I stared at them.

Four men stood ahead of me in an arc, each one with a calm face and stoic demeanor. Their bodies, although varying in size, easily dwarfed my own. And at their sides, each brandished a weapon, massive swords with intricate etching or delicate daggers weaving through playful fingers. Glancing beyond them, more arrived. Materialized instantly from an invisible fog, as though fading into existence, as some of the faces became recognizable.

Eli's brothers.

The realization stole the breath from my lungs.

"Don't be scared." I spoke the words aloud to calm myself and watched as they reacted to them. Some smirked as though entertained. Others sneered as if I'd insulted them.

"Me. Not you," I clarified softly.

"Lilian."

A voice I knew. My eyes flew to its source. "Aurelius." A man I had seen in a thousand dreams.

His mouth opened in response as a blur fell to his side, dust rising around him. I watched as it cleared, and another face seen plainly in my dream peered back at me. As fierce as it had been that last moment I'd seen it. He was slightly bent at the waist, kneeling on one knee, with his sword drawn into the air behind him.

"We are not here to cause you pain," Aurelius said as he stepped toward me.

I stepped back and bumped against a tree trunk. It cradled me gently, resting its hands on my arms.

Hands? Trees don't have hands.

My face turned to look at the large man behind me. He appeared to be South Sudanese. He was strikingly beautiful with a thick neck and a small smile. The corners of my lips turned up automatically in return.

"Well, I can see why you caught Eli's attention." His velvet voice and winking eye caught me off guard.

"I did?"

"And held it." He chuckled.

"We need to finish this. Time is fleeting. He won't be gone long," Lucian said.

Panic gored every cell in my body, and I bolted away from my captor, looking every which way, hoping for an opportunity. But I was slow, and they were too quick. Heavy arms enclosed around my small figure, lunging my torso towards freedom, I called out his name.

"Eli!" My nails were bleeding as they ripped through the bark I tried to anchor myself to.

"You don't need to fight," Aurelius called.

"You're not worth fighting for," Zacarius spoke, masked by a hateful lust. With sick passionate contempt he leaned into me, his smell hot, his eyes dark. "I've seen him with you." He licked his lips. "If given the chance, I would have painted every blade of grass in this forest with your blood."

"You had your chance." I never thought about the gruff words, but they fit perfectly as they were spoken. Some piece of me responded to his threat with unfamiliar bravado. The flash of disbelief crossing his features sparked a sense of vindication and the fury that shadowed his eyes a moment later was welcomed rather than feared.

The man holding me turned away quickly.

"Such a temper, Zacarius," he spoke calmly as he moved me away.

I didn't struggle in his arms and the urge to thrash swiftly faded.

"Eli's close. Tend to that," Lucian commanded from the same spot he'd first appeared.

In the distance, I could hear trees crashing. My eyes followed the men that moved casually toward the unseen chaos.

"Come," Aurelius said softly.

"Göbekli then." The olive-skinned man began walking to his right confidently.

"This is a matter for the garden," Aurelius calmly voiced.

"That could be dangerous. What if we're wrong?" A delicate man with polarized irises stepped forward.

"It's the proof we need. No one will doubt if she gets into the garden," Aurelius responded evenly.

Hums of approval swept through the men. What the hell is the garden?

Those that remained moved in a fluid motion, vaulting upwards through the trees as one carried me along. I watched as branches creaked and fractured with each of their steps. I took in the scents, they could be my last, and I wanted to remember my forest before we left it. I forced concentration on Eli's brothers. I remembered every sneer and somber look.

I was shocked as the incandescent blue rings that encircled their forearms suddenly glowed, enamoring me. They burned from beneath the surface of their skin. I was alarmed as the men began to climb through the trees around us.

Leaping high among the branches in an uninhibited dance as they thrust their bodies upwards, giving a mighty push before leaping from the crowning limbs of the looming treetops. Enchanted by them, I sagged against the arm holding me.

I focused on the gargantuan man cradling me with senseless ease. A ripping sound fractured the silence of the night sky. I cringed at the splintering crack that echoed against the stars, a wind whistled past my ears and wispy feathers dusted my arm clutching his thick-chocolaty neck.

What happened to him? Glancing at the others, I realized they all had wings.

An intense burst of understanding exploded in my chest.

"Angels." I breathed the word. The burning blue forearms were their halos; my breathing grew shallow under the profound impossibility.

We were soaring upwards when the sky began to fade into a formidable blackness. So dark, I couldn't see the face of the man holding me in his arms. I was blind, yet still, I tried to discern my surroundings.

I felt a gentle pressure against my body, pushing and pulling me in opposing directions. Muted voices filtered into my ears, speaking in tones and words that sounded unfamiliar at first. The acrid stench assailed my nose followed by a suffocating sweetness, my mouth puckering as it flooded with tartness. I tasted the smoky frost left on my lips.

"She's here," an awed whisper sounded from somewhere in the distance. Where that distance was, I didn't know. We had flown upward to an unseen destination where we stood somewhere that was night.

"Lilian, I'm hurt. You didn't remember me." A dark smile hinting below Aurelius's pout. "Well, you were just a little girl."

I cringed, revolted by his closeness.

"You do remember your father, don't you? He was a pathetic man, pitiful really, only surviving his *soul* for five years. Your current Paladin seems to be more promising…apparently not enough though." He gestured with his hand to our surround, "you are *here*."

"Shut your filthy fucking mouth before I drown you in a tub of lye." I lurched forward spitting into his face.

Corrosive chuckles rippled through the group landing around me.

A sinister look overwhelmed his face, he growled, beginning to walk away from me.

My eyes followed a flowing light as it reflected amongst the foliage around me. For as far as I could see, a path led through a darkened forest, much like my own but vastly different, with weeping willows and sturdy oaks, and trees that weren't native to Colorado. Flowering lilacs and blooming tulips. Japanese maples with their flaming leaves and what seemed to be Hawaiian hibiscus flowers sprouting from the crags of their bark. Puffs of warm air blew over the frail-looking grasses covering the ground. The same brilliant new green as I was used to, but as fine as hair. As I moved along the walkway, I couldn't help but take in the scents and sounds. A loon's mating call caught my attention, followed closely by the essence of lily of the valley, the whistle of a whippoorwill, and the laugh of a hyena. Each seemed to be right beside me. Yet I saw nothing but an ethereal garden before me. Where was I?

"Lily," Lucian's voice carried to me from around a bend.

I forced myself to move on and away from the intrigue of the thicket behind me. Around the curve ahead, I saw Lucian, standing with his back to what looked like a glass wall. As he saw me approach, one wing quietly unfolded out over his shoulder and canopied the path. The glassy wall parted, and I realized it was water.

"Watch your step," Aurelius called from beyond the cascade.

Peering down, I saw why he'd warned. The path beyond the water turned to stones, placed strides width apart through a narrow river. As I gingerly stepped onto the first, I could feel the warmth rising from it. From stone to stone I watched the water, saw through it and to the silt below. Small fish and other aquatics seemed to peer up at me as they moved slowly beneath my feet.

"Stop gawking and quit wasting our time," Zacarius scolded from across the opening ahead.

"In a hurry to get back to hell?" The retort came with a wave of my hand denoting the brand-new world around me. A place lit by a moon that I couldn't see.

"Zacarius, calm. It's nice to see some appreciation from one of them." This new voice belonged to a crisply statured man, with icy white hair despite his youth and mismatched irises.

"Alokin, this girl and her interference need to go back to her prison of the dead."

"Go to hell," I harshly responded.

"Your courage is admirable." Aurelius smiled.

A light hand on my shoulder urged me ahead. They parted in front of me until I was face to face with him.

"He simply should've left," Lucian said from behind me, his voice dull.

"But if Eli truly cared, he would have walked away long ago," Aurelius spoke.

"He did." Doubt filtered into my heart.

"He never truly left Lily," Lucian's voice was a whisper.

"He was too selfish to go," Alokin added.

"Putting you above all of them. All of us," Zacarius rowed.

"His love was never meant for you," Aurelius said as he moved to stand behind me and rested his massive hands on my shoulders.

"That's not for you to decide." Where were these words coming from inside me?

"Fool!" Zacarius fumed.

I could feel their eyes upon me. Felt the burn of each of them as they looked at me. I heard rushed and rambling thoughts as if they were my own, except they were directed at me. As though rushing in with every breath I took. I could taste the fear, respect, and sorrow permeating the air between us. I could see the blue of their halos begin to ignite in time with the beat of my heart.

The ground beneath me jolted. I watched as a large and intricately sculpted table of blackened iron in front of me shook with the force. Felt the gentleness leave Aurelius's hands as they tightened on my shoulders. I tried to follow the direction that their gazes took, only to find broad bodies blocking my view.

"Eli." Expectation made up the sound of his name coming from my lips.

He came into view as they stepped aside. It wasn't relief or even simmering anger that painted his features. It was wrath that veiled him. It dripped from his pores and trailed from his fisted hands.

Nothing felt more welcomed to me.

"You knew how this would end," Aurelius said with warmth in his tone.

"Give her to me," Eli's spoke grimly.

"Elijah, think twice about this," Lucian's pleaded. I watched as he looked at his brother gently, begging for understanding.

"You would turn your back on us? For *her*?" Zacarius refused to hide his bitter hatred as he spoke.

Eli ignored the biting remark.

"You cannot have both, Elijah," Alokin said.

"I want *her* then." There was no doubt in his voice and tears welled in my eyes as his hands revealed a dagger.

"Eli." It fell in a whimper from my lips.

"Don't make me do this in front of you." It was a request from Aurelius, one I imagined rarely occurred.

I felt the prick of a knife at my back and swallowed slowly.

"Don't do it at all." The dagger in Eli's hand turned slowly as he dropped his head.

"She could be a lost one…" a man to my right growled.

"You don't know that!" Eli growled angrily.

"Elijah. Even so, it has to be," Lucian said softly as he rested a hand on the shoulder of my angel. "This is the way it's always been. If one possibly comes into being, there is no choice for us."

"You would slaughter one of my charges because I fell in love with her?" And as his head rose, his eyes met mine, and his wrist twisted quickly. Without pause, the dagger tore through the flesh surrounding Eli's halo. A purpose I didn't understand until I saw heads drop around us. Defeated breaths left their lungs. The action held meaning for them.

"So be it," Aurelius said firmly.

A sharp thrust caught my breath as searing pain shot through my back. I felt every agonizing tear as the blade ripped through the heightened nerves along my spine. Scraping against the bones of my ribs before he tilted the dagger and thrust it straight through to my lung. More pain spread as he carved through the muscles of my back, leaving a trail of searing torment with his swift design. In a mere second, I felt filleted and branded all at once.

"Take her." His voice barely registered as I was overcome by the pain.

I hoped Eli would catch me as I crumbled to the ground.

28

The Legion's Prayer

The wind was rushing past my ears furiously. It sounded like a plane crashing. I was trying to do as he said, keeping focused on his face. My breaths were becoming gasps and the difficulty to breathe was overwhelming. His face was stern, angry even. He never looked back, not even worried for potential followers, his glare a sheer look of malice.

"I'm going to die," I whispered, ending with an uncomfortable whimper as the words escaped my throat. The wind quieted.

"No. They can't have you!" The anger that horrified me rose to the surface.

"I...can't breathe," I pushed.

"Your lung has collapsed, and the wound on your back is significant. You'll most likely need surgery. I'm more concerned about your blood type." His brows furrowed.

"My blood type?" I didn't understand the question.

"Yes. It's rare and your blood loss is severe. If I let you go, you'll lose consciousness, Lily." He looked down at me and his eyes were stricken with pain.

"Eli...if I die...I'm still happy I met you." I smiled a weak smile as tears were starting to creep into the corners of my vision.

"I'm happy being with you too. Don't cry. You'll live I promise." He smiled trying to be encouraging.

"Everything is getting blurry and it's hard to see your face," I sniffed.

He leaned in and kissed me ever so gently, and I smiled. A faint whisper of life on his lips brought the frayed edges of his face into clarity again.

"Does that help?" he asked, the wind almost completely absent.

I nodded lightly and tried everything not to blink.

Another sound was born…birds. We were close to the forest. I knew we were almost there, and I focused on my breaths. I started to think how I wouldn't be able to see Eli again, Jarrett, or my Ethan. The three men I ran from and avoided now were going to be no longer with me. My heart wept at the devastating realization.

Tears streamed down my cheeks, and I could hear the gargle in my lungs. I coughed harshly and a wet echo resonated. My lips tasted salty. My face twisted with sorrow. I loved them. I shut my eyes tight to the thought trying to capture their faces one last time.

Ethan with his boyish grin, and a soft heart despite his actions. Jarrett's unwavering allure that tugged at me when we were away from each other. I choked on their images in my mind.

I pictured August and smiled at her beautiful blond locks, her bright blue eyes that spilled all of her emotions and gave away her secrets. My best friend…my sister.

And here was Eli…the blue eyes that appeared from nowhere, the man that was everywhere I needed him to be. Now he was going to be *here*. Going to be witness to my death. I tried to keep breathing but it was nearly impossible. I looked at him and smiled at his ambitious will to keep me alive. It felt good to know that he had felt this way the entire time and it calmed my soul.

My arms that had been wrapped around his shoulders had surrendered. My left arm was across my chest clutching at my shirt; my other, limply dangled in the wake of our bodies. Strands of hair stuck to my temples from the mixture of tears and perspiration. Every breath was a chore.

His feet crashed into the dirt. A plume of dust rose around us, a warm wind rushed past. The shine of the sun was inviting. I forced myself to open my eyes so that I could watch him until all faded. He was truly striking, glorious, glowing even. His wings spread high enough, so it seemed that they reached the lowest hanging branches.

"Elijah…" I softly whimpered his name. "I'm scared." Another wet cough thrust past my teeth.

Grief haunted his expression. "I promise to keep you alive, Lilian. I'm sorry we couldn't land closer. I had to take you back the way you came. It's the rule of the Garden," he leaned down and pressed his forehead to mine, closing his eyes. "Just keep breathing…" Anguish creased his lids. "Please."

My chin was to my chest, and I looked down. I couldn't see the carnage, I'm sure that was my shoulder and spine, but I could feel the moist blood saturating our clothing. A faint blue glow painted my clothes in the places his arms were cradling me. I stared wide-eyed.

"I'll be fine. It's only flesh," he explained as he started jogging.

I felt nothing, my body wasn't connected. I couldn't feel the pain anymore. In fact, I couldn't recall the pain well at all and I'm sure that he had something to do with it.

Every thought that emerged was fleeting. This wasn't like drowning; the energy to manifest fear was too much. I felt guilty that I would be leaving my mother alone, no matter her distant reserve. I thought of Jimmy and Nell holding each other at my funeral and ached. The Bayne's solemn for once.

It hurt to think of Ethan and the dark place this would send him. I regretted not explaining my feelings and running, or Jarrett and his casual light demeanor that I would depress. I feared for who would take care of August and her apparent ability to forget her heavy hand in life.

Finally, I was most worried about how this would affect Eli and how he would be forced to stand with his brothers, the keepers.

How, in the wake of my death, the situation would be twistedly explained.

I opened my mouth to speak again but the liquid didn't allow it and I choked. My jaw relaxed with the understanding there would be no more words.

I closed my eyes and wept. Not for myself but for the people I would be hurting as all their faces flooded my thoughts.

I listened to the trees as we passed swiftly. Would this be the last time I heard them? I desperately wanted to reach out and let my fingertips graze over the bark, the leaves. To watch the wandering stars that blessed their tips through the night, and how they held strong through even the dimmest of hours.

We weren't going to make it.

"What the hell? Don't fucking move!" a tiny voice screamed.

We halted and fear bombarded my heart. They were here. They had found us. I mustered my energy and sucked in a wild breath opening my eyes to look over. It was blurry and the edges were darkening.

August?

Standing feet shoulder width apart at a weak five feet two inches tall, her blond curls spun around her glassy face in white fear with the wind. Was she holding my rifle?

Oh, for shit's sake August put the gun down I thought. She must have stolen it from the apartment when I didn't come home. How long had I been away? Hours? Days?

"Lilian is so graced to have a friend like you. Unfortunately, I must move," Eli's voice smoothly replied. He never swayed.

"Bullshit! Put her down! I'm going to shoot you and I promise you this." Her vocals pressed a slow burning rage. "I will not miss."

"It won't matter. Nothing you do will matter. You're misunderstanding what's happening here," he attempted a calm persuasion.

"I'm not missing anything! I go looking for my friend who's missing and I run smack into some crazy asshole wandering through the woods cradling my sister, her blood flooding down your chest to your boots." I watched as she raised the barrel and lined up the sights, eyeing Eli's face.

I wish I could say at this moment I was upset with her but that'd be lying. I was proud. A man a million times her size, so passionately infuriated. He was holding a weapon the length of her body swinging from his back that brushed the dirt. She still held a strong stance, the gun steady.

I smiled. *My* August.

"If you move, I'm going to kill you," she breathed. I wish I could see her eyes more clearly. I wanted to reach out and tell her not to be scared.

"August Bayne." Eli drew in a slow, deep breath. "Move."

"Never." I could hear her click off the safety. I realized I could smell his fury. It tasted like hot metal in my mouth.

"She will die if you don't." It wasn't enough time for my slow working blood-suffocated mind to follow. She squeezed back, but Eli was too quick.

He pulled his shoulders back and stood upright taller than I imagined. His broad body was a frightening force and he thrust his chest outward yelling a violent roar. His wings tore from his shoulder blades with a crack, and he thrust his voice down on her with the force of God pushing his every octave.

"I'll kill you, August, to save her! Now move or this *will* be *your* end!" It broke branches behind her and they detonated into the earth around us. His voice alone vibrated the ground we stood on.

"Mother of all that's holy…" I could hear her whisper as she lowered the gun in awe. "I don't understand," she helplessly fumbled. "What happened to her?"

"I chose to be with her." His head fell under the gravity and weight of his truth.

"You too?" she replied in true Bayne fashion.

August was running in a poor attempt to keep up but was failing miserably. I knew she still didn't understand. I didn't understand either. I was so happy she was here. I could feel her reach out when she was near but not enough. Eli kept up a brilliant pace, but I accepted we wouldn't make it in time. I loved them for not stopping. For trying.

I was devastated that my vocals were weak and that I couldn't belt out in joy that I had wanted him too. I wanted to scream at the men who were taking this from me. My heart burned with hatred towards them.

August was quiet surprisingly enough and didn't seem to ask questions but only pondered as she ran terrified behind Eli trying desperately to get me to help. I could hear her gently whisper now and again.

"I love you, Lily."

I drooped every time she spoke the sentence because I could hear the tears in her voice.

I knew the edges of the woods were near, from the smells of the different trees but we were slowing, and then he stopped.

"Why are you stopping?" August panted. "Don't wait for me, just help her," she pleaded. "Keep going, *angel carrying my friend*. We're almost there."

"We can't." His arms tightened.

"Why?" she cried through the broken gasps.

"Because they're here." He rolled his neck full circle.

"Who? The person that did this to her?" She tilted her head to the side in question.

"No. They sent members of the Legion to finish it." He shook his head furiously.

"Finish what?" She raised the rifle again straight ahead.

"Her." He looked at me longingly. "Listen closely because it will be only seconds." He spoke low but firmly, "August, they're going to do anything within their reach to stop her." He shook his head anticipating her interruption. "She's a threat to them. If I let her go, she'll die. I'm keeping her alive, August, do you understand?" His face grew deep with ambitious determination. "I'm better than them. I can win, but I may not be able to protect both of you. You cannot hide from them, I'm sorry," he sighed.

"And you can't protect us both." She thrust a hand in his face. "Please, I'm a Bayne." She marched past him and pressed on.

I choked on my pain. No. This wasn't fair! Unjust! But I was useless. A cold mess of flesh with a barely there heartbeat curled into a bloody heap held together by Eli's arms.

The trees stood still. The silence of their arrival, so vivid.

They were here.

I watched, cradled in his arms, as two women and three men faced us. A burning fire of red ringed their arms and ignited their thighs. Their halos—no, shackles— were tighter than the guardians' halos.

"Aurelius sent us, Elijah," a petite woman with dark hair and lavender eyes spoke. "He gives you an ultimatum."

"I won't finish this for you." He apparently knew what they were getting at.

"Is this final?" a soft-faced man asked. So young he couldn't have been much older than seventeen. His boyish looks angelic in beauty but wrapped in a disgusting thirst for something more.

"They're no longer my brothers," he spoke as grief and anger danced together.

They didn't reply but acted. One reached behind his back and pulled a stunning sword from a holster. His palms blazed bright red, the power of his halo rushing to where he needed it most.

I stared for a breath as Eli's eyes met mine soft and loving, then filled with ferocity as he looked up to meet theirs. He shifted my entire body to cradle it in his left arm. My head lay on his shoulder. August screamed at the sight of my back, which I wished she wouldn't have seen. Their eyes never left Eli.

His right arm reached up behind him and pulled from his shoulder the sword I was only able to see holstered on his brothers.

It was a goliath. The length and width were the size of a small person. Intricate designs were woven and spun through, while ellipses and openings could be seen along it. He swung it in a massive arc overhead and it sang a beautifully wild song as the metal ripped through the air, nearly touching them as it collided with the ground. It seemed the whole world shook.

"You will not win," Eli affirmed.

"We're not trying to conquer you, only end this," the young woman added, drawing her weapon in reply.

The others mirrored, and then they bowed their heads. "May we be merciful, our actions enriched with right, our movements lethal. Lilian, may your soul be on the right side of the garden." They spoke in eerie prayer-like unison, kissing their fingertips before they wrapped their hands around their hilts and charged forward unafraid while the crimson liquid slowly filled my lungs.

The last thing I remembered hearing was the clash of heaven's steel.

The End.